THE TRIDENT CONSPIRACY

KJ KALIS

This is a work of fiction. Names, characters, places, and incidents either are the products of the author's imagination or are used fictitiously. Any resemblance to actual persons, living or dead, or locales is entirely coincidental.

Published by:

BDM, LLC

ALSO BY K.J. KALIS:

The Kat Beckman Thriller Series:

The Cure

Fourteen Days

Burned

The Blackout

The Bloody Canvas

Sauk Valley Killer

The Emily Tizzano Vigilante Justice Thriller Series:

Twelve Years Gone

Lakeview Vendetta

Victim 14

Soon to Be Mine

The Jess Montgomery Thrillers:

The Trident Conspiracy

The Patriarch Code

Never Call Home

The Detective Morgan Foster Vigilante Justice Thriller Series:

West End Justice

Blister

Deep Deceit

The Travis Bishop Espionage Thrillers:

The Moscow Brief

Threat Rising

Tainted Asset

PROLOGUE

Jess stood off to the side, her teeth chattering and soaked to the bone from the chilly rain coming from above; the smell of smoke in her nostrils. Her brother, Chase, had dragged their little sister, Rachel, away from her as soon as Jess admitted there'd been a candle burning in her bedroom before the fire started. Their life would never be the same.

"This is your fault," he hissed. "It's your fault we're orphans."

1

It was getting hard to breathe.

Jess Montgomery shifted her weight from one hip to the other. Sitting on the hard tile floor of the bank was making her back ache. She tried to slow her breathing. The black hood over her head and the duct tape over her mouth made it difficult to do anything other than concentrate on sucking one breath in and letting another one out. When they first put the hood over her head, she strained to hear what the men in the bank were doing. After a few minutes, she realized the only thing she had the strength to do was to concentrate on the next breath.

Jess kept her hands folded in her lap, as she and the others had been told to do. There was nothing she wanted to do more than to rip the tape off her mouth and hood off of her head, but the men she'd gotten a glimpse of when they'd taken over the bank were heavily armed, wearing black from head to toe, including masks and heavy tactical vests. She knew she'd be no match for them. Her heart started to beat a little bit faster, wondering if Abby was still next to her.

. . .

THE MORNING HAD STARTED off pleasantly enough. It was a nice day in Tucson. Not too hot. Jess had swung by her brother's house to pick up her niece, Abby. Abby had just run one of the fastest times in her training for her middle school soccer team and they were headed out to celebrate. After a big pile of pancakes at a local diner, slathered with sweet butter and sticky maple syrup, they had walked outside talking about how Abby had decided she wanted to be a veterinarian, enjoying the morning sun and the dry air.

"Large animal or small? Jess asked.

"Both," Abby said, a grin on her face. "I want to help them all, but not snakes. I don't like them."

Jess smiled. It was just like Abby to want to do it all. "Me neither, though we have a lot of them around here. Is it okay if we duck into the bank for a minute?"

Abby was only twelve, but she seemed a little taller to Jess every time she saw her; her dark, wavy hair caught in a ponytail around the back of her head. Abby never dressed up. She wasn't that kind of a girl, unlike her mother, Piper, who was what Jess's mom used to refer to as "fancy."

Abby smirked, "So, this whole pancake thing was just a ploy to get me to go run your Saturday errands with you?"

Abby's sarcasm was one of the things that Jess loved about her niece the most. From the time she was just a toddler, Abby said what she thought. It didn't matter who was around or what questions they had. Abby could've been standing in front of her favorite boy band and would have told them to shove off if it met her purposes.

Jess grinned, "No, silly. The bank sent me some paperwork that I need to have notarized and turned in by today. Why, I have no idea."

Earlier that week, Jess received a package overnighted to her, the sound of the doorbell rousing her border collie, Milton, who charged and barked at the door. As Jess ripped the package open, grateful for a little break from her work as an intelligence analyst, she found a curt letter from the bank that held the mortgage on the small house she owned on the outskirts of Tucson, "Ms. Montgomery, it has come to our attention that your file is lacking form 1718B. In order to continue to fund your mortgage, we need this form notarized and returned to the closest bank branch no later than Saturday."

By the time Saturday rolled around, Jess had forgotten all about the papers, but saw them sitting on the counter. Groaning, she sent the bank manager an email. They'd gotten friendly over the last few years, Jess always saying hi whenever she went in the bank. Luckily, the diner she and Abby liked to go to was across the street from the South Ridge Bank branch where the papers needed to be returned. "Derek, I'm heading out to breakfast with my niece tomorrow morning. I'll swing by the bank as soon as we're done eating," she wrote back. These bank people are being really pesky, she thought.

WALKING INTO THE BANK, it seemed like business as usual. There were a couple of customers lined up at the counter, smiling and nodding at the tellers in front of them. A man brushed past Jess as she walked into the bank and headed toward the bank manager's office, clearly in a hurry. "How long is this going to take?" Abby said, in her usual sarcastic tone. "I've got places to be."

Jess raised her eyebrows, "And where might that be, missy? Your mom said you didn't have anywhere to be today until later."

Abby's eyes darted to the floor, "Well, I was thinking about going over to Stephanie's house before we go out to dinner. You know, just to hang out."

Jess smiled. She knew that just hanging out meant eating a lot of junk food and watching videos online with her friends. "Yes, I can see how that might be a priority," Jess said, realizing that her tone matched Abby's. "I'll try to make this fast."

Behind her, near the front door of the bank, Jess heard a click she didn't recognize. It sounded like metal on metal. As she turned, she saw four men, dressed in black tactical gear with masks over their faces, charging into the bank, rifles held up to their faces. Her heart started to pound in her chest and Jess pushed Abby behind her. A deafening noise rang through the bank, causing them both to cover their ears and drop to the ground.

"Nobody move!" A male voice rang out, bouncing off the walls of the bank. Three shots from a rifle echoed after him, nearly deafening Jess. "We have now taken control of this bank. You will do as you are told. If you do, no one will be hurt."

The men, using the tips of their rifles as prods, lined everyone up against the teller's counter, facing the front door, while another man used a chain to lock the doors closed. "All cell phones need to go in this wastebasket. If you try to hold onto your cell phone, you will be shot," a man said, striding past each person. His lips were set in a thin line, staring at each hostage as he walked by, a bag in his left hand, his right hand wrapped around the grip of the rifle. Jess tossed her cell phone in the wastebasket and nodded at Abby, whose eyes were wide. Abby dropped hers in as well. Another man walked to the windows and closed the blinds. As Jess glanced around, she saw the faces of the people who were trapped in the bank with her — some old, some young, but none of them as young as Abby. All Jess could hope was that one of the tellers had managed to press the silent alarm before the bank robbers had gotten too far into the building.

Standing against the teller's counter, Jess didn't say

anything, her body frozen with fear. Jess reached for Abby's hand and held it, giving it a little squeeze. How could this be happening to them? After a minute or so, one of the men stood in front of the line of hostages, "We will make this as comfortable for you as possible. You are going to be given a piece of duct tape. Put it over your mouth. After that, you will be given a black hood. Put that over your head. After that, you are to sit down exactly where you are standing and fold your hands in your lap. If anyone gets up or moves, they will be shot. If you need anything, raise your hand. Do not remove your hood or the tape on your mouth for any reason unless told to do so. Is that clear?"

The way the man barked out the orders made Jess think of a drill sergeant. Could the robbers be military? She didn't have a chance to really look at them as they were coming into the bank. She was too stunned, too scared at how quickly the morning had turned from fun with Abby, to well... this. And now that they were about to tape her mouth and put a hood on her head, she'd get no look at them at all.

A short, stocky man started at the front of the line, four people down from where Jess and Abby were standing and gave them each a piece of duct tape. As he handed it to Jess, she glanced at Abby and nodded, trying to encourage her young niece to do exactly as the men had told them. Unless the police arrived quickly, there was little hope they could do anything other than follow the orders barked at them.

A minute later, a second man, taller and leaner than the first man with the tape walked down the line, instructing each person to sit down and put the hood on their head. Jess remembered reading a report one time about hoods used in crimes her boss, Charlie Burns, her boss at the North American Intelligence Institute, had given her to read after a rash of home invasions funded by a terrorist group broke out in South Dakota.

They were meant to be disorienting. It was hard to take action to protect yourself if you couldn't see where you were. On top of that, they had guns and she didn't, not that Jess would know what to do with one anyway. Her dad had been a hunter, but she'd never gone. Glancing up at the man, Jess slid the black hood over her face, the acrid odor of chemicals still clinging to the new fabric burning her nose.

After a moment, the air inside of the hood became warm and damp from the breath going in and out of her nostrils. Jess glanced in Abby's direction, or at least the direction she thought Abby was sitting, hoping to be able to make out at least the silhouette of her niece through the fabric. She couldn't. The weave of the cloth draped over her eyes and nose was tight, making it even more difficult to breathe, little puffs of air moving the fabric out of the way with every breath. A knot formed in Jess's chest. It was getting hard to breathe. Panic rose in her throat. She swallowed the best she could, not wanting to throw up. The nerves at the back of her neck tingled and her mind became foggy as she tried to take long, slow breaths. She'd seen that on a video one time as a way to stay calm. As her breath started to slow, she realized that there was nothing she could do to escape. Breathe in. Breathe out. Jess wasn't going to be able to battle her way out of the bank. It was just her and Abby against men that definitely looked like they had more tactical training than anyone should. Jess didn't know a lot about the training that the men in front of her probably had, but she'd read about it an awful lot. For a moment, her mind tried to lock on to some of her last reports that she'd sent to Charlie. As an intelligence analyst, she was a paper pusher, not someone who knew how to fight. The slow trickle of air in and out of her nostrils made it difficult to concentrate on anything other than breathing, though. Jess fought the urge to reach a hand towards Abby. Her nails bit into the palms of her hands. She tried to relax, but the pounding of her heart rang in her ears. She knew the best thing she could do would be to sit and wait. The police had to know there was a robbery in progress, didn't they?

After what seemed to be about twenty minutes, Jess heard the muffled sound of sirens blaring in the background through the hood. The police. Jess felt a wave of emotion wash over her. Relief, then a new wave of fear. Someone had managed to get off a silent alarm before Jess, Abby and the rest of the people in the bank ended up sitting on the floor with duct tape over their mouths and black hoods over their faces, waiting politely for men in combat gear to decide whether they should live or die.

With the hood on, it was difficult to hear what was going on behind them. Jess wondered if that was intentional by the robbers, whoever they were. She could make out low murmuring toward the side of the bank where the bank manager's desk was, and a few sniffles from some of the people sitting nearby. Jess closed her eyes for a moment, not that she could see anything anyway, and tried to remember how many people were in the bank when she and Abby walked in. From behind the tape, Jess chewed her lip, realizing there was no way for her to focus well enough to even try to remember. Were there eight hostages? Ten? Jess felt like her body was coated in needlelike prickles, fear running in waves over her again and again, not knowing what would happen next. Wondering if Abby was okay was eating away at the inside of her, bit by bit.

Shifting on the hard floor, Jess realized it had been a while since anything had happened. The sirens outside had gone silent. Occasionally, she thought she could hear the sound of boots walking by her, but she wasn't sure, the darkness of the hood muddying everything around her. Losing her sight, she expected. Not being able to hear and not be able to breathe was something completely different. Without warning, Jess heard the men start to move around in the building, heavy footfalls passing her. It sounded like they were running toward the back of the building. She straightened up against the teller's counter. Were they leaving? Where were they going? Jess's mind raced. It took everything she had to not reach for Abby, to not rip the hood off of her face and the tape from her mouth, to see what was going on. But she had no idea what they would do to her if she did. They said they'd shoot people, but would they? Jess's heart started to pound in her chest again. The bank robbers said when they entered the bank that no one would get hurt if they all cooperated. She thought about Abby, her round face and her big eyes. How would Abby ever get past what was happening to her?

Before Jess could finish the thought, a voice boomed out and echoed against the walls of the bank, "Get up!" It sounded like the first man again, his gravelly voice grinding into her ears. Jess struggled to her feet. Her body had gotten stiff from sitting on the hard floor, nervous tension coiling her muscles into tight knots.

The voice came again, "Listen up! So far, all of you have done exactly what we asked you to do. That's good. Let's see if we can keep the streak running. If you don't cooperate, then you know the consequences. We won't ask questions. We will just put a bullet through your brain." There was silence in the bank for a moment, the breath caught in Jess's nostrils. By the bark in his voice, there was no doubt in Jess's mind that the man meant every word he said. Prickles of fear ran down the back of her legs. Her arms hanging limp, Jess tried to slow her breathing again. The last thing she wanted to do was cry.

The voice interrupted her thoughts, "In a few minutes, we will have you turn to your right and follow the person in front of you. One of my men will come by and put another person's hand on your shoulder. Do not move until we tell you to do so. When we tell you to move, you will do so without argument or drama."

From behind where Jess was standing, she could hear more

murmuring and the bank phone ringing. It had to be the police. Had the robbers talked to them yet? The muffle from the hood made it nearly impossible to hear anything except for the words of the man who barked at them. Jess did a quick calculation. Depending on which way they turned the hostages, Abby would either be behind Jess or Jess would be behind Abby. Jess's mind reeled, trying to get her bearings. Which way was the entrance? She'd been in the Catalina branch of the South Ridge Bank a million times, but for some reason, her mind couldn't grasp which direction was which.

The man's voice boomed again, "Okay, get up!"

Jess heard a shuffling noise behind her as if feet were moving slowly on the ground. They were being lined up. Where they were going, Jess didn't know. The breath caught in her chest as she felt a warm hand on her left shoulder. A little bit of pulling and a firm grip around her wrist landed her hand on the shoulder of someone in front of her. Jess felt the fabric, trying to focus on anything other than the fact that she was a hostage in a bank robbery. The fabric felt smooth, the fibers woven flat and tight, as though it was part of a men's suit jacket or something. Whoever it was seemed to be a bit taller than she was, maybe just shy of six feet. It wasn't Abby, that was for sure. Jess focused back on the hand on her left shoulder. We're going to get through this, Abby, just hang on, Jess thought, wishing she could say the words out loud.

The booming voice bounced off the bank walls again, "Good. I see everyone wants to get out of today's experience alive. In a moment, we will ask you to move. You are to move forward until we tell you to stop and then stand still. If you don't, you know the consequences."

A moment later, Jess felt a push from the hand behind her. Was that Abby? It had to be the signal to move forward. Looking down, Jess realized she couldn't see her feet. The hood was cupped underneath her chin, so the best she could do was shuffle forward. She dragged her feet on the ground, the soles of her tennis shoes making an occasional squeak on the tile. "Okay, everyone, stop," the voice said again. "No one move, until we tell you to do otherwise. Understood?" Jess nodded in what she hoped was the response the robbers wanted. She hoped Abby nodded too.

They stood in the line for what seemed like another fifteen or twenty minutes. Jess's arms dangled at her side, her body limp. The murmuring from behind her disappeared and then there was silence. Jess wondered if her ears were playing games. Why is it so quiet? The sound of her own breath going in and out through her nostrils echoed in her head. As best Jess could tell, a few more minutes went by before there was noise ahead of her, yelling and shouting, then a loud bang that dropped Jess to her knees. Hitting the hard ground, pain shot up through her legs. There was the sound of boots running past her, yells of "Police!" everywhere. Jess rolled over and sat on the floor, not moving, unsure what to do. Did the police really come to rescue them or was this the robbers just testing her to make sure that she wouldn't move?

A moment later, Jess felt a warm hand on her shoulder and heard a female voice, "It's okay, ma'am. I'm with the police. I'm gonna pull the hood off."

Jess blinked as the light in the bank constricted her pupils, blinding her. What seemed like a warm and friendly place to do her financial business had now turned into a war zone. Police officers, dressed almost exactly like the bank robbers, except for the yellow letters emblazoned across their chests that read "Police," were stationed at every corner of the bank, their tactical helmets strapped under their chins, their eyes scanning. Jess heard crying to her left and glanced over, to see an older woman who couldn't seem to get off the floor. Two police officers were kneeling by her, one of them waving toward the front door. A team of paramedics ran by, their medical bags slung over their shoulders. Jess reached up to touch her face, pulling the strip of tape away from her mouth. Exhaling, she felt fresh air pass her teeth. The female police officer was staring at her, not saying anything.

"Abby? Where's Abby?" Jess said, staring at the officer.

The officer shook her head a little bit. Jess noticed her name badge read Sullivan, "Abby? Who's that?"

"My niece. She was in the bank with me. I thought she was right behind me," Jess glanced to her left and right, feeling another wave of fear crash over her. She scrambled to her feet, "I have to find her."

Sullivan nodded, a few wisps of hair coming loose from the bun neatly tied at the back of her neck. She put a hand on Jess's arm, "I'm sure she's outside. That's where all the hostages are. Let's go look out there."

Jess pushed Sullivan away and ran past a couple of the police officers. The doors of the bank had been propped open with the entry. Just outside, Jess stopped, blinking in the sun. The street in front of the bank, between where she and Abby had breakfast and where they'd been held had turned into a small city, a mobile command unit was set up near the corner, three news vans were set up behind that, their long satellite booms jutting into the air. To her left, Jess saw a tent and a line of ambulances and police cruisers. The entire street was clogged with them. There was no moving around except for by foot. Jess looked behind her and saw Sullivan, "Where are they?"

Sullivan pointed at the white tent near the ambulances, "Over there. All of the hostages and the detectives are over there."

Jess's heart pounded in her chest and she took off at a run. She had to find Abby. The hot Tucson sun was pouring down onto the street, the canvas from the tent flapping gently in the breeze. "Abby?" Jess yelled, stopping just outside of the tent. "Abby? Where are you?"

A man dressed in jeans and a shirt approached Jess and stood right in front of her. He was about five inches taller than Jess, making him maybe five feet ten inches, with a shaved head and small eyes, "Ma'am, I'm Detective Jamison Saunders. Who are you looking for?"

"My niece, Abby Montgomery. She's twelve. We went to breakfast," Jess said, whirling around and pointing at the diner across the street, the words coming out of her mouth in a tumble, "and then I needed to go drop off some paperwork at the bank. She was right next to me when the robbers came in. Where is she?" Jess whirled back around, her heart skipping a beat, her hands clammy.

Saunders stood in front of her like a tree, not moving, "We've transported a few people to the hospital, but I'm not sure about anyone who's twelve. Are you sure she was at the bank with you?"

Heat rose in Jess's cheeks, "Are you kidding me? Are you actually asking me if I imagined my niece was in the bank with me? Yes, she was in the bank with me. Now, where is she? What have you done with her?"

Detective Saunders stared at Jess for a second, then glanced at Sullivan. Jess saw Sullivan shake her head slightly as if she was letting Saunders know that Abby was nowhere to be found. Saunders reached out a hand toward Jess's arm, the skin tan and brown from the desert sunshine, "I'm sure she's here some-where, ma'am. Just give me a couple minutes to find her. In the meantime, why don't you sit down and we'll have our para-medics take a look at you, and then I'll ask you a few questions for our report."

Jess could barely hear the words coming out of the detec-tive's mouth. Walking past her was a team of FBI agents, their badges swinging from their necks. Another team of paramedics rolled a gurney toward the bank. Jess couldn't stand still -- she kept scanning the crowd for Abby. Saunders said something to her, but Jess couldn't make out the words. Bile rose in her throat. Abby had to be here, somewhere. She was right next to Jess when the robbery happened. Jess scoured her memory. It was all broken apart, like a vase that had fallen on the floor and shattered into a million pieces. Jess remembered going into the bank with papers in hand, Abby behind her, then the commotion of the robbers, Jess pushing Abby behind her to protect her. It was a mother's instinct, although she didn't have any of her own kids. Her brother, Chase, barely trusted Jess with Abby. It had taken years for him to agree to let Jess take Abby out without him or his wife present. Now Abby was missing.

Jess blinked a couple of times in the bright sunshine and then glanced at Saunders and Sullivan who weren't saying anything. They were just watching her; like they were waiting for her to calm down or change her story. For a second, Jess wondered if that was some tactic they learned in the police academy to calm victims. The problem was Jess wasn't calm. She wouldn't be until she found Abby. "I have to find her. I've got to go," Jess said, taking off at a run towards the bank of ambulances that were parked off to the side, their lights flashing.

From behind her, Jess heard shouts from the detective, "Wait! Let us help you!" But she didn't listen. Going from ambulance to ambulance, Jess looked inside, grabbing the arm of one of the paramedics. "How many people have gone to the hospital?" Jess said, "I'm looking for my niece."

"I think three, ma'am. They told us to be ready for a few more. I guess there's an older lady in the bank that's having trouble breathing."

"Any of them a young girl? Dark, wavy hair, twelve years old?"

The paramedic shook his head, "Not that I know of. You

might want to check with command under the white tent. They can probably help you better than I can."

Jess glanced back at the white tent, the cluster of people still standing under it, trying to stay out of the hot sun. She turned back to the line of ambulances. Maybe Abby had darted in one of them, trying to stay safe after the police broke into the building? Jess ran past five more ambulances screaming, "Abby? Abby? Where are you?"

She wasn't there.

At the end of the ambulances, Jess turned back towards the command center at a half walk, half run. Her entire body felt like it was poised on the brink of collapsing, the adrenaline surging and receding as she realized she couldn't find Abby. Saunders was still standing in the same position she'd left him, taking down notes on an old-fashioned pad when Jess ran back under the tent, "I can't find her. Where is she?"

Saunders blinked and then closed the notebook, shoving it in the back of his jeans pocket, "Come on. I'll take you back in the bank. Maybe she's hiding in there somewhere that we don't know about."

Jess nodded and followed him, trotting behind his long strides. At least he seemed like he might believe her. Inside the bank, there was a lot of movement. Paramedics and police officers were still working on clearing out the last of the victims. The woman that had been having trouble breathing was now on a gurney, strapped in, an oxygen mask on her face, her lips pale and her eyes closed. The team of FBI agents had fanned out all over the building, the bright yellow letters on the back of their T-shirts letting everyone know the feds had arrived.

Just inside the door, Saunders stopped, looking at another officer, "Any idea how these guys got away?"

The officer shook his head, "Not yet."

Saunders looked at the young man, "This woman is looking for her niece. She said they entered the bank together, but I don't have any record of anyone under the age of sixteen in the bank. Do you?"

The officer shook his head, "No, sir. I watched all the hostages as they came out. Nobody looked to be any younger than about thirty to me. I could be wrong though." The officer shrugged.

Jess's stomach cramped. The officers were making her feel like she was crazy. Abby was with her. That was a fact. She stared at them, wondering what she'd need to do to get them to believe her. "Where are the cell phones? They took all of our cell phones."

Saunders pointed at the teller's counter, "Looks like they might be working on them over there."

Without thinking, Jess ran over to where a forensics expert was taking pictures of all of the cell phones. They were lined up on the counter. Jess scanned the phones and then pointed, "That one!" Jess pointed to a pink case with a Hello Kitty sticker stuck to the back. The sticker was a joke. Abby didn't like cats and she certainly didn't like Hello Kitty, but for some reason, she thought it was funny. "That one is Abby's."

Detective Saunders gave a slight nod to the tech, "I need this phone..." he said.

"And that one, too," Jess said. "That one is mine."

The forensics technician, a small blonde woman with her hair tied in a low bun behind the back of her neck took a few more pictures and flipped each phone over with rubber glove hands. "Want me to dust these for prints?" she said.

Before Saunders could answer, Jess said, "You won't find any. They had gloves on. That much I remember. Until they put the hoods on..." Jess swallowed hard remembering the feel of the dark fabric sliding over her face, the chemical smell of the new fabric as it flowed into her nostrils. "I gotta go."

Jess grabbed the two cell phones from the forensics tech

and started to leave, when Saunders called after her, "I still have questions for you. I can help you find Abby."

Jess didn't wait. They couldn't help her find Abby. Until a minute ago, Detective Saunders hadn't even believed Abby existed. She ran out of the bank and disappeared into the crowd, knowing that finding Abby was up to her.

2

Jess darted between two buildings, dodging the blinking lights and the police tape that had been practically wrapped around the entire block where the bank was located. Her heart was pounding in her chest and her hands were still clammy, but she made her way down an alley, darting left and then turning right behind another building before weaving her way back to the parking lot where she'd left her car. A lump formed in her throat. What if the emergency vehicles blocked her car in and she couldn't get out? As she slowed down, she pulled her phone out of her pocket. She needed to call Chase. He needed to know what happened and that it wasn't her fault.

Jess shoved Abby's phone in the back pocket of her jeans and pulled up Chase's number. Her hands were shaking and the phone bobbled. She nearly dropped it. Out of the corner of her eye, she spotted her car. With the phone pressed up against her ear she glanced left and right, trying to see if she could get out of the parking lot. There were no police cars with flashing lights or yellow tape anywhere to be seen. That was a break, she thought, thinking back to just a few hours before when she and Abby had arrived in Catalina on the outskirts of Tucson's downtown. It wasn't always easy to find a parking spot.

As Jess got in her car, she felt her heart race again. Chase hadn't picked up. Jess chewed her lip, scrolling through her contacts, trying to call Piper, Abby's mom. No luck. Piper might not even accept her call. The two of them hadn't always gotten along that well. Piper wasn't exactly someone Jess would hang out with, with all of her fancy, designer clothes and lunch dates with her friends. Jess was a bit more rough-and-tumble, sometimes even more so than her brother, who was frequently buried in books or some sort of research. Piper's phone went to voicemail. Jess pushed her shoulder-length, straight dark hair behind her ear as she left a message, "Piper, it's Jess. I was at the bank with Abby and there was a robbery. I don't know where she is. Call me when you can."

Jess threw the car into gear and pulled out of the parking lot, nearly sideswiping another vehicle at the end of the row, "Easy, Jess. You're not going to be any good to anyone if you get yourself killed," she muttered. Of course, the detectives were going to do everything they could to get Abby back, but they were more focused on securing the bank right now than anything else.

Out on the road, Jess traveled down Canyon Pass and took a right onto State Street, hitting the merge onto highway seventy-seven. As she drove, she thumbed through her contacts, going back to Chase. She called him twice more, but he didn't answer. Typical. She couldn't leave him a message on his phone like the one that she left for Piper. She couldn't bring herself to do it, not after what happened.

Memories of years before surfaced in Jess's mind as she gripped the wheel a little harder, willing Chase or Piper to call her back. Jess remembered the week after the house fire. They'd ended up staying with their next-door neighbor until their aunt could come in from Boston to get them. Jess had snuck out early the morning after the fire and climbed into the heap of blackened rubble that had killed their parents and sat in the space that used to be her bedroom and cried. It had still smelled like smoke, even after the fire department had doused it with thousands of gallons of water. She'd never told anyone about it. The fire had ruined her relationship with Chase, who was sure a lit candle in Jess's room had caused the blaze that burned their parents alive. Even the reassurance from Fire Chief Andrews, who told them they'd found faulty wiring in the furnace, didn't change his mind.

They had all lived together with their Aunt Bonnie in Boston for only two years. Chase had gone to college after that and Jess and her brother hadn't spoken while he was away, Chase was furious at Jess for the damage he thought she did to their family. Nothing had been able to change his mind, not until Abby, his daughter, had been born. Rachel, their much younger sister had stayed with Bonnie when Jess went to college. She never went back.

And now Chase's most important possession, his daughter, was missing because Jess hadn't been able to keep track of her.

Jess gripped the wheel a little harder. It had only been a few minutes since her last attempt at contacting Chase, but she tried to call again, passing a semi-truck on the freeway going breakneck speed. "Chase, pick up," she yelled. He didn't.

As Jess passed the outskirts of Catalina, she tried to relax, staring out the side window for a moment. Catalina was what most people would expect to find on the outskirts of any semi-major city. A few grocery stores, two movie houses, a few parks, and lots of restaurants with homes dotted in developments up and down the flat areas of the desert and peppered along the dry mountainsides.

Jess refocused on the road and racked her brain, trying to figure out where Chase might be and why he wasn't answering her calls. He knew she was with Abby. Wouldn't all of her calls alert him that something was amiss?

When Jess had picked up Abby that morning, Chase hadn't come out to the car. Neither had Piper. Abby just skipped out the front door as if she'd been watching for Abby by the front window. The only information she had from Chase was a text saying to make sure she dropped off Abby by three o'clock. They had dinner plans as a family that night. Piper wanted Abby home to make sure she had time to get ready to go. Knowing Piper, it was probably one of her fancy friends and their kids going out to some pricey restaurant where they served tiny amounts of food on bleached white porcelain plates. Not that there were a lot of those in the Tucson area. It was far more common to find a burger joint or barbecue place. Piper stuck out like a sore thumb.

Frustrated, Jess tossed her cell phone back on the passenger seat. Chase wasn't picking up. That meant one of two things — he was either at home, outside where he couldn't hear it ring, or he was at work in the middle of a project. Jess knew she had a fifty-fifty shot of figuring out where he was. Still on the freeway, just past the exit where she'd get off to go to Chase's house, she kept traveling north, towards the campus at Trident Labs. Jess only hoped that her guess was right, before it was too late.

3

"What kind of execution was that?" Landon Walker said, pulling the mask off his face and tossing it on the floor of the van as it rumbled onto highway seventy-seven, going south out of the city. "We trained for this. We train for this kind of mission all the time. You guys are getting sloppy. I won't have it."

With the surge of anger draining out of him, Landon looked down at his watch. They were three and a half minutes off schedule. That three and a half minutes could have gotten them caught. He felt the bile rise in the back of his throat again. He had chosen Alvarez, Baker, and Reinhardt because they were his best guys. Staring out the front window of the van, he wondered if maybe they weren't anymore.

Landon's phone pinged. It was his boss, Harrison Foster, the man that founded Zeta Tactical Consulting. Foster was not a man to be trifled with. A former Army Ranger, Foster had a sixth sense about him for people who were lying. Landon and Foster had met on a mission in Afghanistan, where Landon had watched Foster cut a man's neck from ear to ear without so much as blinking an eye. Foster was brutal and precise. "On the road?"

Landon texted back, "Yes."

"You are behind schedule."

Landon bit his lip. Foster insisted they use the highest level of technology available, including a GPS system with pinpoint precision. There was no point in arguing. Foster knew the truth and he was right, "Yes, but we've got the daughter."

Landon waited for a moment, waiting for Foster's response. None came. He was sure that Foster would have words with him about the delay in their exit during their after-action briefing, but that wouldn't come for a few days. Landon slid his phone into the side pocket on the pants of his uniform and glanced in the back. Alvarez had secured the package in the van. For some reason, Abby Montgomery, was different than he imagined, more mature for a twelve-year-old kid. Not that they had planned for her. Landon smiled. Foster would be happy they got Abby instead of Jess. Maybe Foster would forgive him the extra exit time with the upgrade in the subject they acquired.

When Foster gave them the mission a few weeks before and explained the target was the Montgomery family, Landon had something else in mind. When he'd read about Abby, Landon had in his mind someone small and frail. Abby was not that. In fact, she'd kicked at them so hard when they took her out of the bank that Landon was sure at least a couple of his guys would have bruises on their shins.

At the moment, the young girl sat quietly. Landon watched as Alvarez leaned over and adjusted the hood on her head. As he did, Landon saw Abby flinch. When they'd gotten her to the van and started moving. Alvarez had cable-tied her wrists together and then momentarily removed her hood, stuffing foam earplugs in her ears so any conversations they had in the van couldn't be overheard. Now, the young girl sat, blind, deaf, and mute with the tape still over her mouth from the robbery. Landon wanted to feel bad for her, bad about the years of therapy she'd likely need if she made it out of the situation alive, but he couldn't quite work up any empathy for her. After all, she was a casualty of war, like so many others he'd seen in his career. He was doing a job. That was all.

"How far out are we?" Landon said, glancing at Reinhardt, who was driving the van.

"Eighteen minutes."

"Roger that. Let's see if we can make up some of that time we lost on the extraction."

Reinhardt nodded but didn't say anything. Landon felt the van press forward a little faster on the highway.

Leaning back in his seat, Landon thought through the morning, the adrenaline in his system finally starting to settle down. Not that he had much of a problem with an adrenaline surge. None of his men did. Zeta Tactical Consulting didn't hire operators that had issues with staying calm. That could jeopardize a mission faster than nearly anything else. But Landon had noticed that there was a certain window of time as he finished a mission when his edginess needed to dull a little bit. That was a good thing. If Landon tried to stay razor-sharp all the time, he'd burn out. He didn't want to do that. Harrison Foster had big plans for Landon and his team, plans that made him excited about the future and his opportunities with Zeta. The abduction this morning was just phase one, if the rest of the mission was successful.

Landon wiped sweaty palms on his pants and ran through the next steps of what would happen once they got to the warehouse. The fourth man on their team, Baker, would exit the white bakery van they were driving, go into the warehouse and raise the garage door within twenty-two seconds of them arriving. The entire area where the warehouse was had been scrubbed of surveillance. One of Harrison Foster's countersurveillance teams had gone in the week before and installed signal jammers and video repeaters on the buildings nearby. If one of the companies nearby had an active security team, they would simply be looking at either static or the same scene over and over again for the rest of the day. Landon knew the plan was to turn it on thirty minutes ago, ensuring that no trace of the white van would be seen on any recording device, unless it was something like a cell phone, but the warehouse district they were in near Mesa Springs, didn't have many workers there on a Saturday. If all went according to plan, Landon and his team would be leaving the site in just a few short hours, their mission accomplished.

The thump of the van's tires over railroad tracks caught Landon's attention. His body swayed in the seat as they passed over them. They were close. Landon glanced out the windshield and saw a billboard advertising jobs in manufacturing. It was weathered by the sun and hadn't been replaced. He wondered if the advertising company had forgotten about it or just didn't have anyone who wanted ad space in a practically abandoned business district. From the mission plan, he knew the warehouse was approximately one minute from the railroad tracks. Just a little bit longer and they'd be at their new home base, at least as much of a home as it could be for the moment. Landon looked in the back of the van and nodded at Baker, who edged to the back, his hand on the van's door, ready to jump out. "Ready?" Landon said. Baker gave a short nod.

As the van got close to the warehouse, the corrugated brown steel door came into view. Harrison had helped Landon pick the safe house himself. It wasn't something that Harrison normally did, giving his senior operators the latitude to do as they saw fit. But in this case, the mission was so critical that Harrison had been involved in nearly every aspect of the planning — from the timing to the preplanning, to the execution itself. Landon knew Harrison was watching with great attention to how the day went down. In any other situation, Landon might be aggravated, but in this case, with a promotion on the horizon, he relished the opportunity to prove himself. He set his jaw, ready for the next phase.

Reinhardt slowed the van as they got close to the warehouse door. It had barely paused when Baker pushed the door open and slammed it closed behind him. From the side of the van, Landon saw Baker's stocky frame sprint at the side door, tap in a six-digit code on the keypad, and disappear inside. Three seconds later, the metal garage door started to lift off the ground. Ten seconds later, the van was inside, bathed in the darkness of the abandoned warehouse, the door clattering to a close behind them.

Landon got out of the van and nodded at Baker, "Good hustle. Keep it up."

At times, Landon felt like he was somewhere between a football coach and a field general, vacillating between the two roles, encouraging his men and then facing the brutality of war as regularly as people ate their breakfast cereal.

"Let's get her out and secured in the cage," Landon said as Alvarez slid out of the back of the van, the butt of his rifle banging against the metal doors. "Reinhardt, give him a hand." As Landon walked to the front of the van, hearing the garage door clatter closed behind him, he looked at Baker, "Let's get the systems booted up, okay?"

The men fanned out of the van, their boots moving almost silently on the rough concrete floors of the warehouse. Landon stood for a second, staring out. It was the first time he'd been in the warehouse in person. Foster had insisted they run drills at another offsite location to limit their exposure to prying eyes. Landon glanced left and right, realizing the setup was identical to the one they'd practiced on. It was no surprise. Foster was precise that way. He knew, as all the operators did, that any variation from the original mission plan could cause issues.

Life and death issues. Landon walked over to the hood of the van, ripping the Velcro apart on the sides of his tactical vest. At the time they planned the bank robbery, Baker argued they didn't need to wear the heavy, Kevlar-plated gear, but Foster had insisted. "This is a mission like any other," he said. "It's my responsibility to make sure you're able to complete it. Wearing the gear is part of the job." There was no more discussion after that.

The heavy vest off of his shoulders for the moment, Landon walked over to the makeshift operations bay Foster's team had managed to smuggle into the warehouse when they did the setup. How they got the equipment into the warehouse, Landon didn't know. All he knew was that when they ran the operation, what they needed would be there for them, everything from technology to snacks to toilet paper. As he slung his gear onto one of the desks that held computers and monitors to help them with on-site surveillance and communications with Foster and the base team, Landon looked over his shoulder just in time to see Reinhardt and Alvarez walking Abby to the cage, their hands gripping her elbows, one on either side of her small frame, her hood still covering her face. She stumbled for a moment, but they didn't let her fall. Landon didn't walk towards her. He didn't need to. His men would handle it with the professionalism that was expected by their boss. Even though what was happening to Abby was horrific, and they all knew it, there was no reason to make it worse than it was.

A spotlight hung over the metal cage that had been erected just inside the garage door. A small bench had been bolted to the floor where Abby could sit if she wanted to. Landon heard the jingle of the gate open and watched the men as they half carried and half dragged her inside. The girl had to be scared to death, Landon thought. Alvarez tugged the hood off of her face and pulled the earplugs out of her ears. Landon could see her blinking in the bright light. From across the warehouse,

Landon heard Alvarez say, "Now, we've taken the hood off. If you can stay quiet, I'll cut the cable ties off your wrists and we can take the tape off. Sound good?"

With wide brown eyes, Abby nodded. Alvarez drew a K-bar knife out of his belt and cut the cable ties from Abby's wrists. "You can take the tape off now." Alvarez said, nodding at her. "We will put the restraints back in place if you don't cooperate. Is that clear?" The young girl nodded and backed away from the man, sitting down on the bench.

Now that Abby was secure, Landon refocused on the work Baker was doing. All of the computer screens — there were five in total — were lit up, running through their boot-up procedures. Foster had promised the systems would be top-of-the-line so it wouldn't take any time at all to get hooked up to the secure satellite link at Zeta headquarters. The systems were as good as Foster promised. Within thirty seconds, all of the screens had settled in, their connections flashing green in the corner of the screen. Landon and his team could speak directly with Foster at any time and for any reason.

Baker, who was leaning over the last of the systems, stood up and looked at Landon, "We're all set up. Now what?"

"We wait a little bit and then make contact."

4

At the last second, Jess decided to head toward Chase's house. At least she might have a chance of catching either Chase or Piper if they were at home. Glancing down at her phone as she was doing seventy-five on the freeway, neither of them had called back. Jess slammed her hand against the steering wheel. If she had a child, she'd make sure someone would always be around to answer the phone. But she didn't. She didn't know if she ever would.

Two miles down the road, Jess exited the freeway on Mesa Boulevard and headed out into the desert. Chase and Piper had bought an upscale house in a development called Desert Palms, western-style ranch houses on sculpted lots of land in a nice neighborhood with a homeowner's association. Jess was sure all of it was Piper's idea. Knowing Chase, he would've been happy to live in a tent in the middle of the desert, as long as he could do the work he loved to do.

As Jess wove through their development, the houses became a little bit bigger and a little bit more elaborate towards the back. That's where Chase and Piper lived. As Jess pulled up, she saw the stuccoed side of their house, the beige front, accented by tasteful desert plantings. Unlike many of their neighbors, Chase and Piper had decided to plant grass. It was something Chase complained about constantly, the fact their water bill was through the roof trying to maintain even broad-leafed scrub grass in the middle of the desert. But it was what Piper wanted. Many of the other neighbors had opted for rocks and native plantings instead of struggling to keep grass growing. For some reason, Jess thought if Chase ever got rid of Piper, the first thing he'd do would be to tear out the grass at the house.

As Jess pulled up in the driveway, she jumped out of the car, leaving the keys in the ignition. She ran to the front door and pounded on it with her fist, trying to look through the small windows next to the front door. There weren't any lights on she could see. "Chase? Piper?" she yelled, cupping her hands around her face to look in the windows. There was no movement. Jess stood for a second, leaning her ear against the door. Roxie, the beagle-mix Chase had bought for Abby, scrambled toward the front door, frantically barking, but no one came to the door to let her out.

Running back around the side of the house, Jess looked in the small window that led into the garage. Neither of their cars was home. "Come on!" she groaned, running back to her car. Getting in, Jess threw the sedan in reverse and peeled out of the driveway, nearly avoiding the neighbor's mailbox across the street. "Where are you?" she whispered, a sinking feeling in her stomach.

The only other option she could think of was that Chase was at work. But it was a Saturday. Did he go to work on Saturdays? Jess racked her brain, trying to remember if Chase had ever said anything to her about working weekends. He hadn't, but it would be like him. Chase had almost a singular focus in his life — work and Abby. Jess thought that Chase loved Piper, but watching him as he watched Abby, she knew that his love for Abby was different than what he had for Piper. It made her heart ache a little, wishing she'd been blessed with her own family.

The tires on Jess's car screeched around the corner as she exited the development. She made a right turn, turning away from the development and the freeway where she'd gotten off, glancing at her phone. It was just after nine. Her mind reeled as she stayed on Mesa Boulevard, heading farther out of town to where the industrial buildings were. What had started off as a nice morning had gotten out of control. Totally out of control.

Driving as fast as she could without careening off the side of the road, Jess kept going down Mesa Boulevard for another five miles passing cars and glancing at her phone every few seconds. Where were Chase and Piper? Why didn't they return her calls? Jess squinted as she passed the signs for the industrial complex. All the buildings looked the same, glimmering white against the harsh sun, lots of glass and square corners. As Jess took the final turn into the back of the industrial park, she saw the sign she was looking for — Trident Labs. Chase had worked for them for nearly his entire career, but Jess had only been out to his building one time when he'd been given an award.

Jess put her car in one of the visitor spots and jumped out, running toward the doors. As she grabbed the closest handle, she realized it was locked. She rattled each one of the doors with no luck. She glanced at her phone and then back at her car just as a noise behind her caught her attention. A man had come and pushed the door open, "Can I help you?" the man said.

Jess looked at him. A security guard. "Yes, please," she said, sliding into the building, trying to catch her breath, "My brother, Chase Montgomery, works here. Is he here? I need him. There's been a family emergency."

"Yes, I know him. Come on over here. Let's see if he's upstairs."

Jess followed the security guard, her nerves tingling. If Chase wasn't at the lab, she had no idea where he was. It could be hours before she was able to find either him or Piper. God only knew where Piper was, not that she'd tell Jess anyway. They weren't close. The security guard picked up the handset for the phone and pressed a couple buttons. After a few seconds, he shook his head. "No one's answering in the lab, but knowing your brother, that doesn't surprise me. Give me a second to check the logs and see if he used his key card at some point today."

A second later, the guard nodded, "Looks like he got here at about seven-thirty this morning. Early start for a weekend. As far as I can tell he's still here. Want me to walk you up?"

"Yes, please," Jess said, relief flooding through her chest. It was the first good news she'd had since making it out of the bank. "I've been trying to call him, but he isn't answering his phone. Neither is his wife."

"Is everything okay?" the man said, furrowing his brows.

"I don't know..."

JESS DIDN'T SAY anything more to the security guard as they took the elevator to the second floor. The elevator doors opened with a whoosh onto a long hallway that ran from one side of the building to the next, dotted with doorways. Jess followed the man halfway down the hallway until he used his key card on a door on the right-hand side, "Chase?" the guard called, walking into the lab. "You have a visitor."

Jess pushed her way past the security guard who was holding the door, her eyes wild. Chase was standing at a stainless-steel table, hunched over what looked to be a microscope of some sort. "Jess? What are you doing here? Where's Abby?"

The security guard squinted at Chase and interrupted, "Okay for me to leave you two up here?"

"Yeah, yeah," Chase said, pushing his glasses up on his nose. Chase was dressed in jeans and a plaid shirt, his dark brown hair, the same color as Abby's, pushed away from his face.

As a security guard walked away, Jess darted toward where Chase was standing, "I'm sorry, Chase. I've been trying to call you, but you didn't answer. Abby and I... we were at the bank. We stopped there after breakfast and then there was a robbery..." The words came out in a tumble.

Chase pressed his lips together, "Wait. Slow down. What's happening? Where's Abby?"

"That's what I'm trying to tell you. Abby. She's gone."

As Jess watched the words settle over Chase, she saw his color change, going from tan to gray. "Jess, start at the beginning."

Jess started to pace. "Well, you know I picked her up early to go to breakfast. That's what we did. We had breakfast. Scrambled eggs for me and French toast for her..."

"Get to the part about the bank, please?" The words came out in a rattle. Chase was getting impatient.

"I had some papers to drop off at the bank. They said they had to be in by today. The branch is right across the street and they open early on Saturdays. Abby said it was okay. I thought we'd just run in and I'd sign and we'd leave. But then the robbery started. And now she's gone. I've been trying to get a hold of you and Piper for the last half-hour, but neither of you answered."

Chase looked like he'd been frozen in time, all of his movements slowing to a crawl. He sat back on a metal lab stool in front of the bench he was working on and closed his eyes for a moment. "Wait, so what you're telling me is that you and Abby went out to breakfast, everything was fine and then you stopped at the bank across the street and there was a robbery?"

Jess nodded.

"And when they let the hostages go, everyone was there except for Abby. Is that right?"

Jess nodded again, the same wave of emotions she'd had after her parents died circling around her, "I'm so sorry, Chase. I don't know what happened. The police don't know what happened either. They thought I was crazy, but then I showed them this." From out of her back pocket, Jess pulled Abby's phone, feeling a slight shudder run through her body. "They made us give up all of our cell phones before they put tape on our mouths and hoods on our heads. I managed to go back into the bank with one of the detectives. They didn't believe me that Abby was gone until I showed them her phone. See, I'm not crazy." Just as the words came out of Jess's mouth, her phone rang. It was an unknown number. Her heart started to pound in her chest, and she glanced at Chase before answering it, "Yes?"

"Jess Montgomery?"

"Yes. This is she."

"Jess, this is Detective Saunders from the Tucson Police Department. We met this morning at the robbery scene?"

His voice sounded so calm. Jess felt curiosity rise in her. Was he always this way? "Yes."

"I was wondering if you could come down to the station so we can get your statement from the robbery this morning? Have you found your niece?"

A wave of fury passed over Jess. "Thanks for reaching out, but I don't have time now." Jess ended the call without saying anything more.

"Did you just hang up on the police department?" Chase asked.

"Yes. They aren't helping."

Chase got up from his stool and started pacing, his hands

shoved deep into the pockets of his jeans. Jess watched him, knowing by his pacing and silence that the reality that his daughter was missing had settled in on him. He walked back and forth in front of the metal table. Jess glanced at his hands. They were shaking. Jess couldn't imagine what he was thinking. "I'm so sorry, Chase. There was nothing I could do..."

He wheeled around, "Nothing you could do? Why did you take her to the bank in the first place? Why couldn't you just do your errands on your own time rather than taking my daughter there and endangering her?"

Jess was startled by his reaction. "I had no intention of putting her in danger. I was just dropping off papers at the bank for God's sake. I'm sure you've taken her to the bank before, haven't you?"

Chase put his hands up, "I'm sorry. I just, I just can't understand what happened. Can you go through it again?"

"Like I said, we went to breakfast then we went to the bank. A bunch of guys in tactical gear came in, taped our mouths with pieces of duct tape, put black hoods over our faces and I thought everything was okay. I thought Abby was right next to me when they walked us to the door," Jess looked down, her eyes filling with tears. "But when they let us loose, she was nowhere to be found. I searched all the ambulances. I ran up and down the street. I couldn't find her. That's when I started calling you and Piper."

"And Piper didn't answer?"

"No."

"She's probably at one of those blasted yoga classes she goes to."

"I even drove to your house. I pounded on the door. Roxie barked, but no one answered. When no one came to the door, I came straight here. I've been trying to call you ever since this happened. I'm so sorry." Just as Jess finished her sentence, her phone rang again. It was Detective Saunders. Jess didn't answer.

"Why would they take Abby? Is that what you think happened?" Chase stared straight at Jess. "Are you sure she's not at the hospital or something? Maybe you just got separated?"

"I don't know what happened. That's why I'm here. Why would they take Abby? Why her?"

Chase sat back down on the metal stool again, rubbing his face with his hands. "I don't know. None of this makes any sense. You guys were just supposed to go out for breakfast and then we were going to go out for dinner tonight with some friends. That was it. That was how today was supposed to turn out. And now, this…"

Jess could tell that Chase was having a hard time wrapping his brain around the fact that no one knew where Abby was. A pit formed in Jess's stomach. She felt the same way. "I hate to ask this, but could it have anything to do with the work you're doing? I mean, I don't know what you're up to here at the lab, but I do know a lot of it is classified. Jess got up and started to walk slowly past the worktables and equipment that peppered Chase's lab. From the one other time she'd been in the building, she knew Chase had a small office toward the back, piled with papers and files.

"My work? Now you're blaming me? Last I checked, a lot of your work is classified, too!"

"I know, but that's not what I'm saying. Someone had to have a reason for taking Abby."

"If they took her. That's a big if."

"What are you saying, Chase? That I manufactured losing Abby? That she's out in the parking lot sitting in my car waiting for us to come out so we can go get ice cream? That's just not the case! She's gone and I don't know where she is. I'm as upset about this as you are."

"I highly doubt that. You're not her father."

The words landed like a punch to the gut. She held her

hands up in the air, "You're right. You and Piper are Abby's parents. What do you want to do?"

"I don't know."

A quiet settled over the two of them, only the murmured beeping of some equipment toward the back of the lab making noise. A faint scent of disinfectant hung in the air, something like rubbing alcohol, but not as strong. Jess crossed her arms in front of her chest and stared at the vials and tubes, autoclaves, microscopes, and mass spectrometers that decorated the lab, cluttering nearly every inch of space. This was Chase's life. Analysis and development. What he used all the equipment for, she didn't know. Jess kept coming back to the fact that someone had to have a reason to take Abby. Her analytical brain kicked in, the same skills she used as an intelligence analyst for the North American Intelligence Institute, where her job was to deal with domestic threats. Only on paper, though. "Who had something to gain by taking Abby? No offense, but it's not like you and Piper are billionaires, if you know what I mean."

"Other than the fact she's a beautiful young girl? I have no idea. Oh my God…"

"What are you thinking?" Jess scowled.

"What if that's why they took her? You know, I was just reading about so many young girls getting taken to be sex trafficked. What if she was targeted? What if they already have her on a plane or ship or something else, headed to some foreign country where she gets auctioned off to be someone's slave?"

"That doesn't make sense, Chase. Why would they go to the trouble of robbing a bank just to nab Abby? I mean, they went to a lot of trouble. They had the whole place staked out. They were dressed in tactical gear; like they were military or something."

"That doesn't explain why they took her."

"I know, but I wouldn't guess it was so they could sex traffic her." Jess started to pace again, chewing her lip. "Maybe it was just coincidental? Maybe they grabbed her when they saw she was a young girl and thought they could use her for collateral in case they had trouble getting away or something?"

"Did anyone happen to tell you how much money the robbers got away with?"

"No. I was so busy looking for Abby, I didn't think to ask. It all happened so fast. I'm not sure they'd even know yet." Jess's phone rang again. It was Detective Saunders. She groaned. "Hello?"

"Are you going to hang up on me again this time?"

"Sorry about that," Jess said, trying to sound apologetic. The last thing she wanted to do was get caught up with a detective and all of his questions. She knew Saunders was trying to help, but for some reason, it didn't seem that way. "I'm with my brother, Abby's father. I was in the middle of telling him that she's gone when you called. Bad timing." The lie poured out of her mouth like honey.

There was a pause for a second as if Detective Saunders was weighing whether what Jess said was true or not, "Okay, I'll buy that for the moment."

Before Detective Saunders could say anything else, Jess saw Chase pointing at the phone, mouthing that Jess should ask him about Abby. "Any news on Abby? Did you find her?"

"I wish I could say we had, Jess. But we haven't. Have you received any ransom demands?"

"Ransom demands?" Jess felt her mouth drop open, "What are you talking about?" The idea there would be a ransom had never occurred to her in her hurry to get to Chase and Piper.

"Whoever these guys are, if they have her, they took her as a hostage. They must want something. The question is what? Is there a place we can meet to talk?"

Jess mouthed the word "meet" to Chase. He nodded yes. "All right. I'm at the Trident Labs building, just off of Mesa

Boulevard. It's in the industrial complex. Do you know where that is?"

"Yeah, I can be there in ten minutes."

"We'll meet you in the parking lot."

For the next few minutes, Chase sat frozen on his stool. Jess tried to catch his eye, but he seemed focused on a single spot on the floor. Where his mind was, she wasn't sure. It reminded her of when they were kids. Jess was always a little bit more outgoing than Chase was. Not that either of them were super extroverts, but compared to Chase's bookishness, Jess was almost outgoing. In high school, Chase spent his freshman year trying to wrestle, thinking the technique around every move was something he could conquer with his mind. But he just didn't have the physical quickness to make it happen. He and Jess ended up running cross-country together in high school, that was, before the fire. The fire changed everything.

Thinking about running brought Jess back to the whole reason for the celebration earlier that morning – Abby's victory in the time trials for her middle school soccer team. Abby had gotten her speed from her Dad, though she used it on the soccer field, not on a trail. Hopefully, she could use it to get somewhere safe and call them.

Five minutes passed and Jess tried to break Chase out of his sullen trance. "Come on. We gotta go downstairs and meet Saunders."

Chase didn't say anything, but stood up, grabbing his cell phone, car keys, wallet, and key card for the building. He opened the door to the lab, letting Jess out, flipping the light switch off. Jess followed him as he walked quickly to the elevator, pressing the button for the lobby. The elevator slid down to the floor below with not much more other than a quiet beep, the whoosh of the doors let Jess know it was time to get off.

Bright sunshine filtered through the two-story windows in the lobby. The security guard that had let Jess into the building was sitting behind a console, playing with his phone. "Everything all right?" he called behind Chase and Jess as they walked away.

"Yeah, it's all good, Sully," Chase said.

"It is at that," Sully said in a gravelly voice, barely looking up.

Outside, the sun had started to heat up the day. It was normal to see people go into work in the morning wearing goose down vests or snuggled up in jackets or windbreakers, just to have to strip them all off by the time lunchtime rolled around. The desert weather did that. The dry air was quick to bring in cold temperatures at night and hot ones during the day. The sun could be so hot that in just an hour or so someone could get sun poisoning. "Let's go sit over there while we wait for Saunders," Jess said, pointing Chase toward a picnic table that was under some palm trees decoratively planted in a landscaping bed just across from the main entrance. "I'm sure he'll pull up here looking for us."

As Jess lowered herself down on the picnic table's bench, a wave of exhaustion covered her. The morning wasn't even half over, and she was more tired than she could imagine. It had to be the adrenaline from the robbery wearing off, she thought, picking at one of her fingernails. She sighed, then looked up, seeing a dark blue sedan with a spotlight attached to the driver's side mirror pull up to the front entrance. As Saunders got out of the car, Jess called him, "Detective, we're over here."

In the chaos of the bank robbery, Jess hadn't really taken the time to look at Detective Saunders, other than to note the fact that his head was shaved clean. He looked like a fitness buff, the muscles in his arms pressing against the shirt he wore tucked into his jeans, his badge attached to his belt. "Thanks for meeting with me. I can't imagine how hard this is."

Jess jumped in before Chase had a chance to say something that might alienate the detective. Her gut told her they might need his help to get Abby back. "Thanks for coming the whole way out here. Detective, this is my brother Chase, Abby's dad."

"Sorry to meet you under these circumstances, sir," Saunders sighed, extending a hand to Chase.

"I just can't believe this is happening. Please tell me you found her."

"I wish I had better news, Chase. If your sister hadn't told us she couldn't find Abby, it could've been hours before we even knew anyone was missing from the bank."

"Where did they take her? Who has her?" The questions tumbled out of Chase's mouth. Jess couldn't blame him. All of the same questions were rattling around in her mind. Was it just a coincidence they grabbed Abby? Maybe they took her as a hostage because she was young and not as strong as the rest of them?

"That's what we're trying to figure out. Can you guys walk me through what happened this morning?" Saunders pulled a notebook out of his back jeans pocket and started writing.

Chase cleared his throat, "Jess picked Abby up at about seven. It was early, but the diner they like to go to gets crowded and we had stuff to do later as a family. So, after Jess picked her up, they left. I saw my wife, Piper, for a second. She said she was going out. And then Jess shows up at the lab telling me that Abby's gone."

"So, you had no idea about what happened this morning until Jess showed up at the lab?"

"That's right. I have to admit I'm not always good about checking my phone. I get started on a project up in the lab and time just flies by. It's a good thing, I guess, except in situations like this."

Saunders nodded, "Jess, do you have Abby's cell phone with you still?"

Jess nodded and pulled the pink case with the Hello Kitty sticker on it and showed it to him. "Yeah, it's right here."

"Chase, can you confirm that's your daughter's cell phone?"

Chase nodded and coughed a little, looking away. Jess knew he was fighting back the reality that his daughter had been abducted. She swallowed hard.

"I don't understand why they took Abby," Chase stammered at Detective Saunders.

Saunders shook his head, "That part we don't know yet, but please know that Tucson PD and the FBI are all over this. We will not stop until we find your daughter." Saunders squinted at the lab, "Let me ask you this, what kind of work do you do for Trident Labs? You said you work on projects or something?"

Chase shook his head, "I'm sorry. I can't talk about the specific work I do without clearance. It's classified. The best I can tell you is I'm in research and development."

Jess was a little surprised at how quickly Chase had blown off the detective's request for information about his work. The words tumbled out of his mouth sounding like they'd been repeated a thousand times. Normally, her brother was happy to talk about the things he was passionate about. What did they have him working on at Trident labs? What were all those vials and microscopes for in his lab? The last Jess knew, he was working on some sort of water reclamation system for the desert. The thought passed in her mind that perhaps it had been a lie. Chase had always been quiet, but all of a sudden it seemed like she knew little of her brother and his life.

"One last question, if you don't mind. You said your wife's name is Piper?"

"That's right."

"Where is she right now?"

"I have no idea."

5

Piper tried to smile as she left her Saturday morning yoga class. The fragrance of cedarwood incense filled her nostrils as she made her way to the front door, slipping on sandals over her bare feet, one of the many pairs that were stacked by the door. A voice called to her from a short round woman with cropped hair, "Have time for a latte, Piper?"

Piper shook her head at the woman, who was a local art dealer Piper had made friends with over the last few years, "No, I'm so sorry. I'd love to, but today won't work. We've got family stuff going on. Next time, maybe." She tried to sound like she meant it.

Piper walked out to the parking lot, the heels of her sandals making a slapping sound on the underside of her foot as she walked. Her car chirped as she pressed the fob to the convertible's locks. The silver Audi had been a present from Chase the year before for her birthday, but not a real present or a real surprise. Piper had chosen everything about it, from the color to the upgraded heated steering wheel and plush carpet. Sliding into the driver's side, Piper set her yoga mat and bag on the passenger side seat and powered her phone on, her hands shaking just a little. Landon had told her to go about her business this morning, to pretend that nothing abnormal was going on. But trying to concentrate on bending her body had been nearly impossible knowing what he had planned. The instructor, a former ballerina named Darlene, came over to check on Piper a few times during class when she found her resting, "Are you okay?" Darlene whispered, placing a warm hand on Piper's back.

"Yes, just a little tired today. I didn't sleep well," Piper lied.

"Just rest then. No reason to push the body where it doesn't want to go," Darlene said consolingly.

Sitting in the cupholder of the Audi, Piper's phone chirped after it had a chance to sync with the satellites. Her hands trembled again as she picked it up, wondering what she would find, if anything. Maybe Landon had decided not to go through with it? Maybe Abby was out with Jess or she was home already? Piper's fingers were sweaty as she accessed her history. There were messages waiting for her. The phone let her know that Jess had tried to call seven times, there was a message from her dentist reminding her it was time for her next cleaning, and a message from a number she didn't recognize, one that wasn't stored on her phone. Piper opened it up, almost missing the spot on the screen with her finger. As it loaded, she realized there was a picture attached. Piper started to cry softly as she saw it. It was Abby, behind a chain-link fence, sitting on a small metal bench. The message read, "She's safe."

It didn't seem that way to Piper.

6

After Detective Saunders left Jess and Chase in the parking lot at the Trident Labs building with a promise to call them with any updates, Jess watched as Chase stared off into the undeveloped acreage behind the industrial park, "What do we do now?"

Jess wondered the same thing. "I think we should go back to your house. See if we can find Piper. She needs to know about Abby, don't you think?"

Chase nodded.

"Once we find Piper, maybe we can figure out what to do. Maybe by then, someone will have contacted one of us."

"You mean like the police or the FBI?"

"Yeah, but I was thinking maybe the people that have Abby..." Saying the words out loud formed a new lump in Jess's throat. Her mind was still reeling, trying to cope with the details of what had started off as a fun morning. Tragedy was always that way, Jess realized. People would be going about their business and then all of a sudden, a car T-boned you, someone died of a heart attack while eating their dinner or slipped on a piece of ice and cracked their head open, leaving them in a coma. Things could be going along just fine and a second later, the world could nearly tilt on its axis. At least that's how Jess felt.

"Okay. I'll meet you back at the house."

Jess turned away from Chase, walking towards her car. Spending a few minutes with Detective Saunders had been strangely calming although he didn't have any answers. Maybe it was just the process of going through the information that was helping. As Jess slid behind the wheel of her car and turned the key, the engine rumbled to life, she reminded herself that she'd been a victim too. Sure, Abby was gone, but she needed to cut herself a little slack if she wasn't feeling like she was one hundred percent. But I have to be, she thought to herself, a wave of guilt rushing over her as she pulled out of the industrial park. It's my fault Abby's gone. My fault. A wave of what-ifs ran through Jess's head. What if we hadn't gone to the diner today? What if I'd stopped at the bank another time? What if we'd gone just a little bit later? But the biggest what if was the one that was nearly choking her: What if they couldn't find Abby; if she never came home? And even if they did get Abby back, would she be okay? There was no telling what was happening to Abby right now. Jess swallowed, checking her rearview mirror. Chase was behind her, staring straight forward, his lips pressed in a thin line.

Even as a child, Chase had never been very emotional. It was as if the scientific part of his brain had grown way faster than the emotional processing side, Jess thought, taking the turn back onto Mesa Boulevard. Into her memory flooded the image of Chase sitting at his desk when he was eight years old, a line of rocks he'd collected from their backyard meticulously arranged on an old kitchen towel on his desk. She'd come running into the house, crying, after falling off her bike. Chase never even got up. How he would process the kidnapping over time, Jess wasn't sure. She whispered a silent prayer that they were able to get Abby back and that her brother wouldn't hate her forever.

The traffic was light, typical of midmorning on a Saturday in Tucson. Not that there was ever heavy traffic anyway. It wasn't like they lived in Los Angeles or Chicago where the lanes were packed from daybreak far past sunset. The sun was making a high arc over the desert, lighting up the gradations of browns and pinks and oranges of the mountains with an occasional patch of green, the spheres of an ocotillo or the arms of a saguaro cactus jutting up into the sky. The weather was a stark contrast to the feelings Jess was carrying in her soul, she realized, gripping the steering wheel a little tighter.

As Jess turned on the road toward Chase's house, she glanced back. He was still behind her. Jess had the overwhelming urge to keep driving, pretending that nothing had happened, that the morning had gone by exactly as it should and they were parting ways like they had so many other times, a quick wave and a "See you later."

But that wasn't the case.

As they got close to the entrance for Chase's development, Jess's hands started to get a little sweaty. She wiped them on her jeans. She wasn't sure if Chase had taken the time to call Piper on the way from the lab or even if he'd been able to reach her. How Piper would respond, Jess wasn't sure. Piper was unpredictable like that. Jess sighed as she pulled her car up in front of Chase's house, his car passing behind hers, driving to the garage.

As Jess got out of the car, she picked up her cell phone and stared at the house for a minute, Walking up the driveway. Chase met her outside. He nodded his head, "Piper's car is here. I'm going to go in," he said, stopping in midsentence to stare at his phone. He looked at Jess and then held up his phone. The number calling said unknown.

Jess's heart started to pound again, a tightening passing over her chest, "It could be Abby. Put it on speaker!" she said.

As Chase's finger slid across the screen, he said, "Abby, is that you?"

The mechanical voice of a woman was on the other end of the line, clearly, computer-generated. "We have your daughter. She is safe and unharmed. I need twelve vials of ABG and the formula in eight hours. If you don't provide it, we will kill her. If you call the police, we will kill her immediately. We will be in touch."

Jess watched for a moment as Chase froze in the driveway, his eyes wide. Jess leaned toward him, "ABG? What's that? They didn't ask for money?"

Chase's mouth hung open and he started pacing back and forth, rubbing his hand through his hair, pushing it away from his face, "I can't, I can't," he said.

Jess watched him, her eyes locked on him as he paced back and forth, "You can't what? What is ABG?"

"I can't talk about it. I can't give them what they want. They are asking for something that's impossible. I can't do that. Oh my God, what's gonna happen to Abby?"

Jess was confused, "Chase, what's going on? Talk to me."

"This has to be targeted, Jess. They took Abby on purpose. Nobody knows about the work I do at the lab. I never tell anyone. There had to be a leak." The words rattled out of his mouth faster than Jess could understand them.

"No one is saying you leaked information. What is ABG?"

"I can't tell you!" Chase yelled, leaning forward, almost knocking her over. "Don't you understand? It's classified. I can't tell you! I can't give them what they want." Chase started to pace again, running his hand through the top of his hair again, "They're going to kill Abby. My work is going to get her killed."

"Can't you call your boss?"

Chase didn't respond for a minute. Whether he was ignoring her comment or just didn't hear her, Jess wasn't sure. "I have to go inside. I have to talk to Piper. You can come in if you want, or don't. It's up to you."

His words stung. Had Chase forgotten that Jess was in the bank, too? That this wasn't her fault? Jess watched as Chase walked away. Part of her wanted to run back to her car and jump in, going back to her house and back to her life, but she knew she couldn't do that. Chase and Abby, and even Piper... they were family. If nothing else, they needed to stick together.

As Chase walked away, Jess looked down at her phone. Should she call their younger sister Rachel? Jess blinked away tears. She desperately wanted to call their parents. Her heart ached realizing how much time had gone by since they died in the house fire. Standing alone in the driveway, Jess decided against calling Rachel. There was no need to get anyone more concerned until they knew something more. Jess glanced toward the house, weighing her options, and realized she had Abby's phone still in her back pocket. If nothing else, she needed to go in and give it to Chase. She set off up the driveway at a trot, slowing down as she got into the garage. Piper's Audi was making a ticking sound, the kind that happens as metal cools. Jess put a hand on the hood as she walked by. It was warm. Piper had been out while the robbery had happened. But where? Why didn't she have her phone turned on? Jess couldn't imagine a situation as a parent that you'd shut your phone off. What if they needed you? What if it was a day like today? She shuddered, suddenly grateful she didn't have kids... at least not yet.

Jess pushed the thought out of her mind knowing it was none of her business. Eight hours. She checked the time on her phone. It was just after ten. Whatever was going to happen would happen between that moment and six o'clock. Time was ticking.

Jess pushed the door inside of the garage open, stepping onto terra-cotta tiles just inside the back door of Chase's house. She could hear low voices and crying. Walking forward, Jess passed the laundry room and a bathroom into the kitchen. Chase had his back to a bank of windows that looked out on their backyard, which faced part of a golf course. Piper was hunched over the kitchen island, sobs coming out of her body. She glanced up and then looked at Chase, "What's she doing here?"

Before Chase could answer, Jess looked at Piper, "I'm so sorry, Piper. I don't know what to..."

"Do?" Piper stared at Jess accusingly, "If you'd just leave us alone none of this would happen. We'd be fine right now."

Piper stomped off to the other side of the house. Jess looked down and then glanced at Chase, who'd taken off his glasses and was wiping his eyes. He'd been crying, "Chase, I am so sorry."

Jess swallowed. The only other time she'd seen him cry was at the funeral for their parents.

Chase put his glasses back on, "No, I'm sorry. Piper shouldn't have said that. None of this is your fault, Jess. They're trying to get to me, not to you. You just got caught in the cross-fire." Chase slammed his hands down on the granite countertop and bit his lip, "They warned us something like this could happen. I never thought it could. I mean, my research isn't that important, after all. It's not like I'm developing a nuclear bomb or something."

"What do you mean, they warned you? Who's they?"

Chase sighed, "The lab. They warned us. All of us. We have meetings twice a year — security meetings — that warn us about threats. Trident does defense contracting."

"You told me that. That's not a secret."

"Well, you know part of it. The work we do, a lot of it is top-secret. A lot of it I can't talk about outside of the lab. I can't even talk about it outside of the people who are working on the same project I'm working on. And for this project, it's only me. I've been working on this for the last five years."

"And whatever it is you are working on is what they call ABG? That's what the kidnappers want?"

Chase nodded, "Yes. But I can't give it to them."

Jess reeled. How could Chase not give them what they wanted? "What do you mean? Can't you call your bosses and tell them? Maybe they would give you some samples of whatever it is, at least something enough so we can get Abby back?"

"You don't understand, Jess," he said, the muscles rippling across the side of his jaw, "They would never agree. Hundreds of millions of dollars have gone into developing ABG. There is no chance they will give up any part of it. Not even the first chemical in the formula. It wouldn't matter if it was the Queen of England who'd been taken. They will not give in. They have a non-negotiation policy with terrorists. I signed it. I agreed to it. You know what that means? I'm on my own. And there's nothing I can do for Abby." Chase turned away, shutting Jess out.

The gravity of what Chase said landed heavily on Jess. Was he giving up? Jess eased herself down onto one of the barstools that was perched at the edge of the center island in the kitchen, looking down, her hands in her lap, a wave of nausea crashing over her. Was this really happening? She was sitting in her brother's kitchen, her niece had been kidnapped, his wife had accused Jess of interfering in their life, and Chase just told her there was nothing he could do to save his own daughter. How was this even possible?

A memory of Abby wearing a fancy hat caught Jess by surprise. When she'd been eight, Chase and Piper had gone to the Kentucky Derby with friends. Abby had learned about the tradition of wearing hats at the race and had made her own, spending all weekend wearing it around the house while Jess watched her.

Jess blinked a couple times, wishing Abby would walk around the corner wearing one of her homemade hats, but she didn't. She wasn't there. Jess swallowed and then looked at Chase. He was leaning his back against a wall in the kitchen, staring at the ceiling. Jess wondered what he was thinking. She stood up, "What if we contact the lab? You don't think your bosses would be sympathetic?"

"Sympathetic? Yes. Able to do anything? No. All the research I've done has been bought and paid for by the US government. They own it lock, stock and barrel. If I give up any iota of information, even to try to save Abby's life, I'll never see her again. They'll charge me with treason and drag me off into some hole somewhere. She might be alive, but I'll spend the rest of my life rotting in jail."

"Chase, we just can't give up! Don't you have a lab here at your house? Can you make up something and give it to them, so they'll give us Abby back?"

"And then what, Jess? I hand them a shopping bag full of some vials and they smile pleasantly and hand Abby back to us and we go on our merry way? That's not how this works. They want the formula and twelve doses. Even if I could fabricate them, it would take days. And I'm betting they'll test them. If they don't work the way they're supposed to, then guess what, they'll come back for me and for Piper, heck, probably for you, too. We've been told the people like this, don't stop. It's one of the risks of the job. I just never thought I'd have to face it."

Jess sat frozen on the stool, unsure of what to do. Inside of her, it felt like a clock had started running in the back of her head, each second and each minute going by, taking Abby further away, somewhere they couldn't get to her. And now Chase was arguing that it was basically impossible to save his own daughter. Before Jess could say anything else, Piper walked back through the kitchen, her face dry. Only her eyes, just a little puffy, gave any hint that she'd been crying. Jess furrowed her eyebrows, waiting for Piper to start yelling at her again, but she didn't. Piper stared at the two of them, opened the refrigerator door, and pulled out a bottle of water. Closing it, she walked away without a word.

Knowing they had absolutely no options was unacceptable. Jess's mind lurched into action, "We have to figure this out, Chase. We aren't just going to give up on Abby."

"There's nothing we can do, Jess. I told you that."

Jess got up and stared at him, "Chase Montgomery. Are you seriously gonna let someone kill your daughter? What's wrong with you? You're not even going to try to save her?"

Jess stared at the floor and licked her lips, wondering if she'd gone too far, "Where is the ABG or whatever it's called?"

"It's at the lab."

"Where are your research notes with the formula?"

"At the lab, but Jess, I told you…"

"Shut up!" Jess was surprised at the force with which the words came out of her mouth. She was angry. The last thing she wanted to do was yell at her brother, but someone needed to snap him back into reality. "We're not going to give up on Abby! You won't be able to live with yourself, and neither can I. We're going back to the lab. Right now."

Chase stared towards the back of the house, "What about Piper? What if they come after her?"

"Bring her or not. Either way, we're going."

Chase shook his head and picked up his car keys, "She's probably better off here."

Jess didn't say anything. She followed Chase out to the garage and got into the passenger side of his car. As he pulled it out, Chase sent a quick text to Piper saying they were going to the lab. There was no response.

As they got on the freeway, Jess knew in her gut there were options, options that Chase just wasn't willing to explore. Chase had always been a rules follower, very binary. There were only two options for nearly everything in his life — on or off. Jess's work as an intelligence analyst had grown in her a need to be more flexible in her thinking, to look for things that were hidden, things that were secret unwritten motives. Chase wasn't tuned up that way. "Tell me what ABG is," Jess whispered as the car merged into traffic, headed north to the Trident Labs building.

Chase stared straight ahead, his two hands on the steering wheel, giving a slight shake to his head. "I can't."

"Chase, you have to. You have to let me help you. If you won't do it for yourself, do it for me. Can you imagine the guilt I'm gonna have if we can't get her back?"

Another second went by, "It's glue."

"What?"

"Glue. Arterial Blood Glue. ABG. It's for the military. It's to save lives."

"Glue? What does it do?"

Chase cleared his throat, passing a truck and trailer that looked like they were hauling four horses north to Phoenix, "One of the biggest problems the military has is loss of blood. All the soldiers wear Kevlar, but they can't cover their entire body with it. The body has joints, you know, knees and elbows and such. They can't cover every inch of the body with Kevlar because it doesn't bend. You'd basically mummify a soldier. They'd never be able to move. What terrorists have gotten very good at is aiming for the neck and the exposed area on the shoulders and the sides of our soldiers overseas. If a bullet nicks an artery a soldier can bleed out in two minutes. Even the best trauma surgeon at the most world-class hospital here probably wouldn't be able to save their life. ABG, or Arterial Blood Glue, fixes that problem."

Jess stared at her brother for a second, amazed at what he'd been able to accomplish. "And you developed this all by yourself?"

Chase nodded, "Yeah, for the most part. I had a lab assistant that was helping me for a little bit five years ago when I started the project, but he's long gone. He moved on to another company or something. I don't know."

"Exactly how does ABG work?"

"It's a thick liquid, just like the consistency of glue. That's how I got the idea. I figured if there was a way that you could glue the injured area closed under pressure, the body would build and maintain enough blood flow so soldiers could be tended to and then taken for proper medical care. If someone in the field gets shot and it clips their carotid, all they need to do is open the tube and pour the ABG on the area. Basically, what the ABG does is rapidly coagulate the blood, just like it normally would except for the fact that it deals with arterial injuries. They are a little different than a scrape on your knee, for instance. If you cut your finger or your knee, there isn't a ton of blood flow. It basically seeps out than anything else, the purpose being: to clean the wound and seal it and start the healing process. With an arterial injury, the pressure of the blood being pumped by the heart sends the blood out in a spurt, not in a seep. Do you see what I mean?"

Jess nodded.

"So, ABG seals up the hole like if you were in a leaky boat and there was water coming in. Except this time, we're trying to keep the blood in the body, not keep water out. ABG thickens up the blood super-fast and then seals it. It's not a permanent fix — as I said, someone with that kind of injury, whether it's a femoral artery or carotid or something like that, they would still have to seek proper medical attention in short order, but it extends the window. Instead of having two minutes to live, they would have several hours to get treatment."

Talking about Chase's work was a nice distraction from the fact they were racing back to the lab with no real plan, Jess thought. If nothing else, at least she had a better idea of what Chase spent his hours doing. Did Piper know? Jess wondered how much Chase told his wife. Knowing her personality, probably nothing. She seemed to be only concerned about how much money Chase made and what he was going to buy her next. Jess pushed the thought away. True or not, it wasn't going to help them get Abby back.

Pulling into the lab complex, Chase glanced at Jess, "Obviously, you can't tell anyone anything about this. You know that, right?"

"Of course. But somehow someone heard about ABG. How could that be?"

Chase pulled his car into a parking spot and turned off the engine. "I don't know. Only a handful of people know about the project, or at least that's my impression. The thing is, it's not a weapon or anything. Why would someone take Abby over this?"

"I have no idea."

Jess sat in the car with Chase for a minute, the engine running, a cool breeze from the air conditioning pouring out of the vents. Chase had chosen a parking spot under a tree which gave them at least a little bit of shade. It was the first chance Jess had to catch her breath since the robbery that morning. At that moment, it seemed like a faraway memory, like something that had never happened, and yet, she was sitting in the parking lot of her brother's lab knowing that her niece was somewhere with people they didn't know who clearly had evil intent. It was almost more than her mind could process. Jess bit her lip for a second, wishing she was home, staring at her computer screen, rifling through documents and chatter, getting ready for her next presentation. All of it seemed so simple and easy compared to the way the day had been so far. And time was ticking.

Chase glanced at Jess, his hands resting on the steering wheel, "Now what?"

"I have no idea."

7

The metal bench bolted to the floor at the back of the cage was beginning to give her a backache, Abby thought. There was no cushion. She shifted, trying to get comfortable, but she felt like her bones were poking into the metal no matter how she sat. How long she'd been locked up in the cage, she wasn't sure. Her memory was coming back in pieces. Breakfast with Aunt Jess and then a stop at the bank, then the gunmen, then...

Abby pressed her thumbnail into her index finger, giving it a little pinch, trying to distract herself. Every time she started to think about what happened that morning, she got to the part when the gunmen told everyone to stand up. She'd done that. She'd done exactly what they asked her to do. Abby remembered turning, hoping that Aunt Jess was right in front of her until she felt someone grab her wrist and yank her out of line. It was so sudden that she nearly lost her balance, tripping on what she guessed was the transition strip between the tile in front of the teller's counter and the carpet that covered the rest of the bank. The hood over her face made it impossible to see and her heart was beating so loud in her chest that she could barely think clearly. All she wanted to do was go home, see her family and climb into bed.

Abby swallowed and stared at the concrete floor trying to remember more of what happened after she'd been dragged from the bank. There were two sets of strong hands that lifted her up and then pushed her down onto a bench, the plastic from the cable ties eating into the skin on her wrists. It kind of hurt at the moment, their fingers pinching her, the plastic from the cables rubbing her skin raw.

Distracted by the pain, Abby didn't even realize she was in a vehicle until it started to move, a wave of nausea passed over her. She wasn't used to traveling inside of a car and not being able to see anything. A second later, she remembered the hood yanked off her head, foam being stuffed in her ears, and then the blackness of the hood again. While the hood was off, she noticed they were in a van. There were two men in the front of it and two men in the back with her with frowns on their faces.

Time passed. She didn't know if she sat in the van for a long time or just a few minutes. It was hard to tell which.

Then she remembered the motion stopped.

Abby didn't have any idea where they were when the van stopped. All she knew was she felt two sets of hands pull her, half carrying her, out of the van and drag her over ground her feet couldn't quite find. A second later, she'd felt another bench underneath her, the glaring lights of the cage constricting her pupils so quickly it gave her a headache as they pulled the hood off. The men in front of her worked quickly to remove the earplugs and unclip her cable ties.

And that's where she was now.

It had only been in the last few minutes she'd worked up the courage to look up from the floor. She seemed to be in some sort of a warehouse, but the lights above her cage were so bright that it made it difficult to see into the murky darkness beyond where she was sitting. It was as if the cage was draped in light. Everything else outside of it seemed to be murky or black. As she waited for her eyes to adjust, she looked around the cage. There was nothing in it -- no water, no food, nothing. The floor was concrete, but she noticed it had a layer of dust or dirt on top of it. Which, she couldn't tell. Abby dragged her toe, still in its tennis shoe across the floor, a small cinder catching under the tread making the slightest grating noise.

As her eyes adjusted to the warehouse, she noticed what looked to be a bank of computers off to her right. They were set up in a semi-circle, kind of like a gaming room, she thought. Two of the men were looking at what was on the screens, pointing and murmuring under their breath. She was too far away to see what they were looking at. Another man, still in his black gear from the bank, was standing by the doorway just past the white van they must have ridden in to get to the ware-house. The last man was sitting on a folding chair just outside of the spotlights of her cage. It looked like he was watching her, but his head was down.

Abby chewed the inside of her lip and wondered if it was okay for her to stand up. The only thing the men had told her was that she couldn't give them any trouble. Was standing up giving them trouble? She eased the palms of her hands to the edge of the bench and pushed herself up to standing, waiting to see what might happen, butterflies forming in her stomach. The man watching the cage glanced up at her but didn't move. Abby took that as a good sign. Walking closer to the edge of the cage, she glanced at the man again. He wasn't looking at her. He sat leaning against the back of the folding chair, one of his legs crossed over the other, tossing something on the ground after chewing it a little bit. Sunflower seeds. Abby could hear the shells dropping every few seconds, a little pile of what looked like leftover birdseed sitting on the floor next to him. Abby remembered being at the grocery store and asking her mom for a package of them from the checkout line, "Oh no, honey. You don't want to eat those. Too much salt and you have to spit the shells out. Disgusting." Just thinking about her mom made Abby want to cry, but she swallowed. She hadn't cried so far. She didn't want to start now.

Watching the man eat the sunflower seeds made her realize how thirsty she was. "Could I have some water, please?" she whispered, looking at the man through the chain-link fence that separated them, her fingers knotted around the wire. She held her breath. What would he do? Would he open the door and beat her because she asked a question?

The man stood up, abandoning the package of sunflower seeds on the seat of the chair where he'd been seated. He walked over to the two men who were staring at the computer screen, talking to one of them. The man glanced back toward Abby, his hands resting on the desk as he looked over his shoulder at her. He gave a slight nod. The sunflower seed man disappeared farther into the darkness, where Abby couldn't see him. Why had he left? Were they going to do something to her? Her heart started to pound in her chest, the whoosh of blood in her ears again. Abby sat down on the bench, closing her eyes. She'd never felt this nervous before, not even before a soccer game. She tried to remember what her coach said about nerves, but the words wouldn't form in her memory. All she could do was try to breathe in and breathe out.

A minute later, Abby heard a rattle at the gate of her cage. The sunflower seed man was back with a bottle of water in his hands, "Here you go. If you need to use the bathroom, let us know." As he turned away from her, Abby could smell something like sweat, kind of like her dad smelled after he came in from cutting the lawn on a hot summer day. Taking the water in her hands, she turned the cap, the click of the seal breaking. She took a couple of sips. Would they really let her use the bathroom if she needed to? Maybe it was a trap, like something she'd seen on television in one of the movies they watched on the weekends.

After another sip, Abby looked up and glanced around, noticing one of the men had come out from behind the computers. He was walking straight towards her. She felt her palms get sweaty. He stopped outside of the cage, not opening up the door, his voice low and gravelly, "Abby. I know you're scared. No need to be. Everything is going to work out fine as long as your dad does what we need him to do. Do you believe me?"

Abby nodded, not sure if she did or didn't, a wave of fear running through her when he used her name. She looked at the man a little bit more closely but tried not to stare. How did he know her? He wasn't as tall as the man with the sunflower seeds and his hair was cut almost down to the scalp. His lack of hair set off his square jaw. From where she was sitting, she couldn't see what color his eyes were, but his skin was tan and there were lines under his eyes. Why had he taken his mask off? Was that a good thing or a bad thing? Uncertainty left a lump in Abby's throat.

"I'm sure you have a lot of questions about what happened today, but none of those are important. What's important is that you listen to our instructions and do exactly as we say. Understand?"

Abby nodded again, silent. Inside of her, she wanted to jump up and charge the gate, shaking it off its hinges and scream at the men to let her go, but something inside of her held her back. She didn't know if it was the guns, or the way they talked to her, or the way they were dressed, but the words wouldn't form in her mouth. She pressed her lips together and looked down again.

"Good," she heard the man say as he walked away.

8

After sitting in the parking lot for a couple minutes, Jess followed Chase back up into the lab. They each gave a wave to Sully as they passed through the lobby, Chase using his key card to get into the elevators. "We've got to figure out what to do," Jess said as the elevator doors slid closed.

Chase didn't say anything, his jaw set. Jess stared straight forward, listening to the cables above them pull the elevator car to the second floor where Chase's lab was. A second later, the doors slid open, and she and Chase stepped out onto the polished white linoleum floor that led down the hallway to Chase's lab. Without saying anything, Chase used his key card to buzz open the lab door.

Inside, nothing looked any different than when they'd been there earlier. Chase flipped on the lights and a few of the machines, as if on cue, started to whir. Jess stepped inside, feeling a wash of cool air over her. "It's cold in here," she said, crossing her arms in front of her chest.

"Negative pressure system," Chase mumbled, sitting down at his lab stool and opening his laptop.

Jess had read about those systems before in her intelligence analysis. Frequently, people who were working with dangerous chemicals — everyone including drug traffickers, bomb makers, and especially those who were building bioweapons — generally commandeered a lab or space that had a negative pressure ventilation system. The process was pretty simple, really. The system would suck toxins out of the air to a filtration unit as opposed to just circulating them around the room, like a traditional furnace or air conditioner would.

"What are you looking for?" she sighed, walking up behind Chase.

"I'm trying to see if there's anything I can give these people that won't compromise the research, anything at all."

Jess turned away for a second, feeling her phone vibrate in her pocket. She pulled it out, looking at the screen. It was a text from Charlie, her boss. "Ready for your presentation?"

Jess knew she was supposed to be putting the finishing touches on a presentation she was due to give to the top brass at Naval intelligence on Monday. It was on her schedule to finish the presentation today, Saturday, and fly out on Sunday to be ready for Monday. She hated doing the presentations, but her boss, Charlie Burns, the Executive Director of the North American intelligence Institute, insisted. "It's the only way we keep our contracts and get more, Jess," he'd said to her earlier that week. "I know you hate doing these, but it's the way we all stay employed."

Jess gritted her teeth together. There was no doubt in her mind that work was on the back burner, but how was she supposed to tell Charlie it didn't look like she was going to make her presentation? Should she tell him about Abby? Wait it out and hope she could get back in time?

Pushing the thoughts of Charlie and work out of her mind, Jess tried to calm herself. She stuffed her phone back in her pocket. She'd have to deal with Charlie later. If he didn't understand why she couldn't make the presentation because her niece had been abducted, then so be it. She'd let the cards fall where they would. Abby was the focus until they got things resolved. She couldn't let Chase down again.

Chase looked up from his computer, stretching his neck left and right, "I think I might be able to fabricate a fake dose for them," he mumbled, staring back down at his laptop.

Jess's heart skipped a beat, "Are you sure that's a good idea? I mean, you said you thought they would probably test whatever you gave them. If they do and they realize it's not the real deal, they're going to kill Abby."

"You're probably right, but what choice do I have? I have to give them something."

"Give them the real ABG!" Jess yelled. "What's the conflict here? Your daughter has been abducted. Go find the samples you have and let's jot down this formula and get it to these people and get Abby back!" As the words came out of her mouth, Jess felt guilty. She knew giving up the formula and the samples would condemn Chase to life in jail, that was if they were even able to get Abby back. Jess swallowed and held up her hands, "I'm sorry. I shouldn't have said that."

Before Chase could respond, Jess's phone rang. It was Saunders. "Hello?"

"Jess, it's Detective Saunders again. You have a minute?"

"I guess."

"Listen, I was wondering if you could come back downtown. Now, don't hang up on me," he chuckled. "Actually, we found something I think you might want to see. Any chance that might happen?"

By the way he was talking, the words coming out slowly and softly, Jess could tell he needed her to come and meet him but didn't want to push it. "You mean at the bank?"

"Sure."

"Okay, I'm sitting in front of the lab. Is that where you and your brother are?"

For a minute, Jess was confused. How did Saunders know they were back at the lab? "Yes. How did you know that?"

"Lucky guess and I ran the license plate of the only vehicle in the parking lot." There was a pause, "Will you come down?"

"Sure. Give me a minute."

As Jess hung up from the call, she stared at Chase. He hadn't moved. There was information on his screen that Jess couldn't decipher. "Listen, that was Detective Saunders. He found something at the bank he wants me to look at. He's waiting for me out front. Let me know if you hear anything else, okay?"

"Okay."

As Jess turned and walked away from Chase, she had a sinking feeling. She wasn't exactly sure that leaving Chase alone in the lab was the smartest plan, but what choice did she have?

Jess stepped out of the elevator and trotted to the doors, giving a wave to Sully as she ran by, "See you later," he called behind her. Out in the bright sunshine, Jess saw the navy-blue car that Detective Saunders drove right by the front door. As she approached, he got out, leaning his forearms across the top of the car. "Thanks for coming down."

Jess slid into the car on the passenger side and fastened her seatbelt. Detective Saunders must've been driving for a while because the air conditioning was blowing strong and cool. As she settled into her seat, she felt butterflies gathering in her stomach. "What did you find at the bank?" she said, as Detective Saunders put the vehicle into gear. For a moment, she wondered if he'd found Abby's body and wouldn't tell her on the phone. "It's not Abby, is it?"

He glanced at her as he pulled out of the industrial park, "No, nothing like that. It's just that sometimes these cases take time to evolve after something happens. You know, we go in all lights and sirens making sure everybody's safe and secure. After that, the real work begins."

"And that real work helped you find something?"

"It did. It's nothing big, but I thought you might want to see it for yourself." The police radio in the car chirped some information about a traffic stop somewhere else in Tucson that interrupted their conversation. Detective Saunders glanced over at Jess and said, "How are you holding up?"

The fact that someone was concerned about her well-being took Jess off guard. She was used to being strong, toughing things out. She'd had to learn to be that way after she lost her parents. Jess caught a sharp breath in the back of her throat, "I'm okay, I guess."

"You know, it's okay if you're not. You were part of the bank robbery this morning, too."

Jess was surprised at how compassionate he was being toward her. She choked out the words, "But Abby..."

Detective Saunders glanced at her, his eyes soft, and nodded, "I know. I know you're worried about your niece. We all are. Have you heard from the kidnappers yet?"

The question hung in the air. No one knew about the call from the kidnappers except for Jess, Chase, and Piper. The kidnappers had been very clear not to involve the police or tell them or they would kill Abby immediately. Based on what she just saw that morning, she took their threat seriously, not to mention if she told Saunders about the call, that would open the door to having to explain about ABG, which she couldn't do. Jess swallowed, "No, nothing yet. I'm hoping maybe they drop her off somewhere and she can get to a phone and call us." Jess stared and looked out the window, hoping the detective didn't pick up the fact that she was lying through her teeth.

"I really hope that's the case."

Jess looked at Saunders as he drove. He didn't look any

more excited about the drive to the bank than he might have looked going to the grocery store. Staring at his finger, Jess didn't see a ring. "Do you have a family, Detective?"

Saunders glanced at her and then turned back to the road. "I don't have any kids, if that's what you're asking me. Never been married. I have a couple of nephews, but with my job, I don't get to see them very often."

Jess turned toward the window, watching the desert pass along the side of the car, dotted with stores and homes here and there. "I don't get to see Abby much, either."

"That must have made today really hard."

"It did..."

Saunders must have sensed that Jess needed to talk about anything else than Abby. "That baseball field right over there," he pointed, "That's where I play softball with some of the guys from work a couple nights a week."

Jess tried to smile. "What's the name of your team?"

"The Rockets."

"Not very original."

"I know. We were trying to decide what to call ourselves late one night after a few too many beers at the Shiny Cactus. No one had any better ideas, so that was it. Have you ever been there?"

Jess shook her head no, "I know where it is, but no, I haven't been there." She turned back to the window, not wanting to talk anymore.

As Jess and Detective Saunders got closer to the crime scene, she could see that the area was still largely barricaded. It'd only been a few hours since the robbery happened, after all, so it made sense in her mind. The block around the diner and bank were still cordoned off, though there were no more ambulances or firetrucks sitting outside of the bank. Detective Saunders pulled the car up behind a line of other Tucson

Police Department cruisers, blocking them in. As he put the car into park, he glanced at Jess, "Let's go."

When Jess pulled on the door handle and cracked it open, she could hear the murmur of people talking in low voices all around her. The law enforcement personnel at the scene seemed to have formed groups of twos and threes, some of them conferring over tablets, looking serious, and others standing off to the side with what Jess guessed were cups of coffee in their hands, smiles on their faces as if they were sharing stories of their child's baseball game from the night before or the concert they were planning on attending that weekend. The contrast was startling. A little bit of bile rose in the back of Jess's throat. Did they know a child was missing? Why were they smiling? Jess pushed the thought out of her head and turned to look at Detective Saunders. He was waiting for her, standing in front of the car. "You okay?"

"Yes. I'm sorry. Just got distracted."

"This way," he said tilting his head in the direction of the bank.

As Jess followed him down the sidewalk, she caught a glimpse of herself in the reflection of one of the windows of the businesses nearby. Her dark, shoulder-length hair was pushed behind one ear, the light blue striped shirt she'd put on that morning pulled out on one side and tucked in on the other. She looked disheveled. She felt disheveled. As they walked, she tugged her shirt down back into place and tried to stand up a little straighter. It didn't make any difference. Abby was still gone.

Outside the bank, the doors were propped open, both the first set that led outside and the inner set that people passed through in order to get into the lobby. Jess stopped just inside the door, staring at what had been a normal place of business just a few hours before. A memory from before the robbery flashed before her eyes, the small clusters of people at the teller's counter, a bank employee smiling and waving goodbye to a family that was in front of them in line, the manager, hunched over his desk, staring at a computer screen...

Everything was different now.

People wearing FBI T-shirts and gloves roamed around the space. Some of them were kneeling, taking pictures of minute objects, others were interviewing bank employees. Jess saw the bank manager, his head in his hands, sitting at his desk with an FBI agent and another police officer standing over him, asking him questions. Off to her right, there were discarded medical gloves and a couple small pieces of medical tape on the ground left behind from where the paramedics had raced in to care for the woman who'd had the heart attack during the robbery. Near the doors on her left-hand side, there was a piece of duct tape and two discarded hoods wrinkled on the floor. Jess shivered, thinking about what it felt like to not be able to see or speak and having no idea what was going on around her.

Jess felt a warm hand on her elbow as Detective Saunders pulled her toward the back of the bank, glancing at her, his voice in a whisper, "This way." They passed a couple smaller groups of people working, then rounded the corner into a small hallway that led to what looked like the vault. Jess stopped for a second, staring at what she saw in front of her. The vault door looked exactly like something she would've imagined out of a movie — tall and round and at least three feet thick, with large rotating handles on the outside of the door. Inside, there were shelves where money and papers were stacked, but no safety deposit boxes. As Jess thought about it, it made sense. The bank personnel wouldn't want people off the street accessing their safety deposit box in front of millions of dollars. Too tempting. Too many opportunities for loss or error. Banks survived on not making those. Detective Saunders led her inside of the vault and then stopped, pointing, "Here. This is what I wanted to show you."

Jess took a couple steps forward and looked to her right. One of the shelving units, filled with stacks of cash carefully wrapped in clear shrink wrap had been moved off to the side. Behind it, near the floor, there was a hole that couldn't have been more than about two feet in diameter. Jess squinted her eyes a little bit and then looked at Detective Saunders, "You think they got out through here?"

He nodded. "We sent a couple agents through and it comes out on the other side in an abandoned mechanic's garage. They could have easily concealed their getaway vehicle there as well as using it as a staging area."

"You think that's how they got Abby out of the building?"

"I do."

"I want to see for myself." Without thinking, Jess bent down and pushed herself through the hole, ignoring Detective Saunders behind her calling to her to come back.

The hole was narrow and dark for the first three or four feet. Jess pulled her phone out of her back pocket and turned on the flashlight so she could see where she was going. She had to scoot along on the ground on her stomach but just ahead, it looked like things changed.

On the other side of the tunnel that had been dug through the vault, the area opened up into something that looked a lot more like a cavern, probably a void between buildings when the area had been built up decades ago. Jess pulled her body to an upright position, brushing the dirt off her shirt and pants. It smelled like a combination of dust and dampness. A metal ladder was leaning against the side of what looked to be an opening into a dry sewer line. From living in Arizona for so long, Jess knew that the sewers were only there in case of torrential rains, the desert sand unable to absorb any water at all. It could cause major flooding in no time flat. She stared up. A single work lightbulb with a thin layer of dust covering it glowed from the ceiling. From the looks of it, whoever had done the robbery had been working on the hole into the back of the vault for weeks, if not months. Doing some quick calculations in her head, Jess realized the kind of work they did would have needed jackhammers or other power tools. How no one had heard the commotion was a mystery. Whoever had kidnapped Abby had spent many a long night there working on digging the final hole into the bank vault. It was methodical, patient. Sitting on the edge of the hole with her feet dangling down, Jess realized it didn't bode well for Abby. Her stomach sank. Her gut, and her experience as an intelligence analyst, told her these were no common thieves. She and Chase and Abby were caught up in something bigger. Much bigger.

From her left side, she heard a grunt. Detective Saunders came wriggling his way through the same hole Jess did. "Just because I wanted to show you the hole didn't mean I wanted you to go through it." The words came out with a bit of an edge to them.

Jess couldn't tell if he was mad, but it didn't matter whether he was or wasn't. She didn't care if he was frustrated or not. He'd invited her to the bank. What did he expect -- that she'd stand around, cry and wring her hands? That's not who she was. Jess needed to see for herself. "Whoever did this spent a lot of time thinking and planning this out. How much money did they get away with?"

Detective Saunders pushed himself into a seated position, brushing off his jeans, "When the guys said it was a tight hole, they weren't lying." He looked at her, "The money? That's the thing. Best the bank manager can tell, they didn't take anything at all. Not one penny. They've got people from their headquarters coming in to be sure, but that's the initial thought."

A pit formed in Jess's stomach. That could only mean one thing, she realized. They targeted Abby and didn't want to get more than a kidnapping pinned on them if they got caught. It was as plain and simple as day. They were mitigating the situation the entire time. The whole thing had been a setup. Or maybe it wasn't...

Sitting in the dark, Jess realized the robbers had no way of knowing Abby would be with her today. They could fairly assume that Jess would show up at the bank with the fake paperwork she was supposed to drop off — after all, that was the only explanation for the strange request with a tight deadline. But when Abby showed up and they figured out who she was, that must've made more sense to them than grabbing Jess. A wave of nausea rolled over her. If they were this well-planned and this well-rehearsed, there was no telling what they would do to get what they wanted. And that was the ABG.

"I want to see the rest of it," Jess said, putting her foot on one of the rungs of the ladder. Not waiting for permission, she climbed down into a dry culvert that had to be eight feet in diameter. It was almost big enough to drive an ATV through, she realized, wondering if that's how they got the power tools they needed to the back of the bank in order to break through the wall behind the vault.

"If you want to see the rest of it, the FBI agents told me it's just straight down this culvert and up the ladder at the other end. Fairly simple. But listen, you can't touch anything when we get to the other side. You'll contaminate the crime scene. The FBI will freak out."

"You can take my fingerprints so you can exclude me if you want." Before Detective Saunders could answer, Jess took off at a quick walk, still using the flashlight from her cell phone, although the robbers had taken the time to string more work lights the entire distance, or maybe the FBI had, Jess wasn't sure. Each step on the metal culvert made a hollow, ringing sound that echoed off the walls. On the edges, Jess saw a few pieces of debris -- an old soda can, a single shoe, a tennis ball black with mold. For a second, she was surprised that the detective didn't argue with her about seeing the rest of the crime scene. That couldn't be the standard operating procedure, she realized.

A minute later, Jess saw the other ladder. It matched the first one just outside the bank. She crawled up the rungs and found herself in exactly what Detective Saunders had described — a mechanic's garage. There were tools on one of the walls on the side and a car lift on the other, the kind used to do oil changes and change tires. In between, there was a large space, big enough to park two or three other cars. Jess heard Detective Saunders climb out of the hole behind her. "Where is this place?"

"We're in an old, abandoned garage about a block from the bank. The FBI pulled the records already and it went out of business two or three years ago and then was bought about six months ago by another company, but they haven't done anything with it.

Jess was immediately suspicious, "A shell company?"

Detective Saunders cocked his head to the side, "Why would you say that?"

"It's just something I see at work a lot."

"Oh really? And what kind of work do you do?"

Jess wanted to answer his question but not give him too much information. "I do research for a think tank based out of Washington. No big deal. Just organizational stuff." The idea that a shell company would purchase a property they could use for their own purposes was nothing new in Jess's business. It was normal. Standard even. A few years back, Jess had spent three months trying to track down all of the shell corporations and aliases for a grassroots movement on US soil that looked like it could be troublesome over time. Criminals were getting better and better about hiding their identity. Some people thought that technology made everything transparent. In Jess's world, it just made everything even murkier.

"That's interesting. And to answer your question, yes, the

FBI is tracking down the owners of the building, whoever they are. The timing does seem a little fishy, don't you think?"

Jess nodded, looking at the space around her, imagining what Abby must have gone through. Did they let her take the hood off while they moved her through the tunnel? If they didn't, the poor girl had to be terrified trying to crawl on her belly, the hands of the men grabbing at her to pull her through. Jess would have been. A wave of guilt passed over her.

This was supposed to be me.

She had an urge to tell Detective Saunders everything — about the fake bank papers, about how bringing Abby was a last-minute thing, and about Chase and his work, but the artificial female voice of the kidnappers telling them not to tell the police rattled in her mind. They could be watching her right now. She would never know it.

Jess glanced back at Detective Saunders. He was watching her, sizing her up. "Why did you want me to see this?"

"Well, I have to be honest, my intention was to show you the hole, not to take a dive through it, but yes, I wanted you to see this."

"But why?"

The question hung out in the air for a moment, as if Detective Saunders was wondering what to say next. "First, you seem like a person who's more comfortable with the facts than conjecture. I get that. I'm the same way. The other issue I have is that if these people took all this time to commandeer the garage and tunnel into the vault and didn't take any money, why would that be? In my mind, that means the target was your family and I'm wondering why."

Jess felt the heat rise in her face and was grateful for the shadows of the garage, hoping that Detective Saunders wouldn't see her expression. She couldn't tell him anything. Not one bit of it or it would put Abby's life in danger, "I'm not sure."

"Ms. Montgomery, I've been on the job for ten years. Something isn't right. What's going on here?"

Jess's eyes darted back and forth, looking for the exit, not wanting to answer his question. Abby's life depended on her keeping her mouth shut. Jess pointed, "Over there. I'm going to go out that door. I need a ride back to Chase's house. That's where my car is. Can you drop me off?"

Detective Saunders squinted for a second, "All right. I'll drive you. We can finish our talk on the way to your brother's house. I have some questions for him, too."

I'll bet you do, Jess thought.

9

S itting in the detective's cruiser on the way back to Chase's house, Jess stared out the window. Though it was even close to lunchtime, every bone and muscle in Jess's body ached from the strain of the morning. At least a few of the pieces were starting to come together, but it wasn't enough to help her and Chase find Abby, not without someone helping them. So far, the only hope the two of them had was Detective Saunders. Unfortunately, he had more questions than answers, questions that Jess couldn't answer for him. If someone was going to tell him about the demand for the ABG, it wasn't going to be her. She wouldn't be responsible for what happened to Chase's family.

Stopped at a red light, Jess saw the people in the car next to her -- a man, a woman, and a couple of kids in the backseat. She blinked, thinking of Chase's family and wondering if it would ever be whole again. Her eyes moved from the family in the car to a young couple walking on the sidewalk, holding hands, passing a few storefronts — a silver and turquoise jewelry dealer, a coffee shop, and then a bookstore. It was one of the things Jess liked about Tucson the most, the small-town feel even though it was a sprawling city. At least, it used to be until this morning.

Jess looked back at Detective Saunders. He was focused on the road. He hadn't said anything since they got into the car except asking where Chase lived. Jess wasn't sure how to interpret the silence. Was he trying to freeze her out to guilt her into giving him more information? Or maybe he was just giving her some space to process everything that happened in the last few hours? She hoped it was the latter and not the former, though, at some point, she knew she and Chase would have to give him answers of some sort whether they liked it or not.

The cruiser snaked its way back into Chase's development, hugging the corners of the curves as they passed a few other roads in the subdivision before making their way to Chase's house. "That's it right there," Jess said, pointing. "That's my car."

As Detective Saunders pulled the cruiser up behind Jess's car and put it into park, her phone buzzed again. Charlie. Distracted by what'd happened, she'd forgotten to text him back. "Everything okay, Jess?" the text read. Once she got rid of Detective Saunders she'd have to deal with Charlie. She sent a quick text back, "Yeah, everything's okay. Sorry for the radio silence. More later." At least she hoped that bought her some time.

Though she wished Detective Saunders would just drop her off at Chase's house, she heard his door open at the same time as hers. It wasn't actually a surprise that he'd want to follow her in. At least he was a man of his word when it came to questioning Chase.

Before Jess could walk Detective Saunders to the back door, Chase charged out through the garage, his eyes wide. "I just got back here. What happened? Did you find Abby?" he stammered.

Jess shook her head, "No, not yet." She glanced at Detective

Saunders and then back at Chase, "Detective Saunders, you remember my brother Chase?"

He nodded. "I had a couple of follow-up questions and wanted to update you on the information we have right now. What we know is that your daughter was definitely targeted. Why, we're not exactly sure."

Chase squinted at him, "How exactly do you know that?"

"Well, we made a significant discovery just about forty-five minutes ago. No money was taken from the bank, not a dime."

"Nothing? They didn't take any money at all?"

"That's correct. And the act was about as intentional as it gets. They spent a lot of time working on their approach and escape plans. We can tell from the way that they exited the building."

Chase looked back and forth at both of them. Jess chewed her lip for a minute, the thought passing over her that she wasn't sure how Chase would deal with the escape route the kidnappers dragged Abby through. It spoke of such intentionality and planning that it was scary. "Listen, Chase, what Detective Saunders wanted to show me was how they managed to get out of the bank with Abby. It looks like someone, whoever has her, accessed a dry sewer between the bank and an abandoned mechanic's garage about a block away. They used some sort of jackhammers or chisels to break through the wall between the bank and an abandoned space between buildings. They hid the hole behind a rack of cash in the vault."

Chase furrowed his eyebrows together, frowning, "What you're saying is they grabbed Abby on purpose? That's what you're saying? They had this whole thing planned from the beginning. It was never about the money?"

Jess squinted, a little confused at Chase's questions. He knew what the kidnappers were actually after, the ABG. Was this a ploy to get Detective Saunders to back off? Jess wasn't sure. "That's right," Jess said slowly, "Detective Saunders feels like the kidnappers are targeting the family."

Chase blinked for a second and then stared at Jess, "Wait, they didn't know Abby would be with you this morning. How could they?"

Jess nodded. As usual, her brother put the pieces together quickly and easily. "That's right."

"So, you were the actual target, Jess?"

Hearing the words come out of her brother's mouth gave her a lump in her throat the size of a boulder. She wasn't the cause of all of this, Chase's research was, but knowing none of them would be standing here if she hadn't invited Abby out for breakfast settled on her.

Jess glanced at Saunders. He seemed to be soaking in their conversation, looking for nuance that wasn't there. His eyes were narrowed, his lips open just a little, enough that Jess could tell he was memorizing everything they said.

Before any of them could say anything else, Chase looked down at his phone, which he was holding in his hand. It was ringing. He held it up so Jess could see. It was the unknown number again. Jess opened her eyes wide. What were they going to do? Detective Saunders was standing right there with them. Her heart started to beat a little faster. This was exactly what they were trying to avoid. If the kidnappers found out that Detective Saunders was with them, they would kill Abby. There was no question in her mind they'd do exactly as promised and then Jess and Chase would have no chance of getting her back. Jess looked at Detective Saunders and put her finger up to her mouth, telling him to be quiet. He cocked his head at her, suddenly realizing there was more going on than he knew. Chase answered the call.

The same computer-generated female voice they'd heard earlier crackled through the air, the high pitch sounding like it almost belonged to a child, the words stunted and clipped. "We hope you've been making progress on getting us what we asked for, Chase," the voice said sweetly. "You currently have six hours left before time runs out. Remember, no police or we kill Abby. If you do not cooperate, everyone will pay the price. We will be in touch." As the call ended, Jess heard another chirp on Chase's phone. Jess watched as Chase tapped on the screen, his hands shaking, his color becoming ashen in the bright sunshine as he opened it and held it up for Jess to see. It was a picture of Piper and Abby. It looked like they were walking together somewhere, both of them smiling, Abby's dark wavy hair cascading out behind her, a broad smile on Piper's face, her purse tucked under her arm.

"That looks like a picture I took of them downtown a couple of months ago!" Chase's face went slack, "What does that mean?"

"I think you could fairly say that whoever is targeting your family has just expanded the threat to include everyone," Detective Saunders said dryly. "Now, would someone care to tell me exactly what is going on here?"

Jess's mouth was suddenly dry. "I think we better get inside of the house. Detective, you should probably move your car out from in front of the house in case they're watching us."

Detective Saunders looked at Jess and gave a brief nod, "Okay, if that means I can get some of my questions answered."

While the detective was outside moving his vehicle, Jess ran up the driveway trying to catch up to Chase. He'd charged back inside the house. He and Piper were in the kitchen, leaning over the counter. Piper barely looked up at Jess when she walked in. Apparently, even the kidnapping of one of their family members hadn't softened her attitude towards Jess. "Jess, can you tell Piper how they got Abby out of the bank?" Chase said.

"Yeah," she sighed, looking down and realizing there was dirt all over the front of her shirt and her pants. She tried to brush it off, but scooting on her belly through the tunnel had ground it into the fibers of the fabric. "The kidnappers broke a hole through the wall between the bank and some sort of an empty void between buildings. Then they broke through the floor and accessed a dry sewer culvert. When I walked through the culvert…"

"Wait? You walked through the culvert? What are you, some amateur detective now?" Piper said sarcastically.

Chase covered his wife's hand with his own, "Honey, I know you're upset. We all are. You need to hear this. It might help you understand what happened to Abby."

Piper's eyes widened, her face in a grimace, "I don't want to understand what happened to Abby! I want her back. Why aren't the police and the FBI investigating? I don't understand it! You and your sister," she pointed a long-manicured finger at Chase, "the two of you are always in cahoots. And you," Piper turned her ire at Jess, "you are always figuring out ways to worm your way into our family. It's not your family! It's ours! Can't you understand that?!"

Jess's face burned with the pain of the words. She always knew that Piper didn't really want her around. Piper hadn't been that obvious until today. Until now, Piper had reluctantly agreed to let Jess be part of their life, at least a little bit. Jess turned and walked outside, slamming the door behind her. She wasn't going to sit in the kitchen and let Piper scream at her. Abby was her family, too. What Piper didn't realize was that Jess was the actual target. Not Abby. Walking out into the garage, her eyes stinging with tears, Jess realized Piper probably would be happy if she knew that Jess had been the one the kidnappers wanted until they saw Abby. Jess imagined Chase giving Piper the news, "Oh honey, Jess's been taken by kidnappers. I'm worried about her…"

Jess imagined Piper's response, "Oh, that's nice. I have lunch with my girlfriends at noon today. See you later!"

Jess sat down on the back bumper of Chase's car, wiping the tears from her face and bracing her hands against the cool metal. She had the urge to storm out of the garage, get in her car and go home. If Piper was going to be that cruel, then maybe they could figure out how to get Abby back on their own. After all, Chase had what the kidnappers wanted, and it wasn't Jess. It was the ABG.

But something kept Jess seated on that bumper.

A moment later, Detective Saunders walked up to the garage. Jess noticed he'd pulled his shirt out of his pants, covering his badge. "All set. I put the car around the corner at a clubhouse or something."

Jess knew where he was talking about. The development that Piper and Chase lived in had a small clubhouse with a pool, a weight room, and a party room. A few years back, they'd had Abby's eighth birthday there, the room was decorated with balloons and streamers and a big cake. It had mostly been a fun afternoon. Jess remembered she and Piper circling each other at opposite ends of the room like fighters preparing to do battle, but not coming out of their corners.

"Where are Chase and his wife?"

"In the house. You can go through the back door." Jess pointed over her shoulder, sniffling a bit.

"Okay. Will you be out here in case I have follow-up questions?"

"Yeah, sure."

Saunders turned back, "Are you okay?"

"Okay enough."

Jess heard the back door close behind Detective Saunders as he went into the house. Being so far from the kitchen, she couldn't hear what was going on. Was Piper being nicer to Detective Saunders than she'd been to Jess? Part of her wanted to get up and go in the house to see what was going on, but part of her didn't. Piper's comments had cut Jess to the core. She didn't want to worm her way into Chase's family. She just wanted a relationship with her brother and her niece. Jess stared down at her hands. Her knuckles were white from gripping the bumper. Jess didn't have her own family, not yet. She'd never found the right guy, though she thought she'd been close a couple times. Her work made it difficult for her to concentrate on a relationship much past the initial stages of flirting and eating out. Just the mental brainpower it took to do what Charlie needed her to do sucked up most of her time and her energy.

From the edge of the garage, Jess heard a noise. She looked up to see Roxie, Chase's beagle mix standing at the edge of the garage, panting. Roxie came over and nuzzled Jess's hand, looking for a back scratch. Jess happily obliged. It was the most normal thing she'd done in hours. The little dog looked up at Jess with watery brown eyes as if asking her if everything was all right. "No," Jess whispered to Roxie. "Things are most definitely not all right."

A few more minutes passed by with nothing happening inside the house that Jess could hear. She got up and started to pace, hoping her mind would kick into gear and help her figure out something, anything that would help them get Abby back. But it didn't. She sat back down on the bumper, wondering if she should stay when the back door closed behind her. It was Detective Saunders. He had a scowl on his face.

"Your brother said he doesn't want my help. He doesn't want any help at all. Said this is a family matter and that I should leave."

From the look on the detective's face, Jess could tell he was angry, the skin pulling his features taught, his lips thin. Jess held her hands up, "I'm sorry. It's his daughter. I don't know what else to say."

"I think this is a mistake, to be honest. And I might leave peaceably, for the moment, but I don't think the FBI is going to be quite so cooperative since the kidnappers broke into a bank vault to get to her." From his back pocket, he pulled out a business card and handed it to Jess. "If you change your mind, give me a call. Day or night."

Jess nodded, looking at the card as he walked away, "Detective Jamison Saunders" it read. She stared at the letters as Saunders disappeared down the driveway. Jess's eyes followed him as he turned down the street, walking on the sidewalk to the clubhouse where he'd parked his car. She felt her heart sink a little bit. Detective Saunders, Jamison, had been fair with her. He'd let her give him the information at her own pace without pressuring her and he even let her crawl through the escape route without pulling on both of her ankles and yanking her out of the hole and slapping handcuffs on her before she got too far. He seemed like a patient man, but she wondered what would happen if his patience ran out.

Before Jess could think about it much more, she heard the back door open and close behind her, watching Chase come down the two wooden steps into the garage. "I'm so sorry about that, Jess. It's just, Piper, she's under so much strain right now."

Jess jumped up, heat running to her cheeks, "From what? She's always treated me this way, Chase. She doesn't work, so exactly what kind of stress is she under? And she wasn't in the bank robbery this morning. I was. It would be nice if she could show a little bit of compassion at least once in a while." The words came out in a tumble. Jess hadn't meant for them to do so. She'd always been careful about not putting Chase between the two main women in his life — Piper and Jess. Piper didn't seem to have any problem with their younger sister, Rachel, but dealing with Jess was an entirely different issue.

Chase blinked and then looked at Jess. "You're right. I'm sorry. There are times she's just insufferable. No, she's not being fair to you. Yes, she should show a little bit more compassion. I'll talk to her. That's all I can do."

"And what about Abby?"

Chase glanced around the garage before answering, "What happened to the detective?"

"Jamison?"

"Oh, so now you two are on a first-name basis?"

"Not really. He just gave me his business card before he left. His first name is on there."

"We didn't tell him anything," Chase sighed. "I think Piper was about ready to, but then she clammed up all of a sudden. It was strange."

"Where is she now?" Jess wanted to be prepared in case Piper decided to come screaming out of the back door of the house for another round of the blame Jess game.

"She's locked herself in the bedroom. Said since the actual target was you that you and I have to fix this."

It was just like Piper to push off the responsibility onto someone else. "No pressure, right?" The fact that Piper would insist that Jess and Chase somehow go up against a well-planned kidnapping plot was somehow funny to Jess. She shook her head.

"Right." Chase leaned against the back of his car, standing next to Jess, his arms crossed in front of his chest. Neither of them said anything for a second, both lost in their own thoughts. Jess's mind cycled through the memory of crawling through the hole at the back of the bank, to the presentation she was supposed to be working on that morning, to Piper screaming at her. She felt like her emotions were on overload, as though someone had charged her skin with a current of electricity. For a second, she wondered if she'd ever be able to sleep again. She shook the thought away. Abby. They had to figure out what to do about Abby.

Jess sighed, "So, since it is up to us," she said sarcastically, "What do you want to do?"

"I don't know," Chase said, pushing himself off of the car

and turning to face her, "I think I'm going to have to call my boss and tell him what's going on. See if they'll give me the ABG so I can get Abby back. We don't have that much time left."

"But you said they wouldn't do that. You said it was a matter of national security, right? What would make them help you now?"

Chase started to pace, his arms crossed in front of his chest, "I don't know! What else am I supposed to do?"

Jess sighed. No answers were coming to her. "We've got to think this through. These guys have apparently spent months planning this. There's no telling how deep the leaks go. And, if you call your boss, they may lock everything down. That won't leave us with any options at all."

"I feel like I've become part of one of your intelligence briefs."

Jess raised her eyebrows. What he was saying wasn't entirely false. "Well, maybe that's the way that we need to look at this. I remember a case from a few years ago. It had to do with a leak in the FBI office in Oklahoma. Tulsa, if I remember right. Anyway, there was an organization that had spent years getting people in place so they could get information on moving terrorists into the United States through the southern border. I mean, these guys went to such great lengths. They had people at every level of the organization — we found a janitor, a landscaping company, electrical contractors, and even some people in catering that had ties to a cartel from Mexico. On the face of it, it looked like nothing, but when you put the pieces together, it was like an octopus that had tentacles everywhere in the organization. By the time we figured it out, so much information had been leached out of that office they had to shut it down temporarily, send in some FBI specialized task force to remove bugs and other surveillance equipment and then reopen the office. It was a nightmare."

"And you think that's what's happened here?"

"I have no idea. I'm just telling you to think of what's possible. Look, they managed to fabricate official enough looking mortgage documents that it made me show up at the bank this morning. And I do this stuff for a living! Who knows if they've been surveilling you in the lab or what else has been going on."

Jess could tell the idea was settling in on Chase. Although he wasn't as up to speed with intelligence gathering and analysis as she was, the thinking he'd done to develop ABG was much the same type of mental exercise. As she waited for him to speak, Jess realized there was no telling how deep the plot had gone. Quiet settled around the two of them. Off in the distance, she could hear a dog bark. It wasn't Roxie, but down the block, maybe. A car passed by, the tires crunching on grit from the desert breezes on the road. Jess started to think about the ABG again. How was it possible that anyone knew about the ABG if it was a classified project and only Chase was working on it? "You said the ABG is classified, right?"

"Yeah, that's right. It's more for medical use than anything else. I can't figure out why they want it."

Jess shook her head, "Listen, that's not the right question to be asking. The right question to be asking isn't why they want it, it's who wants it. Who comes before the why. Whoever is looking for the ABG has a problem and they're looking for something to solve it. And it must be a pretty serious problem for them to go to these lengths."

As Jess watched Chase absorb the information, he became a little paler, as if the idea that the people who'd taken Abby were far more dangerous than he ever imagined. Jess didn't want to hurt him with the information, but she needed to make sure he understood exactly what they were dealing with. The pieces started to click together in her mind — the bank paperwork, the carefully executed escape route, the overly cheerful computer-generated voice that communicated with them, and now the picture of Abby and Piper together. It was a clear-cut escalation campaign, designed to keep Chase teetering on the edge. It wasn't enough to make him shut down, but it was definitely enough to get his attention and keep him moving forward to meet their demands, not to mention question himself.

And that's what the kidnappers needed Chase to do... question himself.

In some of the most difficult cases Jess worked, the difference between whether the classified intelligence got out into the community or didn't was the amount of uncertainty the target experienced. More uncertainty meant more control. There wasn't much more control than holding the life of a child in your hands. Jess swallowed and then looked hard at Chase. He was staring down at the ground, pacing back and forth. Three steps one direction and then three steps back. It was something she'd seen him do when they were young when he was trying to solve a problem. Habits die hard, she thought.

A second later, he spoke through gritted teeth. "I understand what you're saying, Jess. But where does that leave me? What am I supposed to do? How can I possibly get Abby back?"

"I think we need to go back to the lab. See if you can quickly fabricate some samples. I think we need to be prepared to give them what they want, or at least some version of it."

"What about the detective? What are we gonna do about him?"

"Technically, you sent him away. I don't think he can pursue the case from the kidnapping angle, at least not too much, without your permission. He can look at the robbery, but with nothing missing, he's kind of stuck. Saunders needs our cooperation. We might not be able to stop him, but we don't have to give him any information. Now, if the FBI catches up with us, that might be something completely different. We are gonna have to cooperate at some point, but maybe we can put it off for a while."

"What you're saying is we have to outsmart the kidnappers and outrun the police."

"Something like that."

Chase nodded and sighed, "All right, let me go in the house and tell Piper we're headed back to the lab. I'll see if she wants to come, but I don't think that's very likely."

Jess didn't say anything. She just watched as Chase turned toward the door into the house, weaving his way between the two cars, one of the steps giving a little squeak as he put his weight on it. For a moment, quiet descended over Jess. She checked the time on her cell phone. How had only a couple hours gone by? Time was moving alternately very fast and very slow. Time that could tick down to the end of Abby's life if they weren't careful.

The image of Abby's smiling face popped up in Jess's mind again. Jess remembered the last soccer game she'd attended. Piper had been out of town visiting friends and Chase had invited Jess to come. She stuffed her pockets with candy and showed up at the game with two yellow pom-poms in Abby's school colors. She found Chase perched up in the stands, his eyes never leaving his daughter. As she passed him a box of licorice she'd bought at the local drugstore, she didn't say anything, absorbing the sweet moment of watching her brother watch his daughter.

Jess stared down the driveway as a landscaping truck passed by, the engine rattling and thrumming as the trailer behind it bounced along on the pavement, branches sticking out from inside. It looked like the tanned crew had been trimming trees nearby, two of them in the truck and two of them sitting down inside the bed. They must not be going far, Jess thought.

Around her, she could hear birds chirping and the rustle of some small critters in the landscaping on the side of Chase's driveway. Her breathing slowed, but the weight of Abby's disappearance still set heavy on her. They had to get Abby back. They couldn't turn to the police or the FBI because the kidnapper said they would kill her. Unfortunately, Jess believed them. These were the kind of people that had a contingency planned for every circumstance. Probably military or former military, Jess thought, doing some quick calculations in her head. They'd been outmaneuvered before the game ever started.

Jess chewed her lip. It was one thing to do intelligence analysis on paper, but she'd never worked as a field agent. Her stomach sank a little bit. What if they couldn't find Abby? What if somehow in the next few hours, she lost her nerve or forced Chase to make a wrong decision? Uncertainty poured over her. A child's life was in her hands. Jess knew that Chase wasn't in the mindset to make decisions. It was all on her.

Chase still hadn't come out of the house. Jess started to pace. What was he doing inside with Piper? Were they having an argument? Her palms sweaty, Jess sat back down on the bumper of the car, and drew in a deep breath, trying to still the pounding in her chest. She never felt this overwhelmed before. She knew the pieces of the puzzle were coming together, but not enough that anything made sense yet. Would it? Would they be able to figure out enough information to make enough of the right moves to be able to save Abby? Time was ticking and they were on the clock. Jess shook her head and held her breath for a second, feeling the air stopped in her lungs. What if the kidnappers killed Abby? Jess stood up. She couldn't focus on Abby dying. She had to focus on Abby living. And the only people that could make sure it happened were her and Chase.

10

By the time Chase's footsteps went back down the hallway, it was nearly one o'clock. Piper sat on the edge of the bed, dabbing at her eyes. She sat for another moment, listening and staring at the painting that had been hung on the opposite wall. It was one she'd found at an art show on the outskirts of Tucson a few years before, an oil painting of the mountains at sunset. When she saw it at the show, her first thought was that it matched the colors in their bedroom. Then she realized that looking at the mountains gave her peace. Not that she was an outdoorsy-hiking-in-the-desert-kind-of-gal, she thought, standing up and tugging her leggings up a little bit higher around her waist. But she did like the way it looked.

Piper walked to the window, pulling the curtain aside just a little bit, enough that she could see the corner of the street. If Chase and Jess were really leaving in a second, she'd see one of their cars through the corner of their yard, going down the street. There was only one way to exit their development, so they had to pass the window where she was standing. Licking her lips, she stared as she saw Jess's car go by.

They were gone.

Piper went to the bedroom door and opened it, feeling the rush of air on the other side. She looked towards the kitchen and turned the other direction, her bare feet making a quiet padding sound on the cool tile. Down two doors on the left, the door was closed. Abby's room. Piper put her hand on the doorknob and turned it, pushing it open.

Sunlight was pouring through the large bay window throwing sharp shadows on the carpet, lighting up the white walls with a golden glow. A pair of soccer cleats sat on the floor next to Abby's bed, even though Piper told her to keep them in the garage. Somehow, they always ended up in the house. The door to the adjoining bathroom was open. Piper wandered in, passed through the bedroom, and stopped in the bathroom, where Abby's toothbrush lay off to the side. She touched the handle of it and pulled her hand back, her stomach clenching in a knot. What had they done to her daughter?

Piper turned and walked to the bedroom, swallowing hard. She bent forward a little, tugging on the comforter on Abby's bed. Abby was pretty good about making it every day, but not always very good about doing it well. There were wrinkles, always wrinkles.

She couldn't spend one more minute in Abby's room. Everything about it looked and felt and smelled like Abby, slightly sweet and clean, like the floral shampoo she used. Piper went back to the bedroom she shared with Chase, except for those nights he didn't come home when he was cooped up in the lab, leaving the door open. When Chase was gone, she didn't mind it. A little alone time wasn't ever a bad thing, she reasoned. She sat back down on the edge of the bed, crossing one foot over the other as she pulled her phone out of her pocket. Looking at the screen, she found the phone number that had sent her a picture of Abby and dialed.

"I was wondering if you'd call," Landon said.

"Yeah, they just left. I'm not sure where they're headed. But Chase and Jess are together, just as you predicted." Piper glanced around the room for a second, "How's Abby? Is she okay? She's not hurt or anything, is she?"

"No, she's been a real trooper. I can tell she's scared, but who wouldn't be."

Piper swallowed, "I miss you. I want to see you. I can't wait for all of this to be over." The words came out of her mouth in a rush, far faster than she wanted them to. She and Landon had met by chance a few years before at a restaurant when Piper was out with her girlfriends. Piper thought it was some innocent flirting, after all, she was a married woman, but for some reason when Landon asked for her phone number, she'd given it to him. Not that she ever expected him to call.

The first call came about a week later. He asked if they could meet for coffee. Said he was having marital problems and that she seemed like someone who had her head screwed on straight. Piper remembered stammering on the phone a little bit, "I'm not sure. I don't know if my husband would be okay with this," she said to him.

"I just need some advice, Piper, that's all. I'd prefer to do it in person if that's okay with you."

Landon sounded so sad and lost at the time Piper didn't feel like she could refuse.

A few hours later, Piper met Landon at a local coffee shop. He told her the story of his wife and how they didn't have any children and had fertility problems and now they weren't getting along. What did Piper think he should do?

Two weeks later, after another one of their coffee dates while Abby was at school and Chase was at the office, Piper found herself in Landon's car doing something she never planned to do.

And now she was in love.

Landon was everything Chase wasn't — strong, courageous,

a man of decisiveness. Chase could barely decide what to order for dinner, let alone exude the kind of strength that Piper needed in a man. After meeting Landon and spending time with him, Piper wasn't sure why she married Chase. At the time, she thought his quirkiness and scientific brilliance were attractive. He was so cerebral, so different than so many of the other men she'd met.

Then, three months ago, things had changed. Piper had told Chase she was going on a weekend trip with a couple of friends from college he'd never met. There was no trip. It was a weekend away with Landon. They'd driven up into the mountains, to a little resort with tall pine trees and long walking trails. It was there that Landon said he wanted to spend the rest of his life with her, but there was something they needed to do first. When Piper first heard the plan to abduct Abby in order to get the ABG from Chase, she balked. "No, I can't do that to my family," she said to Landon, sitting up on the edge of the bed they were sharing. "How can you ask me to do that? Abby would be traumatized. And I have no way of knowing how Chase will respond."

"Piper, honey, you need to understand. This will save lives. Chase has a formula that could be out helping people right now, but he won't release it. I needed to protect my men, to protect lives in the field. All we're going to do is scare him a little bit. And, I promise, we won't hurt Abby. She'll walk out of the whole thing thinking it's a fun experience. I'll make sure she knows I know you. She'll have so much to tell her friends about."

Now, sitting on the edge of the bed, Piper wasn't so sure Landon was right. How could she have believed him? What kind of a mother was she to allow this? She tried to refocus on the conversation she was having with Landon. His gravelly voice penetrated her thoughts, "Where are you right now?"

"At the house still. What else do you need me to do? Landon, I'm lonely and scared."

"I know, baby. This will all be over soon. There's not much going on here. Want to meet?"

Piper's heart skipped a beat in her chest. Meeting Landon might be exactly what she needed. At least she could look into his eyes and make him promise her that Abby was okay. "Yes. I think that would be good."

"Okay. I'll see you in an hour. Saguaro Pass?"

Piper nodded. They'd met there before. It was a small park at the top of a canyon with a picturesque view of a big stand of Saguaro cactuses below. "Sure."

As the call ended, Piper checked her phone. It was about a half-hour drive from the house to the park where Landon wanted to meet. Piper suddenly felt sticky from her morning at yoga and decided to take a quick shower.

Ten minutes later, Piper opened the door to the bathroom, sliding into a pair of jeans and a loose top, her long blonde hair braided down her back. She dabbed on a little bit of makeup, some dark eyeliner, a couple coats of mascara, and pink lipstick. There wasn't time for much more.

Piper grabbed her purse and keys from the kitchen and went out to the Audi, starting it and checking in the rearview mirror before backing out of the driveway. There were always landscaping trucks and swimming pool maintenance people passing by. The last thing she needed to do would be to crash into one of them on her way to meet Landon.

As the road curved before her, Piper gripped the wheel a little bit more tightly. Her stomach was in knots. She stopped, waiting for the traffic to clear so she could pull out onto Mesa Boulevard, heading south, toward the freeway. Saguaro Pass was far enough away from home she didn't have to worry Chase would find her and Landon together. But now, driving the Audi, she felt a wave of nausea pass over her. She was a married woman who allowed her own daughter to be kidnapped by her lover. What had she become?

Piper turned off the air conditioning and rolled down the window; as if somehow the fresh air might blow her feelings away with the wind. Merging onto the freeway, she turned on some music. It was hip-hop, from the last time Abby was in the car. Piper swallowed and tapped the screen, switching to a pop station. Music filled the little car and Piper stared straight forward, keeping her eyes on the road.

The Saturday afternoon traffic had thinned out quite a bit, just a few cars scattered here and there, traveling north toward Phoenix or to some other destination. A couple of the cars she passed had rental stickers on them, families or couples who had come to Arizona to enjoy the hot, dry weather, defrosting from wherever they lived. Piper glanced off to her right, seeing the desert change a little bit as she drove. Tucson was largely flat, with mountains around it, much like Phoenix. A long time ago, Abby had done a report on why people settled near the mountains in Arizona. Piper chewed her lip for a second. Third grade, maybe? She discovered that people settled near the mountains because of the runoff of rainwater. Living in the desert wasn't easy, especially not back then, when drilling wells and siphoning water off of the Colorado River was nearly impossible.

A semi-truck passing her Audi startled Piper back into concentrating on the road. She checked the signs above — Maxwell Street, and then Tombstone Road, where she needed to get off. She felt like her heart skipped a beat. The closer she got, the more she was excited to see Landon, but she couldn't shake the feeling that she was just a little bit angry at herself for letting him take Abby. When they'd talked about it, Landon assured her that it would be like a field trip for Abby, but now that the day had come, Piper wasn't so sure. Abby had never met Landon. How could she? Piper was still married to Chase.

Chase.

Piper sighed and steered the car with one hand, trying to relax in the seat. What had happened to her marriage with Chase? Probably nothing from his end, she realized. Chase was just, well, Chase. He got up in the morning, ate the same breakfast every day, and then went to work. That's who he was really married to, Piper realized, his job. She straightened up in her seat. It's practically marital neglect, she realized, putting the blinker on to get off of the freeway.

On the ramp, she tapped the brake to slow the little Audi down. Butterflies formed in her stomach as she realized she was just a few minutes out from seeing Landon. He was the one she was meant to be with. Maybe when all this was over, maybe she'd leave Chase and take Abby and they could go live with Landon. Yes, that was a plan.

The Audi's engine automatically downshifted as she hit the first rise, going up the side of the mountain. The spot Landon chose for one of their rendezvous was beautiful. The road curved around the side of a low mountain, the desert below sweeping in front of anyone who stopped to look. It wasn't much more than an extra lane on the side of the highway with a placard explaining that Saguaro cactuses were protected and that the pass had one of the best views of many of them growing naturally in all of Arizona.

At the next stop sign, Piper looked in the rearview mirror, running her finger under her lip to clean up a little bit of pink lipstick that wasn't where it should be. She used her hand to fluff up her bangs and check to make sure there was no lipstick on her teeth. Chase didn't seem to care about how she looked anymore, but Landon did.

A minute later, her phone chirped, "Here. How far out are you?"

"Two minutes," she said into her phone, sending the text remotely.

Another set of butterflies formed in her stomach. Maybe this was a time to talk to Landon about moving in together. She was ready to leave Chase. She knew it.

Piper slowed the Audi down because the curves in the road were becoming more severe as she drove; the mountainside hanging over the left side of the road leaving no room for error, a drop-off on the right. It was a two-lane road, but just barely. Piper put two hands on the wheel and slowed down even a little bit more, not wanting to fly the Audi off the side of the road. If she swerved left, the Audi would go into the side of the mountain. If she swerved right, it would go off the side of a cliff and drop at least one hundred feet down to the desert floor.

As she pulled up at Saguaro Pass, Piper checked her rearview mirror. No cars behind her. That was a good sign. She put on her blinker anyway, hearing the clicking and seeing the light on her dashboard. She pressed the brake and pulled to the right. Landon's car was already there, parked off to the side. She saw the muscles of his back through his shirt as he stared out across the desert, looking away from her. Pulling the Audi up next to his car, she shut off the engine, just in time to see him turn and smile at her. All the misgivings she'd had on the drive over about letting him take Abby disappeared in that second. She knew she was supposed to be with him.

Sliding out of the car, she slammed the door behind her and ran over to him, giving him a hug and a kiss. "I'm so glad you had time to meet today. How are things going?"

He stepped back from her just a little bit, "Fine. We have everything under control."

Piper grabbed his hand and gave him a tug toward the single bench that was positioned to take advantage of the view out into the desert. Piper plopped down, letting go of Landon's hand for a second, staring out into the desert. The Saguaros stood tall, their arms growing out of the side of a central trunk. There were hundreds of them dotting the landscape as far as she could see. She glanced at Landon. He wasn't looking at her. He seemed preoccupied. "How's Abby? I've been really worried about her today."

"She's fine. She was a champ."

"Does she know?" Piper felt bad asking the question, but part of her wondered if Landon had pulled Abby off to the side and told her this was just a ruse, just a way to get her dad to cooperate and that he was friends with Piper. Part of her hoped he did because it might make her less afraid.

Landon furrowed his eyebrows as if he was mocking her, "Now, why would we tell her?"

"That's what you told me you were going to do, to make her feel more comfortable."

"You heard wrong. I wouldn't do that. This is an operation, like any other. She's only gonna know what she needs to know. She doesn't need to know that I know you."

The comment struck Piper as a little strange, but she tried to ignore it. "So, what's next? I know we talked about the details, but I'm just feeling a little unsure. I was wondering if you could run me through it one more time? And," she said, looking down at her fingers sheepishly, "I also thought that maybe we should talk about what happens after this. Like I was thinking on the drive here that maybe I leave Chase and then you and I could live together, and we could have Abby come and stay with us." Piper glanced up at him, but Landon wasn't looking at her.

"I don't know about that."

"Why?"

"It could be because I'm in the middle of an operation. Don't you get that?"

"Of course, I do, but I just thought..."

Landon stood up, "When I'm on an operation, that's really all I can concentrate on, Piper. I thought you understood that."

"I do, I do. Will you at least tell me where Abby is? Can I

talk to her? I think that might make her feel better." As soon as the words left her mouth, Piper saw a change in Landon.

A muscle rippled across his jaw, "No. We're not going to call Abby. I'm not going to tell you where she is."

Piper stood up and crossed her arms in front of her chest, "Why? I'm her mother. You told me that you would share what was going on with the operation. What's going on here?"

Landon stood up and walked over to her, pulling her close. He kissed her. When she opened her eyes, she expected to see his features softened, but they weren't. They were as hard as stone. He whispered, "You don't understand, do you?" Piper felt his hand grab the back of her hair, his fingers encircling her braid. Pain ripped through the back of her head. All Piper could do was tip her head back on her neck, hoping to loosen his grip. He felt her shove at her back from behind and growl, "Let's go. You want to see your daughter. Let's do exactly that."

The next minute or so was a blur. Landon pinched the skin of her left arm with his hand and pushed her toward his car. She tried to wrestle free, but all that did was make him grip harder. She winced in pain. His fingers were so strong it felt like a vise; like her skin was being torn off the muscle. He pushed her face-first into the side of his sedan; the hot metal stinging her skin, and leaned his body weight into her, not letting go of her hair. The sun was right in her eyes, so she closed them, hoping he would let her go. "Please," she whimpered, "I don't know what's going on here, but please, just let me go. I promise I won't tell anyone anything."

"I don't believe that for a second," Landon hissed in her ear. She could feel his hot breath on the side of her face. Before she could say anything else, she felt something tight around her wrist. Landon let go of the grip on her hair long enough to catch her right arm and force the other wrist into a cable tie. Piper sucked in a breath. Was this actually happening? Landon pushed her off to the side, opening the back door of the sedan.

"Get in," he said. Piper realized she couldn't do anything other than comply. She was out in the middle of the desert on an abandoned roadway where there was no traffic. She didn't have a gun or a knife or the training to get away from him. She and Abby now had something in common. They were both his hostage.

Landon fastened the seat belt across her chest and then opened the front door to the vehicle. He pulled out a roll of duct tape, using his teeth to tear off a piece. He slapped it over her mouth and then added a black hood. "Lay down. If you sit up before I tell you to, you will never see your daughter again."

Terror filled Piper's chest. She felt like electricity was passing through her body. Had Abby gone through this same thing? Questions started to roll through Piper's mind as she heard the car start and pull away. Surely, someone would find her car and come looking for her. She used her fingers to press at her back pockets, realizing her phone was left in the car. So was her purse. Someone would be able to figure out it was her vehicle, but without her phone, she couldn't call for help. Whatever Landon had planned, she was now part of it.

After a couple minutes, Piper's breathing started to slow down a little bit, the initial surge of adrenaline wearing off. She tried to focus on what she did have left, her hearing. Other than the road noise, she could hear Landon humming. A second later, she heard a faint beeping, as if he was dialing a phone. "We're on our way in. I'm five minutes out. Be ready," was all he said.

Piper sucked in a ragged breath through her nose, taking in as much oxygen as she possibly could through the hood. Is this how Abby had felt this morning? Had she been able to breathe okay? And they were five minutes out from what? Where were they going? Maybe Landon was just taking her to see Abby, and these were all precautions? Part of Piper wanted to believe that's all it was, but the way he handled her at the park had surprised her. He'd never been that rough in the past. Maybe it was all just a misunderstanding? Maybe he was trying to keep her in the dark about where they were going? But why had he been so rough?

A couple minutes later, Piper felt a bump in the road that was enough to jostle her from where she was laying on the seat. Railroad tracks? She tried to adjust herself on the seat. Her right arm and shoulder had fallen asleep from being pinned behind her for the ride. Her right leg had a cramp in it. All she wanted to do was sit up and move her arms and look around a little bit, but she couldn't even ask for that because Landon had taped her mouth closed.

Another bump from Landon's car and some quiet rattling overhead and murmurs of voices got her attention just as the car came to a stop. Piper heard the driver's side door open and then close, feeling the car shake a little bit. A second later, she heard the door that was closest to her feet open and Landon's voice coming through the car, "Get her out and put her in the cage. If she's calm you can take the cable ties off of her. If not, leave them on."

Piper heard boots walking away from her as she heard another voice say, "Sit up."

Piper struggled to do that, trying to swing her legs back down onto the floor of the car, but without using her hands it was difficult. She felt someone with a strong grip pull at her and then say, "Put your feet on the ground." Piper tried to feel with her feet for the edge of the car and leaned forward, trying to get out. Whoever was speaking to her pulled on one of her arms and put his hand on the top of her head so she wouldn't bump it. Not that it made much of a difference. The pain in the back of her head from where Landon had grabbed her braid was so tender she was fighting off a headache. She stifled a few tears, sniffing under the hood that kept her in the darkness, worried she wouldn't be able to breathe and not wanting to give Landon the satisfaction. She couldn't cry. She just couldn't.

Piper stood for a second, trying to get her balance. Without being able to see, it was hard to figure out where she was. She felt one hand on her left elbow and another on her right. Two men? One on either side of her? She wasn't sure. The voice she'd heard a moment before said, "Walk forward." He barked at her like someone in the military, probably someone that worked with Landon. Piper shuffled her feet on the floor, not wanting to trip on anything. The two strong hands on her tugged her forward, trying to get her to walk a little bit faster. Ahead of her, she heard the rattle of something that sounded like a gate being opened. There was the squeak of some hinges and then she felt herself being turned around, facing the way she'd come in.

A second later, they removed the hood, the bright lights causing her to squint. There were two men standing in front of her. "I'm going to take the tape off now. Let me just tell you there's no point in screaming. You're in an abandoned ware-house. There isn't anyone other than us for nearly a mile. If you scream or make a fuss, we'll put the tape and the hood right back on again. Understand?"

Piper nodded.

As the man pulled the tape off, the adhesive stung her skin, taking her lipstick off with it. Piper blinked a couple of times, trying to get her bearings. Her hands were still cable-tied behind her back, but at least she could open her mouth. She drew in a couple of long deep breaths while the men stared at her. "Good," the man said, staring at her.

Now that her eyes had adjusted to the light, she could see there were two men staring at her, both wearing black from head to toe. They were outfitted like they were in the military or something, long-sleeved polo shirts and black cargo pants letting everyone know that they spent a lot of time at the gym.

Of the two of them, one was shorter and stockier. The other one, who stood off to her left, seemed to be taller and thinner. Both had the same grim expression on their face, the same square jaw. The shorter man was staring at her. After a second, he said, "The boss said I can take off your cable ties if you can stay calm. If that's what you want, nod your head once."

Piper was afraid to do anything other than what they asked, so she nodded. Just once.

The man looked at her, "Okay. But understand, if you cause a fuss, the restraints go back on."

Piper nodded again, just once.

The taller man pulled something out of his waistband and flipped it open. It was a knife. Piper held her breath for a second, wondering what he was going to do, then realized he was going to use it to cut the cable ties off her wrists. She heard a snap and then another and felt her arms drop back to her sides. She shook them and looked at the men. The shorter one looked at her and said, "Now, go sit down."

As they stepped away, Piper turned around. A huddled form sat on the bench behind her. "Abby!" she whispered.

Abby looked up, her eyes wide and sad, "Mom? What are you doing here?"

11

Something wasn't right.

Charlie Burns sat at his desk in his office at the North American Intelligence Institute in Washington, DC, and swiveled his chair to stare out the window. Outside, he had a not so lovely view of the back of a cluster of office buildings. If he stood up, he could see the tip of the Capitol building, but that was it in terms of view. He tugged on his shirt, pulling the collar away from his neck. Something definitely wasn't right.

Jess Montgomery was his best analyst. There was no one that even came close to her ability to piece together chunks of information that weren't connected and make sense of them. It was Saturday. She was supposed to be finalizing a presentation and getting it to him so he could review it. Jess was due to travel the next day, Sunday, and give the presentation to some of the Navy brass on Monday. This wasn't just a run-of-the-mill presentation — it was one that could land the think tank millions of dollars in consulting fees from the government, wider-ranging responsibilities, and probably a big promotion for Jess.

But where was she?

Charlie checked his watch, a gold one with a large face that had been given to him as part of an award he won a few years before. The back was engraved "Honor, Commitment, Courage." It was four o'clock in Washington, which meant it was one o'clock, or just after, in Tucson.

Charlie tugged his pants up as he walked toward his desk, crossing his arms in front of his chest. He shook his head just a little. There wasn't really anyone else in the office today given that it was a weekend. He saw two low-level analysts were at their desks when he wandered in two hours before, their heads hunched over their desks, their laptop screens glowing as they stared at the information in front of them. Charlie's mind raced. Why do I let Jess continue to work in Tucson? It would be so much easier if she was here in this office with the rest of the team, Charlie thought.

As Charlie turned back toward the window, he saw a few cherry trees blooming in the distance. Spring came fast to Washington, and with it, lots of tourists, people who wanted to walk the National Mall, visit the Smithsonian, and go to the White House, if they could get an invitation into the building. The rest of them hung outside on the metal fence that at least gave them a glimpse of where the President lived and worked, but that was all. Charlie liked the constant hum of Washington, the politics, the intrigue, and even the meetings. And there were lots of meetings.

A scowl on his face, Charlie turned back toward his desk, noticing his door was open. He usually kept it closed so that he could get some work done, but on a day like today with no one in the office, it didn't really matter. The only person he was concerned was working this weekend was Jess. He chewed the corner of his lip, leaning back on the windowsill. Something didn't seem right this morning. He couldn't put his finger on it, but his gut told him that there was something going on.

In all the years he'd known Jess, she wasn't the type to blow off requests from him. He'd mentored her and they had built up a good working relationship. If anything, she would over-explain what was going on, "Yes, I'm working on the presentation. I had to step out for a second to go to the grocery store, but I'll be back at my desk in forty-five minutes." That was the kind of communication he was used to from her. Why was she being squirrely? Charlie tried to shake off the thought. Maybe he was just reading into something that wasn't there. Maybe he caught her at a bad time. It was possible, he tried to convince himself.

The presentation she was putting together for the Navy was complex, an analysis of ongoing border threats, both from the north and south and how US waterways and territorial waters were being used to allow sex traffickers, cartels, and most importantly, terrorists and espionage into the United States. When Jess and Charlie had talked about the presentation and him handing it over to her, he explained how many moving parts there were. They weren't just talking about one section of one small border and how that impacted a state, they were talking about every inch of every mile of border and territorial waters that surround the continental United States, plus another analysis that covered US territories, Hawaii and Alaska. All of those required separate analyses. Jess had been working on the project for three months. Charlie had no idea how many thousands of hours she had into it, but her prelimi-nary work had been good, very good. Now, if he could just get her over the finish line.

Charlie sat back down at his desk, waking up his computer, staring at the screen. No new emails from Jess, either. Some-thing was wrong. Something was very wrong.

12

J ess turned in her seat, checking to make sure her backpack was in the backseat of Chase's car. It was. At the last second, she decided to grab it. She'd stowed it, complete with her laptop and cables of different sizes and connection types in her car on the way out to pick up Abby that morning, just in case Abby asked her to spend the afternoon. Not that Jess wanted to work while she was trying to spend time with Abby, but there was that presentation she needed to finish.

The presentation.

It was nearly impossible for Jess to think about what was going on with her work at the moment. Finding Abby had eclipsed everything else in her life. "So, do you think you can fabricate something to give the kidnappers?"

"What time is it?" Chase said, not taking his eyes off the road.

"Almost two."

"I have no idea. I'll know more once we get back to the lab."

Jess stared at the road again, wondering if they had any options. The bare bones of a plan formed in her head — have

Chase formulate some sort of fake ABG and then use that to get Abby back, but she wasn't sure it would work. There was a lingering question of why the kidnappers were so convinced they needed ABG. It just didn't make any sense to her.

"This ABG, Chase, you said it can be used in the field to stop arterial bleeds?"

"Yeah. That's what it was designed to do. Kevlar will stop bullets when they hit center mass, but if somebody gets clipped in the neck and their carotid is exposed, we can lose them in about two minutes. ABG seals up the hole long enough for the blood flow to be restored to the brain and heart. It's not a permanent solution, that's for sure, but it's enough to give the medics and the trauma surgeons a real chance at saving lives." Chase glanced at her, "This is probably the most important work I've done in my entire career, Jess. It could help hundreds of thousands, if not millions, of people. And now these thugs, whoever they are, they want to take it away from me. I just don't understand it!" Chase pounded his fist on the steering wheel.

Jess frowned. She almost asked him how it was possible he was more upset about his work than Abby, but she held back not wanted to upset him more. Jess knew Chase loved Abby. He just loved his work, too. "Okay, try to stay calm. If I'm going to help, I need more information. Here's what I don't understand, why would someone leverage Abby to get the formula and samples of ABG?" As soon as the word leverage came out of her mouth, Jess felt bad. It was a word she used in her work. It probably wasn't the best choice when talking about her niece who'd been kidnapped.

Chase sighed, "I have no idea, honestly. The military's been interested in this because of the application. It means fewer lives lost in the field. Even though we're not in an active war with any country, you know as well as I do there are operations running around the globe all the time. Our military and special operations units are always exposed, and the enemy is just getting more and more sophisticated. We have to keep up."

Jess knew that probably better than Chase did, she realized. "Are there any other applications for the ABG? Anything you haven't told me about? Any drawbacks to it? Any way it could be used offensively as opposed to just for medical use?"

Chase turned the car down the side street that took them into the industrial park where the lab building was. Jess had never made so many trips in and out of Chase's lab in one day. She realized he probably hadn't either. "I don't know exactly how to answer your question. I mean, what ABG does is it quickly clots the cells in the area, creating a flexible shield. It's almost like a silicone patch once it's applied."

Jess shifted in her seat, "So it creates superfast clotting? Like blood clots?"

"Well, I hadn't thought of it that way, but I guess so. It just covers the area so that the blood can't escape from the system. With those kinds of wounds, that's how people die. It's not the wound itself, it's the loss of blood."

"Is there any other way that it could be applied?"

"I don't think so. Right now, it's a liquid. We've talked about how to package it, and I'm thinking the best way is a small squeeze vial. The medic would simply pop off the lid and squirt the ABG on the injury. It would be like using superglue. Right now, it's a liquid, but we can turn it into a gel, which might be easier to use. Anyway, once it's on, within about ten seconds, the area would be sealed, the medics could stabilize the injured soldier, and then they could evacuate and get more help." Chase pulled the car into a parking spot, the same one they'd parked in earlier that day, and turned off the engine. "What are you thinking?"

"I'm not sure. Something isn't right here. I need to do a little bit more research. It just doesn't seem like ABG is something worth kidnapping someone over. I mean, it's a lifesaving product, not something that I'm thinking could be used offensively. Or at least you haven't said that's the case." Jess unclipped her seatbelt, "Can I take a look at some of your research papers while you're in the lab?"

As Chase got out of the car, he called over his shoulder, "I guess. At this point, the cat is out of the bag."

Chase took off at a trot across the parking lot. Jess followed, slinging her backpack across her shoulders, trying to keep up with him. She caught the door as it started to close, Chase was a couple of steps in front of her. Chase broke down into a quick walk, waved at Sully, who was still perched behind the security console staring at his cell phone. Chase was already inside the elevator by the time Jess caught up to him. They rode in silence up to the second floor, the elevator beeping as the doors opened. Chase trotted off down the hallway, opening the lab door. He'd already flipped the lights on by the time Jess walked in. She stood for a second, staring. She needed a place to work. "Is there a conference room or something on this floor?" With the amount of equipment in Chase's lab, there wasn't even an inch for her to put her laptop down.

"Yeah, across the hall. It should be open."

Jess stepped back out into the bright hallway and saw the door that Chase was talking about. She opened it, flipping the lights on, the expanse of a long wooden table stretching out in front of her. Jess took a seat facing the door, just in case Chase or someone else walked in so she wouldn't be startled by them coming up from behind her. She opened up her backpack, pulling out her laptop and a charging cable, quickly plugging it into the wall. If nothing else, at least Charlie could see she was online. That might buy her a little bit more time.

While her computer warmed up, Jess started to pace. Something about this entire day didn't make sense, she realized. A lot of things, actually. She started to make a mental list. First, how did the kidnappers know that Chase was developing ABG?

Second, who were they? Third, why did they want it and to what end? Jess realized she needed all that information in order to do any type of calculation on their odds of getting Abby back. As she thought about it, she realized it sounded so cold, so analytical. But that was her job, analysis. Pure and simple. She just hoped that the skills she developed in her career would be enough to help save Abby. There would be time to be emotional later, to hug and cry if they were able to get Abby back. That time wasn't now.

As Jess sat down in front of her computer, she thought back to the pictures that the kidnappers had sent. The first one was just of Abby, clearly wherever they were holding her. The second one, though, was more interesting to Jess. The picture of Abby and Piper together implied there was ongoing surveillance. Whoever had taken Abby knew about the family and had taken their time gathering information about them. They were well planned and methodical. Disciplined and analytical. Jess stared off at the blank wall in the conference room. Maybe they were tracking the movements of Abby and Piper before the kidnapping? They had to be in order to get the picture of Abby and Piper they sent. They certainly had to be tracking Chase, too. Jess scowled. How was it possible that Piper and Chase had no idea someone was following them? Before the question could fully form in her mind, Jess already had the answer. Chase and Piper weren't trained in countersurveillance. Very few people were. Jess wasn't sure she could evade someone who really wanted to follow her. Clearly, she hadn't, because they had found out where she did her banking and lured her there pretty easily. She chewed her lip. If only she'd noticed there was something fishy with the bank papers. If only...

But maybe that was the way to find the people who took Abby, Jess realized. Maybe she could counter their countersurveillance. Through her work, Jess had access to all sorts of surveillance databases and video feeds from around the world. It was one of the best ways to make connections between people and organizations. Could she use the same technique to help figure out who'd taken Abby? All of a sudden, it felt like Jess's heart skipped a beat in her chest. If she could figure out who had Abby, they might have a real chance of getting her back.

Jess ran across the hall, shoving the door open and yelling for him, "Chase!"

He was hunched over his laptop, typing away, "What?"

"I need the license plate numbers from your car and Piper's. You know them?"

Jess held her breath for a minute. Most people didn't know their plate numbers, but it was the best way for Jess to track them. Chase stopped for a second, stared at her, and then scrawled something on a piece of paper. Jess heard the paper tear as he ripped it off the pad, "Here you go. Mine's the one on top."

Chase didn't bother to ask why she needed them. Jess was grateful for that, not sure how her brother would feel about Jess peering into their personal life with a great amount of detail. Jess ran back to her computer and sat down in the chair, swiveling it back into place. She typed in Chase's license plate number into a video surveillance program that NAII had access to. It was a pretty simple program actually. All it did was log a license plate when a car passed a reader. Most people didn't realize it, but there were LPRs, or license plate readers, placed strategically all around the country, with tighter clusters in each urban area. Federal law enforcement was using the technology the most effectively at the moment, but local law enforcement was starting to figure out how use the information to help solve local crimes.

A small round wheel appeared on Jess's screen while the request processed. About ten seconds later, Jess had all the data on Chase's car from the last two weeks. She went into the dashboard of the program and squinted, adjusting the time frame, extending it to a month. Jess guessed the surveillance had to be going on at least that long. These guys were too well-planned to have pulled this off in just a couple days.

The wheel spun on her computer again, and then pulled up a map covered in dots. They were all the places that Chase's license plate had registered over the last thirty days. There were clusters in several spots — the LPR on Mesa Boulevard about a quarter-mile from the lab, another cluster about five hundred feet from the entrance to his development, and then another cluster near Abby's school. Other than that, there were very few dots. Jess hovered her mouse over the map, looking at some of the outliers. While she couldn't tell exactly where he'd gone, she could expand the map and then see what was nearby. She moved her cursor over one of the dots and expanded the selection. There were three hits in that area, with a drugstore nearby. It seemed reasonable that Chase would have visited the drugstore over the last month or so, probably picking up things for Piper or Abby on his way home from work. She hovered her cursor over another dot, a single one, and realized it was near a movie theater. For the next few minutes, Jess sat and checked all of the outliers over the last month. Every single one seemed plausible, a dot near a car dealership, another one near a school where Chase had told Jess Abby went for a soccer camp. There were a couple other dots near restaurants, but that was it. Jess knew she could pick up video of his car passing those areas, but nothing seemed out of the ordinary. She chewed her lip. Maybe checking the countersurveillance was a dead end? Her chest tightened.

Jess pressed her lips together for a moment. She had to stay focused. She had to treat what was going on in her brother's family like it was any other analysis. That was the only way they had any chance at all to save Abby. Jess looked down at the conference room table where the scrap of paper Chase had given her was sitting. She keyed in Piper's license plate number, adjusted the duration for the track to thirty days and waited. About a minute later, the results popped up. Jess squinted at the screen, trying to make sense of where Piper's car had been over the last thirty days. As she enlarged the screen and checked the results of the LPR, she saw some of the same locations she saw in Chase's results — dots around Abby's school, the local grocery store, and hits on the license plate reader just outside of their development.

She stared at the screen for another second. Something caught her eye. There were quite a few dots on the edge of the screen, almost out of her view. Jess dragged the view down and noticed there were a series of registrations north of Tucson at the Tombstone Road access off of the freeway. Jess furrowed her eyebrows. That didn't make any sense. She used the map feature to determine what was in that area. Nothing. There was a tiny town about five miles from where the reader had caught Jess's car, but her car hadn't registered in that area. Not that it was impossible that's what her destination was, but why so many dots in that area? What was out in the desert for Piper to visit? The only thing in that direction was the mountains. Jess pulled a pen out of her backpack and made a note on the piece of paper with the location. It was something to ask Chase about. Then she caught sight of another set of dots, more than ten of them, once again north of the city, but this time northwest. A lump formed in her throat. From the looks of it, wherever Piper had gone was at least a forty-five-minute drive from their house. That wasn't an insignificant drive. Jess enlarged the area and saw that the LPRs had pinged Piper's car in Desert Springs, a suburb north-northwest of where they were now. Jess chewed her lip. That was strange. Why was Piper so far from home so many times over the last month?

Desert Springs apparently had several LPRs already

installed. Zooming in on the area, Jess could see that all of the data that had been collected was downtown, or at least as much of Desert Springs you could call downtown. Jess looked up at the ceiling for a second, remembering the one time she'd been there. She'd gone with a girlfriend for the day. They'd walked up and down the streets, wandering in and out of boutiques and bakeries, stopping for a little lunch in the area. Desert Springs was nice. A little touristy, but a fun place to visit. Jess tried to picture Piper walking through the town. Was she alone? With a couple of girlfriends? Jess frowned. It seemed like it was too many trips over the last thirty days. Ten trips put her at a little bit more than two per week. That was a lot, given the fact that it was forty-five minutes from home. Maybe Piper had gotten a job Jess didn't know about? Jess shook her head, realizing how unlikely that was given how much she loved to be seen as a woman with status. Jess pushed the thought away and then enlarged the area on her screen again. All of the dots were in basically the same area, the most populated section of Desert Springs. Piper clearly hadn't gone very far out of the area. It was like she'd driven directly to Desert Springs and stopped there. But what was there?

Jess enlarged the view a little bit more, enough so that the buildings had labels on them on the map outline of the license plate readers. Jess quickly spotted the restaurant where she and her girlfriend had gone while visiting, Cactus Trio, and then a few of the boutiques. She studied what was on the street. There were a couple of clothing stores, a bookstore, another store that looked to be upscale home goods, and several restaurants. On the edge of the screen, there was a larger building. Jess moved the view on her computer so she could see what it was. A hotel. The Whispering Sands Hotel.

A sinking feeling passed over Jess. A hotel? Was it possible Piper was having an affair? Jess sniffed, picked up her pen, and quickly jotted down the dates and times the LPR reader had flagged Piper's car on the piece of paper next to her. Jess needed to know what Piper was doing in Desert Springs. Why was she there? Who was she with? It might have nothing to do with Abby's disappearance, but something told Jess Piper's stay in Desert Springs might be the key that unlocked who had taken Abby and why.

Jess opened another application on her computer, this one with access to video surveillance. It was a program that came in very handy in her work. If she had concerns about a particular target or members of a particular group, she could access all of the public cameras that were available all in one program. It was something that was used by the FBI, local law enforcement, and certain organizations with classified status, like NAII. She had to give credit to Charlie, Jess thought, keying in the ZIP code for Desert Springs to bring the videos online. He always found a way to get his team the very best tools to do their job. For a moment, Jess thought about the presentation she was supposed to be working on. She pushed the thought away. Nothing was more important at this moment than getting Abby back. She'd have to tell Charlie at some point but now wasn't the time. She couldn't afford to get distracted. Knowing he was going to be disappointed weighed heavy on her. She'd worked way too hard to let him down, to build trust between the two of them, and to prove herself, but family was family. Even if Piper didn't like her, Jess loved Abby. Inside, Jess knew Charlie would understand – he'd probably even offer to help – but she could do this on her own. She needed to.

Sifting through all of the videos of what had gone on in Desert Springs over the last month could take weeks. Jess knew she didn't have that much time. She rechecked her notes on the exact locations and times Piper's car had pinged on the license plate readers and keyed in a few parameters, hoping it would narrow the video search enough for her to find something, just a quick view of Piper darting into a boutique with a friend, or something. Anything that would tell Jess why Piper was in Desert Springs so many times in the last month.

Staring at the screen, Jess tried to catch a glimpse of Piper's blonde hair. The program gave her six different views all at one time, all of them from up and down the main street in town. What was the street called? Palmdale Avenue. A few minutes of searching gave her nothing. It was like Piper arrived and somehow disappeared off the grid. I'm gonna give it just a couple more minutes, Jess thought, then I'll go check on Chase and see if he's come up with anything.

Just as Jess was about to give up, she saw a blonde braid walk by on the screen. Piper wore her hair like that sometimes, she thought. Jess paused the video and then reviewed it again, going half speed. She leaned near the screen, trying to see better, enlarging the single view. In front of the store that was next to the hotel, she saw Piper. She was smiling, wearing a short sundress and flats. It looked like she was dressed up. Next to her was a man. It wasn't Chase.

Jess swallowed. She went back to the multiscreen view and watched as Piper and whoever the man she was with moved from one camera angle to the next. Piper was laughing and smiling, holding the man's hand. He was smiling back. This wasn't a platonic visit to Desert Springs. Jess froze the video and took a screenshot of the man's face. He was a little bit taller than Chase and well-built. It looked like he spent time at the gym, with square shoulders and short, cropped hair that was nearly the same color as his tanned skin. He had on a short-sleeved, button-down shirt that was hanging out of his shorts. He and Piper looked like they were having a good time. He moved with purpose, like a man who knew where he was going.

Her stomach clenching, Jess used one of the NAII databases to send the man's picture to facial recognition. The database had driver's license pictures of everyone who was a registered driver in the United States. Hopefully, the guy was in the system. Was Piper's affair somehow connected to Abby's disappearance? Questions swirled through Jess's head. Chase was a good husband. Jess had seen him with his family. And he'd given Piper everything she could possibly want — she had a nice house, a nice car and they had a beautiful daughter together.

By the time Jess walked back and forth in front of the conference room table a couple of times, her hands clenched together, the identification program pinged. She had a hit. Jess's heart skipped a beat. Who was this guy? Jess clicked on the results. The program pulled up the screenshot Jess had provided alongside a driver's license. The information read Landon Walker of Catalina. Jess squinted at the image. It definitely looked like him, not that she was going to argue with the program. The technology they used pinpointed almost one hundred pieces of data on someone's face to match it up to at least ninety-nine percent accuracy. So, according to the program, the man that Piper was with was definitely Landon Walker.

Jess stared at the door to the conference room for a moment, catching a glance of the lab door behind where Chase was working to get a solution for Abby's kidnappers. Jess felt the pull to tell him about Piper and about Landon, but she hesitated. What did she really know about this Landon anyway? If Piper was just having a fling, then this might not be the best time to tell him. On the other hand, if Landon Walker was somehow tied to Abby's disappearance, then she did need to tell Chase, but not without more information. She stared at the lab door for a moment, thinking through her options. She turned and sat back down at her computer, pulling up the NAII background check programs. Her chest tightened a little bit. Using the think tanks resources for personal use was something that could get her fired, if not prosecuted. People that worked for Charlie were only given access to the information to use on official, approved projects. Figuring out who Landon Walker was didn't exactly qualify, but Jess hoped Charlie would understand.

Jess typed in the information she had from Landon's driver's license including his name, address, and driver's license number. The results came back just a minute later. Jess scanned the screen, raising her eyebrows. Landon was former military, dishonorably discharged from the Army. He was one of their high-level operators but had gotten kicked out three years before. The background information didn't say why. Jess knew that information would be housed in the Army's database, but she didn't have access to it. Her belly cramped. The guys that had robbed the bank that morning were clearly military. They had to be, by the way they moved, by the way they spoke, not to mention their planning. Was Piper somehow involved in all of this? Jess blinked a couple times, finding it hard to believe that a mom would do that to her child. Her heart sank a little.

Reading further down on the page, Jess saw that Landon was divorced, with no kids. A brief financial overview showed that he was currently employed by Zeta Tactical Consultants. That struck Jess as strange. How was someone who was dishonorably discharged doing tactical consulting?

Jess flipped over to an Internet search engine and pulled up the website for the company. On the homepage, there was a picture of a grim-looking man. The caption below it read "ZTC's CEO, Retired Colonel Harrison Foster." Jess scanned the rest of the information on the page. She'd looked at websites like these before, hundreds of them. After the Blackwater scandal, it seemed like off-the-books operators hiding behind what looked to be legitimate companies had popped up all over the globe. While most people thought they only operated outside of American borders, they couldn't be more wrong. Everything operators did overseas, they also did right here at home. Some of the time, it was sanctioned work by the FBI or another government agency that simply didn't have the expertise or the manpower to handle a threat, but sometimes it wasn't. There had been a few cases, Jess remembered, of companies and their leaders that had been taken down for things they couldn't be prosecuted for, sins against the government that couldn't be tolerated and needed to stay hidden, away from the public's eye.

Jess shook her head and went back to the video of Piper and Landon. She ran it back and forward over and over again, watching them walk down the street, hand in hand, smiling at each other. She picked up another camera angle, this time one from across the street from the hotel at a bank, and saw them walk back in, probably going upstairs to spend more time together. How was this possible? She felt her jaw clench. Piper was cheating on her brother.

Before Jess could wrestle with any more of the information, her phone buzzed. She looked at the screen. It was Charlie. She glanced up at the ceiling for a second, closing her eyes. She knew she needed to talk to him, but she didn't want to. Not now. She couldn't very well ignore his calls though. "Charlie?"

"Hey Jess, how's the presentation coming?" Charlie's voice sounded more quiet than usual; like he was being careful what he said.

As she answered, Jess's voice cracked. She cleared her throat. "Well, it's coming along. I'm taking a little break right now, but I will be back at it here in a couple hours, I think. I'll be sure to have it over to you later on tonight." The words tumbled out of Jess's mouth. As they did, she wondered whether they were the truth or a lie.

"That sounds good. Did you have any specific questions you need me to answer? Any sticking points in the presentation? I know you had some concerns about waterway security in Guam, right?"

Jess stood up and started pacing, the phone pressed to her

ear, staring at the floor. "No, I think I've got those handled. Like I said, I should have something back to you in the next few hours, I'm hoping. You know, just doing the final run-through -- that kind of thing..." The words drifted off.

There was silence on the other end of the phone for a moment. "Jess, is there anything you'd like to tell me?"

She stopped walking and stared ahead of her, "No."

"Are you sure?"

"I'm sure. Everything's fine." As the words came out of her mouth, Jess realized they sounded a little too happy, too chipper.

"Okay. Would you like to tell me why you're accessing classified information on Zeta Tactical Consulting?"

Jess's heart sank. She knew that Charlie got notified whenever the team was working in one of the classified databases, but she always assumed he didn't really pay much attention to it. After all, he had dozens of analysts that were constantly accessing the databases that NAII had access to. "I, ah, I'm doing some background research for another part of the report." Jess felt heat rise in her face, like she'd been called to the principal's office after cutting class, only the principal was on the phone, not in front of her.

"Jess, let's try this again. Zeta Tactical Consulting has nothing to do with your presentation. What's going on? This isn't like you."

Jess sighed and slumped down in one of the conference room chairs, "I don't know what to say, Charlie."

"How about the truth, Jess?"

She could tell he was losing his patience. "Okay. Listen, I picked up Abby this morning to take her to breakfast. I got some weird paperwork from the bank I needed to drop off across the street. When I did, there was a bank robbery. Abby and I were stuck in the middle of it..."

"Oh my God! Are you guys okay?"

"Yes, I'm fine, but Abby... Charlie, they took her. We don't know where she is."

"What do you mean?"

Over the next couple of minutes, Jess told Charlie the story, starting at the beginning, giving him all of the details about that morning — the way the kidnappers had come into the bank, the hoods over the hostage's heads, the tape over their faces, the tunnel that ran out of the back of the bank and her interactions with Detective Saunders. She paused for a second, a wave of relief coming over her. It was nice to tell someone, someone who was on her side. "I was using the databases to try to figure out where the surveillance had come from. You know, the LPR database?"

"Yeah, what did you come up with?"

For a second, Jess was surprised Charlie didn't chastise her for taking advantage of the information she'd be trusted to manage. She got up and started to pace again, "Well, Chase looks clean. Honestly, I love my brother, but he's so up in his head with all of his science stuff that you could probably follow him around the city, and he'd have no idea. But then I pinged his wife's car. She's made a lot of trips out to Desert Springs with a guy named Landon Walker. I ran his background and found out he was dishonorably discharged from the Army and now works for Zeta Tactical Consulting."

"That explains why you were in the databases then."

Jess couldn't tell if Charlie was mad or not. "I'm sorry, Charlie. I didn't know what else to do. The kidnappers are demanding part of Chase's research and if they don't get it, they're going to kill Abby. We can't go to the police for exactly the same reason. Honestly, I have no idea what we're up against, but I'm afraid. These guys seem really serious. It wouldn't surprise me if we lose her, and time is running out. I'm not sure I can bear that." Her stomach sank a little. She wasn't trying to hide anything from him, not really. Jess just wanted to try to handle her personal problems on her own, like she always had.

When Charlie spoke again, his voice was lower. Jess had seen him in this mode before; when other analysts were upset by the information they'd found, or they'd had a disaster in their own families. "Jess, I understand the actions you've taken. And it's okay. Can you tell me what the kidnappers are demanding?"

Jess swallowed. If she did, she wondered if she would put Chase in harm's way. After all, no one was supposed to know about the ABG. Not her. Not Charlie. A wave of emotion passed over her. She'd been strong up until that point, but hearing Charlie's voice and the way he was speaking to her it was like he could see inside of her, see how afraid and sad she was. He reminded her of her dad. She bit her lip, the metallic taste of blood in her mouth. There was nowhere to hide. She wiped a couple of tears from underneath her eyes as her voice cracked, "I don't know, Charlie. It's some classified medical treatment. Chase said it's called ABG. I guess he's been developing it for the last few years. It's something the military medics can use out in the field to stop arterial bleeds. He said there's no downside to it, no way to weaponize it." The words came out in a tumble. The tears did, too. The robbery. Losing Abby. Crawling through the dark, terrifying tunnel with Saunders behind her, knowing that Abby had to do the same with a hood over her head was shattering what was left of Jess's strength. "I wasn't supposed to tell you that. He said it's so classified that if it got out, he'd go to jail."

"Okay, now we have something to work with. At least they've made a demand. That's a good sign."

"What do you mean?"

"Well, in cases like these, if the kidnappers never make contact, that's not a good sign. That means that whoever they took will likely be killed, is already dead, or they have other plans for the person. But the fact they made contact means they want to give you guys a chance to buy Abby's life back with the ABG."

Jess shook her head a little bit, feeling the tension in her chest ease enough that she felt like she could breathe again. Charlie was able to look at the case clearly, even a little dispassionately. It was something Jess hadn't been able to do over the last few hours. It was like someone was blowing the cobwebs out of her mind. "What do we do now? I've got Chase in the lab across the hall from me. He's trying to fabricate some samples or something we can give to them as a trade."

Jess heard typing in the background. It sounded like Charlie was on his computer. "You said this stuff is called ABG? Does that stand for Arterial Blood Glue? Can you remember?"

"Yes."

Charlie sucked in a breath, "Jess, you really need to listen to me very carefully. Under no circumstances are you to give the ABG to the kidnappers. You can pretend to do so, have Chase work up some sort of other samples or something else, but you can't give it to them."

"Why? I mean, according to Chase, all it does is stop arterial bleeds. And anyway, how do you know all of this?"

"I'm accessing the files right now."

"How? He said this is all classified."

"You have a classified clearance, don't you?"

Jess blinked for a second. For some reason, it hadn't occurred to her that the same classified clearance she had for the work she did with NAII could get her information on the things that Chase was working on. "Wait. My clearance would've gotten me information on ABG?"

"Not exactly. Let's just say I have access to some other databases for projects the government is working on that the rest of the team doesn't. Anyway, I'm just scanning this right now. I'll need some time to digest it, but you guys can't give the ABG to the kidnappers. No matter what. Can you take the phone to Chase? I want to talk to the two of you."

"Okay." Jess walked across the hallway with the cell phone in her hand, tapping the screen to put it on speaker mode. Pushing the door to the lab open, she saw Chase was still hunched over his laptop in the same position she left him twenty minutes before, a scowl on his face. A machine had taken up a violent whirring in the back corner of the lab. "Chase? My boss, Charlie Burns, is on the phone. He wants to talk to the two of us."

"All right."

"Chase, it's nice to meet you. I'm sorry it's under these circumstances. I'm the Executive Director of NAII. Jess has filled me in a little bit on what's going on."

Jess watched Chase as the words came through the cell phone. A look that started as confusion on Chase's face became anger. He glared at Jess, "I told you not to tell anyone! You're going to get Abby killed!"

Before Jess could say anything, Charlie interrupted, "Chase, calm down for just a second. First of all, I already have access to all the data from your projects. I always have. Your name came up on Jess' background check and we work for some of the same people. I can't give you their names, but you'll have to trust me on that one." Charlie paused for a second. Jess could hear more typing in the background, "I have a high level, top-secret clearance from the work that we do with the government. Mine is a couple of steps above Jess's, and to be honest, it's above your clearance as well."

"How did you know about what happened this morning?"

"Well, that didn't come from any good espionage work, that's for sure. Jess is supposed to be home working on a major presentation for the Navy brass on Monday, but when she blew me off this morning, I knew there was something going on. I just called her bluff and that's how we ended up on the phone right now. Can you tell me what happened so far?"

For the next minute or so, Chase ran through the details — the shock he felt when Jess told him Abby was gone, the initial contact from the kidnappers demanding the ABG, and the second contact from them when they sent the picture of Piper and Abby together. Hearing Chase walk through the information again sent chills up Jess's spine. She still couldn't believe it was happening. Any of it. Her mind was reeling. The robbery, running through the crush of ambulances and police cars after it was over trying to find Abby, the fear and frustration at not being able to find Chase or Piper — the day had gone very wrong. Very wrong.

"Hold on for one second. I need to check something." Charlie said.

Jess stared at Chase for a second while they were waiting for Charlie. She mouthed the words, "I'm sorry. I didn't have a choice."

"How could you?" Chase said, staring back at her.

Jess's stomach turned into a tiny knot. The look on his face was the same look he'd had the day of the fire. His expression – one of disgust and betrayal mixed together – was burned in her memory. The weight of it on top of everything else was nearly unthinkable. Jess felt heat well up in her face and tears sting her eyes. She looked away for a second as Charlie spoke again. "Chase, I'm gonna tell you the same thing I told Jess. Under no circumstances are you to give that ABG to the kidnappers. I don't care if you bottle orange juice and give it to them as a substitute, but we can't give away the ABG. Through the research that Jess is done, this group that has Abby, we've been looking at them for a long time. This is our shot to get them. Now listen, I'm gonna rope some other people in, some tactical people who can help us get this done..."

Charlie didn't get a chance to finish his sentence. Jess interrupted him, "Charlie, we can't! We can't rope in anyone else or any other agencies. They will kill Abby. They already told us that. And by the looks of the plans they've made and how detailed they are, they are serious. We can't take that chance."

Chase scowled, "You guys are talking a foreign language," he said. "What group are we talking about? Have you guys figured out who the kidnappers are?"

Jess took a second and quickly filled in Chase on the research she'd done. She swallowed as she asked him to follow her back to the conference room where she still had the pictures of Landon Walker and Piper together on her computer. The last thing she wanted to do was to hurt her brother even more, but he needed to know the truth. Glancing at the phone, she said to Charlie, "Give me a second. I just want to catch Chase up on what I found." Charlie mumbled something in the background, something about he'd be waiting for them and would hold on.

"Chase, I started doing a little digging around about where you and Piper have been in the last thirty days or so. I figured these guys are so well-prepared they probably were surveilling you and you had absolutely no idea. Everything about your scans came back clear. I could easily figure out where you were going to and from, but Piper's were a different story." Jess bit her lip, her heart pounding in her chest. Why was she always the bearer of bad news for Chase? "I found out that Piper has made a bunch of trips out to Desert Springs. That confused me because there's not a lot out there. I thought maybe she'd gone out there with girlfriends, but it was too many trips in too short of a time, like almost a dozen over the last thirty days. So, I started pulling up the video surveillance from the banks and stores on the street and this is what I found."

As Jess tapped the play button on the video of Piper and Landon walking hand in hand in front of the hotel, she watched his face. A frown turned into a scowl and then she saw him wince, like a shot of pain ran through his body. "And you think this is the man that took Abby?"

Jess nodded. "At first, I wasn't sure it was connected, but then I did a little digging. His name is Landon Walker. He was in the military, dishonorably discharged. He now works for a civilian operator group called Zeta Tactical Consulting. Given the precision with which they ran the operation this morning, the fact that they have surveillance photos of Piper and Abby together, and probably ones of you and me as well, it wouldn't surprise me if this is who's behind the kidnapping." As the words came out of Jess's mouth, she felt bad. She sounded more like she was delivering points in a briefing or presentation than she did breaking the news to her brother that his wife had been cheating on him with the man that had probably kidnapped his daughter. She swallowed, trying to chase the lump of guilt back down into her stomach.

Charlie cleared his throat, "As I said, we've been looking at Zeta Tactical Consulting for a while, but haven't been able to pin anything on them."

Jess frowned, "Since when does NAII go after criminal targets, Charlie?"

"We always have, Jess. It's just not something that's been part of your purview. As I said, this group is a team of really bad dudes. The whole company is a front led by a retired Army colonel, Harrison Foster. He was honorably discharged, but just barely. He's got a lot of black marks on his record and the Army was more than glad to retire him and get rid of him. I'm betting that if we did a little bit more research, we'd see that Landon Walker and Harrison Foster worked together at some point during their time overseas. Anyway, Foster's guys work under the guise of being a security group offering executive protection to Americans traveling abroad, but in reality, based on the research we have, we know they do a lot more than that."

"Like what?" Chase said, leaning over the conference room table.

"Like assassinations, kidnappings, theft of sensitive material both from the US, our allies, and our enemies. They get a job and then sell whatever they're able to find to the highest bidder. It doesn't matter who it goes to — the Chinese, the Russians, the British. These guys have somehow lost their moral compass along the way."

"Which is why they had no issue taking Abby..." Jess said, standing up and walking toward the window, staring out.

"That's right," Charlie said.

Chase stood up, throwing his hands open, the palms of his hands slapping on his thighs as they dropped to his side, "Okay, that's all well and good, but what are we supposed to do now? These kidnappers, this Landon Walker, or whoever it is, they have my daughter and I want her back. What am I supposed to do? I'm here. My wife is waiting at home. Those are all the cards we have to play!"

"As I said, Chase, you can't give them the ABG."

"Well, we can't go to the police either. They will kill Abby."

"Given who we are dealing with, there is a high probability that would be exactly the case," Charlie said.

"So, I'm going to ask exactly the same question again — what do we do now?"

Charlie cleared his throat, "Keep doing what you're doing. Try to fabricate something that's close to ABG, but not quite it. Maybe it works long enough for them to test it, but it degrades as soon as they hand Abby back to you. I don't know. If you're half as brilliant as your sister, you'll think of something. I'm certain of that. In the meantime, I'm going to do some more research on my end and see what we can come up with that doesn't involve the police. Jess, I'd suggest you keep doing what you are good at — research. Put the pieces together. Try to figure out what they're going to do with the ABG and why they want it so badly. Think about it, this is a pretty radical step in order to get something that's only meant to save lives. There has to be another reason." He paused for a second. "Before I hang up with you guys, let me ask you a couple questions. Can you tell me a little bit more about Abby? Her description, what she was wearing, anything like that?"

"As best I can remember, she had on a pair of shorts, a T-shirt, and a jacket. It was still a little cool when I picked her up this morning," Jess said, her gut clenching. From her work she knew that details mattered. She just wasn't thinking they'd matter as much in her own life.

"Yeah, I told her to grab it when she was walking out the door," Chase said. "She had on tennis shoes, too. She hates pretty much any other kind of footwear."

"Was she wearing anything else? Did she have a cell phone with her or a Fitbit? Anything like that at all?"

Chase shook his head, "I think she had her cell phone with her when she left this morning, but no, we haven't gotten her a Fitbit yet."

"How old is she exactly?"

Chase cleared his throat. Jess could tell he was getting emotional, "She's twelve, Charlie. She's about five foot two, dark wavy hair. She's an athlete. Plays soccer. Loves to run. She just did her forty-yard dash time for soccer tryouts and was the fastest one on the team."

"Okay, that gives me a little bit more to work with. I'll be in touch as soon as I know anything more. And if the kidnappers reach out to you guys, let me know right away. Jess, you can use our secure communication channels for that. That way they won't know we've been in contact. I'll be in touch."

As the call ended, Jess's phone gave a little beep. She stared at Chase, who had flopped down in one of the conference room chairs. He ran his hand through his hair, pushing it away from his face, "I can't believe this. First Abby's gone then I find out

Piper's been running around on me with the guy that likely has my daughter. This is a nightmare. How are we ever going to get out of this?"

"One step at a time. That's how we're going to get out of this." For some reason, talking to Charlie had poured a reserve of strength into Jess. "Listen, Charlie Burns is one of the most brilliant people I've ever met. Do what he says. Go back into that lab and focus like Abby's life depends on it. Find a way to give the kidnappers the ABG but render it useless. How, I have no idea. But Chase, get it done. I think that's the only way."

Chase stood up, staring at Jess, "And Abby's life does depend on it."

"That's exactly right."

13

Detective Saunders spun in the chair in front of his desk a little bit, not full circles, but quarter arcs he could make without moving his feet. It was something his coworkers knew he did when he was frustrated by a case. And frustration didn't begin to describe the feelings he was having around the robbery that morning.

"Anything new on the robbery case this morning?" The voice over his shoulder belonged to Lieutenant Ferguson, his boss.

For a second, Jamison wanted to tell the lieutenant everything he knew, everything including the part about how a ransom demand had been given to the Montgomery's, how they'd refused his help and basically kicked him out of the house. How frustrated he was by it and how he knew that a young girl's life was in danger. Wasn't that what the city was paying him to do, to solve cases just like these? "Nothing," he mumbled. "The FBI has pretty much taken over the entire case." Something about Jess and Chase's desperation to keep everything quiet left him wondering if he should too. With any luck, he'd be able to get them to cooperate without telling

Ferguson, but Jamison knew time was ticking. If Ferguson found out Jamison didn't pass on all the information, he could get himself in hot water. The fallout, especially if they didn't find Abby in time, could cost him his job. He needed a little more time, he told himself. Just a little more.

Ferguson grunted and tugged the back of his pants a little higher on his waist, "That figures. Bank robberies are their jurisdiction. Any news on the girl?"

"Another nothing. I went over to the mom and dad's house to check into things. They haven't heard anything yet. They are checking with her friends. Think she may have gotten frightened during the robbery and ran off afterward." It was a bald-faced lie, but for some reason, Jamison wasn't ready to tell Ferguson that Jess and Chase had pretty much kicked him out of Chase's house, telling him they didn't want his help.

As Ferguson lumbered off, Jamison stared back at his computer, the blank report form on the screen staring back at him. He'd never had a case during his tenure with the Tucson Police Department where a family had refused his help. Even the ones that were the most scared and the most upset seemed to settle down when he arrived on the scene. Lots of people got worked up when the police arrived, but those were just the bad ones, the people that were headed to jail. For people that truly needed help, Jamison had seen over and over again through his career how his presence and the presence of the other officers calmed the people around him.

But not so in this case.

Jess Montgomery and her brother had gone off the reservation. Something about Abby's disappearance caused Chase to shut down, preventing Jamison from doing his job. He stared at the ceiling for a second, and then looked down. His gut told him it was more than the fact Abby had been taken. Something the kidnappers had communicated to Chase had spooked him. It apparently was enough that Jess went along with the program, agreeing enough that she'd done nothing to keep Jamison in the loop. He shifted in his seat and logged into his computer, running quick searches on Jess, Chase, and Chase's wife, Piper. Not much came up that he didn't already know. Jess worked as an analyst for the North American Intelligence Institute, Chase worked as a researcher at Trident Labs, and from what he could tell, Piper was a stay-at-home mom. The cursory search didn't reveal anything that would explain why kidnappers would target Abby and go to the lengths they did to acquire a property near the bank, access the sewers, and then spend what had to be at least a week chipping away at the concrete in the block between the void in the buildings and the vault to build the escape tunnel. The execution of the kidnapper's plan was brilliant. Too much so for it to have just been a robbery. Not that there actually was a robbery, Jamison thought, rolling his head from side to side, trying to get his neck to crack. Nothing had been taken from South Ridge Bank. Not a dime. That only left Jamison with one possibility — the Montgomery family had been targeted. But why?

Jamison pulled up the video surveillance the bank had sent over. He knew the FBI would take the lead on the case, but there was something about it he couldn't let go of. He tapped on his keyboard, enlarging the video to full screen and then hitting play. He ran through it a couple of times seeing the robbers come in the front door, the chain they put around the door handles, the way they quickly got control of the people in the bank. Another minute or so went by and he saw them hand out tape and hoods to everyone who was seated against the teller's counter.

A voice came over his shoulder startling him, "What you watchin'?" It was Ferguson again.

"The bank just emailed me the video surveillance from the robbery for our records. I was just watching it to see if I could spot anything they might have missed."

"Run it. I'd like to see this. Heard these clowns didn't even bother to take any cash. Who does that? Let's see what happens with the girl." Ferguson slid a chair up next to Jamison so they could watch on the same screen. Jamison tapped the keyboard again, starting it from the beginning.

They sat in silence, watching as the video ran through. About two minutes into the video, Jamison increased the speed to two times so they could get through it more quickly. They passed the spot where the kidnappers had handed out the tape and the hoods and then watched as the kidnappers grabbed the bank manager and dragged him to the back. Jamison paused the video for a second, "I'm thinking this is the point at which they take the bank manager to open the vault."

"Makes sense to me," Ferguson grunted.

Jamison tapped the screen again, restarting the video. About a minute and a half later, the bank manager reappeared, nearly falling as they put him back in line against the teller's counter with the rest of the hostages. Jamison stopped the video again, "See there?" he pointed. "That looks like Jess Montgomery and her niece, Abby, right there."

Ferguson nodded.

Starting the video again, Jamison squinted at the screen. It looked like there were four men in total in the bank, dressed in black tactical gear, the kind that Tucson's SWAT team wore, but without the police lettering on it. Their faces were covered in black ski masks which made them indistinguishable from each other except by their body sizes. It was an old-fashioned way to protect their identity. Each of them had on a pair of black gloves with a rifle strapped across their chest and a pistol on their hip. "Wearing those gloves means there are no fingerprints."

"And those ski masks mean that the FBI is going to have a heckuva time trying to get fibers," Ferguson said. "Without their heads exposed, it's not likely any of them dropped any hairs, not that identifying a single hair in the building filled with people would be easy anyway."

They got into the part of the video where it seemed like the kidnappers were getting ready to leave the building. As Jamison started it again, he noticed that two of the men stood conferring with each other, looking in the direction of Jess and Abby. What were they saying? One of the men pointed toward Jess and then moved his finger toward Abby. The other man, a shorter version of the one pointing, nodded. Jamison stopped the video for a second. "Doesn't that seem a little strange to you, Ferguson?"

Ferguson nodded, "Well, it's like they'd planned for Jess, but were surprised by Abby. What kind of people take a child instead of an adult? Sure, if they are trying to get to the Montgomery's, taking the daughter is a better bet, for sure, but why risk it? Kids are more fragile and more unpredictable. For how methodical these guys are, you'd think they would've stuck to their original plan." Ferguson stretched in his seat, putting his hands up on the back of his head, his elbows winging out from each side.

Jamison nodded, "I hear you. It does seem like they made a decision on the fly to take the daughter instead of the sister, doesn't it?"

Ferguson stood up, tugging his pants up again, "I guess, but I don't think you need to worry too much about this, Jamison. With the FBI taking the lead, I just need you to fill out a report and file it. Just link the video and note on there that the FBI has taken over and we'll put this one to bed."

Jamison nodded as Ferguson walked away. The video in front of him was stopped at the part where the men were pointing back and forth between the two Montgomery women. Ferguson was right about one thing — the kidnappers had taken the riskier option by grabbing Abby as opposed to sticking with what Jamison assumed was their original plan, to grab Jess. How had they identified her so quickly?

Tapping the keyboard again, Jamison let the video continue to run. Once the kidnappers were done conferring with each other, they started standing the hostages up, turning them toward the front door of the bank. The taller of the two men that had been talking pulled Abby out of line, away from her aunt. He saw the other men adjust the line, placing the hostages' hands on each other's shoulders, moving them toward the front door. But only two men were working on that. Jamison saw as two other men grabbed Abby by each elbow and moved her out of the camera angle. Jamison frowned. There had to be another camera in the bank, one that focused on the vault. He clicked over to his email and checked. The bank has sent a separate video. This must be the one with the vault angle, he thought, clicking on it and watching the progress bar as it loaded.

While Jamison waited, he stood up and walked over to the coffee, pouring himself a fresh cup. In the chaos of the morning, he'd missed lunch, not that he was hungry. Something about this case had his full attention and he wasn't sure why. Sure, they didn't get a lot of cases this complex – usually, just domestic issues and some minor robberies as Tucson was pretty safe – but this one had more layers to it than an onion. Jamison took a sip of his coffee and hoped he'd be able to help Jess and Chase in time.

By the time Jamison got back to his computer, the second video had loaded. His chair gave a creak as he sat down on it, clicking play on the video. As soon as he did, he saw the black-masked kidnappers half walking and half dragging Abby into the vault. One of them kept his hand on her arm, like she was a prisoner in a jail, while the other one knelt down in front of the shelving unit that he now knew concealed their escape route. The man in the vault pulled and tugged until the shelving unit gave away, exposing the hole. He returned to where Abby was standing and pushed her forward. One of the men turned towards her, his mouth moving. A second later, he saw Abby kneel down. The same man that had given her the instruction to kneel pulled the hood off of her head. Jamison saw a wisp of hair float across her face. As she looked up, the camera caught her face in full view. She was a beautiful girl, Jamison realized. Wide eyes, wavy hair. He couldn't imagine what she was going through. The men pushed her forward. The first man entering the tunnel, the second man staying behind, pushing Abby to follow him. At least they let her see where she was going, Jamison thought. He couldn't imagine how she would navigate the tunnel without any sense of sight at all if they'd kept the hood on. He'd done it and it was terrifying enough when you weren't being coerced. How Abby managed to get through the tunnel and follow the men, he wasn't sure. It had to be pure terror, her body just running on adrenaline, fighting for survival.

Jamison stood up, shoving his hands in his back pockets, pacing in front of his desk. He knew he should just let the FBI handle this. They probably had agents all over the Montgomery's house and Chase's lab already. But there was something about it, something about the desperation Jess had shown that caught him by surprise. Was it her shock at not being able to find her niece? Sure, people got concerned when they couldn't find their loved ones, but it was something more than that, something deeper. It was as though something precious had been trusted to Jess and she'd lost it. Jess had searched for Abby with the desperation of a mother. Jamison sat back down at his computer and ran another search on Jess. A second later, pulling up her records, he realized she was unmarried with no kids. Her attachment to her niece still seemed just a little over the top. He wasn't that close to his own family. Maybe there was a painful family history he didn't know about? An issue between Chase and Jess? Jamison shook his head. There'd be no way to figure any of that out if he couldn't get the Montgomery's to talk to him.

Looking down at the floor, Jamison realized he only had a bare-bones knowledge of the facts on the case. He knew there'd been a well-planned kidnapping of a twelve-year-old girl, no money stolen from a bank, an extraordinary level of planning and execution, and a family that didn't want to cooperate. The whole thing smelled funny, and he wanted to know why.

14

"She's secure?" Landon grunted at Alvarez as he walked back to the command center.

"Yes, sir."

Landon glanced over at the cage in the center of the warehouse where Piper and Abby were now locked up. Piper had her arms around her daughter, one of her hands stroking Abby's face and pushing the hair out of her eyes. What they were saying, Landon couldn't quite hear. He was sure it was some emotional mumbo-jumbo, the kind of stuff that Piper loved so much. He wasn't that kind of guy, but he'd played along, at least long enough to get her to trust him. The sex hadn't been bad either. She came at him like a starved rabbit, which told him pretty much all he needed to know about her relationship with Chase. But Piper wasn't the kind of woman he ever wanted to spend more than a night or two with. She was part of the mission, that's all.

When Colonel Foster had approached him about acquiring the ABG, Landon had listened quietly to the framework of the mission Foster had put together. Adding Piper into the mix had been Landon's suggestion, his way of making sure they had complete control over the family. "The fewer options Chase has, the better," Landon had said to Foster after they'd spend about a week of planning.

And now the day was here...

It remained to be seen whether Chase would cooperate and give them the ABG or not. Landon looked down at the tactical wristwatch he had on. He'd had it since he was in the Army. Never took it off. It was black with a black strap and read the time whether it was night or day or underwater or in a plane. The thing was nearly indestructible. It was like him. The Army had tried to destroy him with their rules. They said they were written in stone, but they weren't. When Landon had bent them a little bit to get the mission he'd been assigned done for Foster, a promotion-chasing JAG attorney decided to charge him. A sour taste filled his mouth remembering the trial, which had only lasted two hours. A dishonorable discharge. His attorney told him to be happy he didn't get jail time. They'd given him the watch back at the end of his case once he'd been released from his holding cell. He'd kept it on ever since to remind him to never trust anyone. No one. He could only trust himself.

Looking at the time, Landon realized Chase only had a few hours left until the deadline. From what they could tell by the tracker on his car and the cameras they had planted in the parking lot, it looked like he was at the lab. That was good news. If he was sitting around at home that could signal a problem. Landon glanced over to Baker, who was leaning over the computer screens, jotting something down on their mission log. "Location on Papa Bear?" That was the name they'd given to Chase. Not that they really needed target names for this small of an operation, but it was the way the men were used to working, so Landon kept it in play.

Baker glanced at Landon and then sat down in one of the chairs, tapping something on the computer before looking up again. He pointed at the screen, "Still at the lab. I think the sister is there with him. That's good news, right?"

"That's only good news is if he's packing up the ABG to hand it over to us."

Landon stared again at Piper and Abby, his arms crossed in front of his chest. He had no feelings for Piper, none that were real. She and Abby were just collateral damage. The reality was that what Colonel Foster wanted, he got. That's why Zeta Tactical Consulting was growing and thriving. Just in the last month, Foster had told him they'd added another ten operators, carefully screened and trained, the best of the best.

Landon glanced at his team. They were all holding their positions and their roles exactly as trained. Baker was running the command center at the moment. Reinhardt was sitting on a folding chair in front of the cage, watching Piper and Abby, still working on sunflower seeds. Alvarez was keeping an eye on the door to the street outside in case anyone came calling.

Walking out from behind the command center, Landon wandered over toward Reinhardt. As he approached, he could hear the shells from the sunflower seeds hit the concrete floor. There would be DNA all over it, but Landon wasn't worried. Colonel Foster had a cleanup team stationed about a mile away. As soon as they completed their exfil, jumping on a plane to a safe location with the ABG in hand, the cleanup team would come in, remove all the technology and the cage and basically sterilize the entire building. Foster was thorough that way. "How are they doing?" he said to Reinhardt.

"A lot of whining and crying if you ask me," Alvarez said, glancing up at Landon. "I almost taped their mouths again, but then they got quiet."

Landon looked at Piper and Abby. They were sitting

huddled together on the metal bench at the back of the cage. Abby was looking at the floor as though she found something on her tennis shoes to be completely interesting. Piper did not, however. She glared at Landon, her arm protectively around her daughter. "How could you?" she hissed. "I don't know what this is about, but look at her, she's terrified!"

Landon stared back at Piper but didn't say anything. He looked at Abby for a second. She looked nothing like her mother. Her face was rounder, and her hair was the same dark color as her father's. Landon wondered if Abby got as hysterical as Piper did. Landon had met other women like Piper in the past — ones with too much money and too much time on their hands. After a little while, the only thing they could focus on was themselves. That wasn't what he was about. Whether people understood it or not, Landon was all about his country and protecting the freedoms they had. After a while, the Army didn't understand his motives, but Colonel Foster sure did.

Landon gave a slight nod to Reinhardt. As soon as he did, Reinhardt stood up, pulling a single key from his pocket. Landon stood at the gate for a second while Reinhardt undid the lock. He remembered back to a few weeks before when they had discussions on the layout of the warehouse. Colonel Foster's briefing team, which included Foster and two other project managers were sitting around a large conference table, the wall plastered with live time monitors of other Zeta Tactical Consulting missions around the globe. They'd been locked in the planning session for three hours. One of the project managers, a young woman, glanced at Landon, "We're not thinking we're going to have to provide a lock for the cage. After all, you know Piper."

His mind flashed back to the last time he'd seen her. It'd been fun while it lasted, he thought. "So, you're assuming that she won't try to get out of the cage because we are all standing right there in front of her?"

The young woman nodded, "That would be my assumption. Wouldn't you agree?"

"No, actually I think we should run this mission like we would run any other. If we were securing prisoners anywhere else, we would lock the cage. This one should be no different." Landon felt like adding a stinging comment like, "You should know better," at the end of what he said, but decided against it. The woman he was talking to wasn't a slouch when it came to mission planning — she'd been one of the very first females to get through Army Ranger training. It was a mental slip, nothing more.

Standing just outside of the cage, Landon waited for Reinhardt to undo the padlock and chain that held the gate together. Landon glanced up. There was no wire over the top of the cage. Theoretically, Abby or Piper could have scaled the chain-link fence, hopped over the other side, and made a run for the door, but the odds of them making their escape was virtually zero, not unless all four of the Zeta team members were incapacitated. That wasn't going to happen.

The chain dangling on the gate gave a little jingle as Reinhardt pulled it open. Reinhardt stayed in the doorway as Landon walked in. He approached Piper, pulling her up from the little bench she was sitting on, "Let's go."

"Where're we going?"

"To get a lovely picture of you to send to your husband. Wouldn't that be nice?" Landon said, sarcastically.

Just beyond the cage in the opposite end of the warehouse from where the command center was, the setup team had hung a black backdrop on a set of poles. It draped down onto the floor, covering the area where they were standing. There were no markings or landmarks anyone would be able to decipher. Landon dragged Piper towards it, "No, I don't want to leave Abby. Landon, what are you doing!"

"Piper, this will go much easier if you just cooperate."

There was a small table positioned just on the outside of where the draping had been installed. On it was one of the black masks and gloves they'd used that morning. Landon stopped for a second, handing Piper off to Reinhardt while he pulled the mask and gloves back on. They'd learned the hard way a few years before that making sure they were wearing gloves at all times made a difference. An operation in Bulgaria had gone south because one of the team members had a noticeable tattoo on one hand and a scar on the other. The Bulgarians had quickly figured out who they were and found out where they were holding a government official they were getting ready to transport to a CIA black site. The team didn't have a chance to initiate the transfer before Bulgarian special forces breached the building they were in. No one survived. Landon watched the entire thing from the command center. That was the one thing about Colonel Foster, Landon thought, tugging the black gloves onto his fingers, he didn't make the same mistake twice. Ever since then, there'd been a policy that all operations would be done with gloves on and long sleeves, no matter the heat, no matter the situation. Their skin had to be covered at all times.

With his mask and gloves now on, Landon gripped Piper's arm and pulled her forward onto the black fabric. It slipped and slid a little bit underneath his boots as he moved her towards the back. Landon spun Piper around, keeping a tight grip on her arm. He didn't think she'd run or even try to struggle away. She didn't have that kind of personality. She was more compliant, more docile, than the people he was used to working with. Seeing how easy it was to maneuver her, he was glad for the amount of time he'd spent with her prior to the operation. Somehow, knowing who'd kidnapped her made her more cooperative, not less. It was a calculated tactic, one that he and Foster had spent quite a bit of time talking about, Foster tracking every little bit of the relationship between Landon and Piper and how it proceeded.

Standing just behind her in front of the black curtain, Landon could smell the faint scent of her perfume. He remembered Colonel Foster saying, "You're going to have to be aggressive, but not too aggressive. We don't want to spook her, but we're on an accelerated timeline. Get your hooks into her, if you know what I mean, it's time to get on with this."

From a sheath on the back of his belt, Landon used his right hand to pull out a long knife. He stared forward for just a second, keeping the blade behind him so Piper wouldn't see. Reinhardt was standing directly in front of him, holding up a cell phone, ready to take the picture. "Ready," Reinhardt mumbled.

Without warning Piper, Landon wrapped his left hand across her chest, bringing his right hand up, settling the knife right against the tender skin of her neck. He pressed the blade in against the flesh just a little bit. He had no intention of slitting her throat, not at that moment at least. Her body was warm against his, but he didn't feel anything for her. He never had.

Piper didn't try to fight. From somewhere deep inside of her, Landon heard her groan, as though she was going to faint. But before she did, Reinhardt had already taken the picture. "Got it," he said.

Landon pulled the blade away from Piper's throat, noticing a slight red tinge as he shoved Piper with his other hand towards Reinhardt. Reinhardt could take her back to the cage and get her settled. Landon didn't need to. He wiped the blade on the leg of his pants and stuck it back in the sheath, pulling off the gloves and the knit hat and putting them back on the table. He followed behind Reinhardt as he guided Piper back toward the cage, keeping one hand on her elbow. She stumbled a couple times as if she was in shock. As Reinhardt opened the cage door and pushed Piper in, Landon stopped to watch. Piper turned around, a few wisps from the braid she wore down her back having come free, just grazing the skin of her face. Her skin was pale and drained of color, with a grayish tinge. It was common for people who were in shock. She looked at him with a blank stare on her face, her arms hanging limply at her sides. A second later, she lifted her fingers to her neck and touched the area where the blade had been. She looked down at her fingers as if surprised to see they were tinged with blood. Without saying anything, she went and slumped back down on the bench next to Abby.

Landon took in the whole scene. They had Piper exactly where they wanted her. He didn't think she'd fight them, but who knew? He'd had other targets he thought would cooperate the whole time but didn't. No matter the situation, they had to keep her locked up until everything was resolved, and then they'd see if there was any chance for Abby and Piper to go back to their life. Or not. It didn't matter to him which way it went. Violence had never kept him up at night. It wouldn't now either.

Landon glanced down at Reinhardt again, who had resumed his spot sitting on the chair in front of the cage. Landon glanced over his shoulder, looking at the images that Reinhardt had just taken of Piper. "Use that one," he pointed, choosing the second picture out of five. The look on Piper's face was blank, which was good. There was a small trickle of blood coming out from underneath the knife blade, which was even better. If that didn't get Chase moving, he wasn't sure what would. "Keep them quiet, okay? It's probably time to give them some water and a sandwich, too."

As Landon walked back towards the command center where Baker was seated, Landon wondered if he should have said something to Piper, if he should have responded to her to keep her under his control. But his training told him not to. More importantly, Foster had told him not to. "Once you get her to the warehouse, she's a hostage. That's it," he'd said, matter of factly. Hostage takers didn't talk to hostages. The minute you started a conversation, you lost the upper hand. Not talking to them taught them very quickly that they were not much more than a piece of meat. If Piper had thought the relationship was something more than that, she was dead wrong.

15

Jess drummed her fingers on the conference room table. In some respects, she was upset that Charlie found out what was going on, but part of her was glad. He was one of the few people that understood what her daily life was like, who understood the amount of research and data she did and how she thought.

She was alone. Chase went back to the lab, mumbling something about formula degradation under his breath. Charlie's conversation with them had been just enough to get him to focus. That was good.

A second later, there was a knock on the door. It was Sully, the security guard from downstairs. "Listen, I have three SUVs filled with FBI agents downstairs."

Jess's heart stopped for a second, the breath catching in her throat. "The FBI?"

"That's right. Said they want to see Chase. Is he in the lab?"

Jess nodded, a thought passing through her mind, "Sully, do they have to come up?"

"No ma'am. This is a secure facility for only people who

have a classified clearance. Technically, you shouldn't even be here either. I only get to be here because I work security."

"Actually, I do have a classified clearance."

"Well, if that's the case, then you're welcome. But those FBI agents don't have classified clearance as far as I've been told. They need permission. With it being the weekend, getting that permission could be problematic, if you know what I mean."

Jess didn't say anything for a minute. The last thing they needed was a whole team of FBI agents descending on Trident Labs or Chase's house, stalling out the progress they were trying to make. They just didn't have enough time to answer their questions and fill out papers. Jess thought back to the threats from the kidnappers that they would kill Abby at six that night if they didn't have the ABG. Based on how she'd seen them behave and the background Charlie had given them, Jess had no doubt they would be good for their word. Not to mention the FBI definitely fell under the category of police. Jess imagined what it looked like at the front door of Trident Labs, the three shiny black SUVs sitting parked, nose to tail. It would be a dead giveaway to anyone watching them that the FBI was involved. Jess frowned and then grabbed her phone, glancing at Sully, "Tell them you have to get clearance for them to come up to talk to us, okay? Can you buy us some time?"

Sully shook his head slowly, his eyebrows raised, "Listen, I don't know what you guys have going on up here, but I can do that. Chase has been good to me over the years." As Sully started to walk out of the conference room, he leaned his head back in, just inside the doorway, "If you need anything, you call downstairs. I'll come running."

Jess smiled, "Thanks."

As Sully left the room, Jess stared back down at her phone. She opened an encrypted text chain with Charlie, using an app that deleted the messages as soon as they were read. "FBI at Trident," was all she wrote.

"Are they in the lab?"

"No. Still downstairs. We are stalling them."

"I'll take care of it."

Jess stuffed her phone back in her pocket and ran across the hall, shoving the door open. Chase was still hunched over his computer. "Does one of these windows face the front entrance?" she asked.

Chase didn't say anything. He just pointed, as though speaking would interrupt his train of thought. Jess ran to the corner of the lab and peered down. She didn't think the FBI would know enough about the building to be able to identify which window belonged to Chase's lab, so she wasn't too worried about being spotted. After all, they were far away enough that someone on the ground would probably have to be looking for her in order to see her.

Sully had been right. From where she was standing, she could look down and see the roofs and hoods of three black SUVs. Agents had spilled out of the cars. There were at least six of them milling around that she could see. Where the other ones were, she wasn't sure. She trembled. If the FBI managed to get up in the lab, there was no way they'd be able to figure out how to doctor up the ABG in time to rescue Abby. The agents might be trying to help, but Jess knew better. Having them interrupt the process might be just enough to kill her.

Jess didn't take her eyes off the FBI agents that were standing around in the parking lot. One of them, a man with sunglasses on, glanced up in her direction. Jess jerked back from the window, not wanting to be spotted. She stayed at the edge for another second and then looked down again. The man who'd been looking in her direction was now looking towards the front entrance. Jess's phone vibrated. Charlie. "All set."

Jess waited for us another second and then leaned forward. The agents were all doing the same thing, staring at the front door. From around the corner, she could see two more agents walking towards them, one of them raising his hands in the air as if to say, "What was that?" with another one, trailing right behind.

Charlie. Jess breathed a sigh of relief, whispering a silent thank you that she had the relationship with him she did. If they were able to get through this day and get Abby back alive, that would be a miracle. Jess would definitely owe Charlie, that was for sure. A lump formed in her stomach. But nothing was for sure yet. They didn't have a solution for the problem with the ABG. At least, not yet.

By the time Jess turned away from the window, Sully had made his way back up to the lab. Jess met him at the doorway, and pulled him out into the hallway, not wanting to disturb Chase. "What happened?" she whispered.

"I don't know," Sully shrugged. "It was the strangest thing. The agents were giving me a really hard time. I was just about to call our Executive Director to try to get them clearance to come up, or actually to not get them clearance to come up, if you know what I mean, but then one of the agents got a phone call. He walked away, leaving me with another agent who just stood there glaring at me. I heard them talking but couldn't make out what they said. A minute later, the lead agent came back and told the other agent they needed to go. Apparently, their supervisor had called them off, for some reason. I don't know why."

"That's good," Jess sighed. "Sully, you've been a gem. Keep doing what you're doing. By the end of the day, if things go all right, you will have helped us more than you could ever know."

Sully looked confused for a minute and then walked away as if he was afraid to ask any more questions, not that Jess would answer them. As Jess saw him disappear into the elevator, she wondered for a second how many secret and classified things Sully had witnessed over the years, maybe without even realizing it. His job was difficult and easy at the same time —

make sure only the right people got into the building, but he had to keep his mouth shut about what he saw and what was going on. That was a fact. Hopefully, Sully would keep doing what he was doing until at least the end of the day, or at least until they could get Abby back.

Jess pulled her phone out of her pocket again and sent a quick text to Charlie, "Thank you." She glanced toward the conference room but decided it was time to go check on Chase.

Chase was up from his position at his laptop when she walked back in, a scowl on his face. He was kneeling in front of the refrigerator that had a clear glass door, racks of vials inside of it.

"What are you looking for?" Jess said.

"My samples of the ABG. They aren't here." He stood up, a panicked look on his face. "I don't understand it. I sent them out for a test yesterday in Building B, but they should have been back by now." Chase shut the door of the refrigerator and then walked back to his laptop, leaning over it. He sighed, and then groaned, "This isn't good."

"What is it?" Jess had a sinking feeling in her chest. The last thing they needed was something else to go wrong.

"The equipment that they use for the test, it wasn't working yesterday. They had a tech in, but apparently, they didn't get it fixed until the end of the workday." Chase pointed at his laptop. "There was an email in here, but I didn't think to look at it."

"Well, can't we just go and get the samples?"

"No. Building B has a different security clearance than we have here. The security is much tighter. They have some other research they're running over there. Armed guards, that kind of stuff. Sully doesn't work over there, so that won't help us."

"And you don't have any of the samples here at all?"

Chase shook his head, "No, I've been making it in really small batches, but we don't have the time to make more. It takes twenty-four hours from start to finish. Abby doesn't have that kind of time!"

Jess could tell by the tone of Chase's voice that he was getting flustered. Her brother wasn't used to working under this kind of pressure, with this high of stakes. Chase had always been that way, even as a little kid. He'd get things done, but it was on his own timeline as if he lived in something of an alternate reality. As Jess slumped down onto Chase's stool, her shoulders felt heavy, the reality of the situation dragging her down. Maybe Charlie could help? She sent him a quick text, asking him if there was any way they could get access to Building B with his contacts. He wrote back a second later telling her to give him a minute. She looked up at Chase, who was pacing back and forth, his hand on top of his head, his fingers entwined with his hair. "Chase, if we can get the samples, then what? Do you have a next step after that?"

"I think so," he said, biting his lip. He stopped moving. "I actually think Charlie had the best idea. I can coat the inside of the vials with a chemical that will render the ABG useless and then put another coating on the inside of the vial on top of the first layer that will seal the chemical in for long enough for them to test it."

"Two layers?"

"Yes. If I don't do the two layers, as soon as I put the ABG in, it will be inert. Useless. If they test it, they will know for sure. But if I seal it, it will buy us maybe a couple hours to get Abby back." The idea they would only have a couple hours once the ABG was loaded in the vials sent a shiver through Jess's body. She stood up and walked towards a single small window in Chase's lab, crossing her arms across her chest wondering if it would be enough.

"Will a couple hours be long enough?" Chase didn't answer. Jess's heart tightened in her chest. If Chase didn't keep the ABG in play long enough, Landon Walker and his cronies would definitely kill Abby. There was no doubt in her mind about it. They needed enough time to give the kidnappers the ABG, let them test it, and get Abby back. If for any reason, the ABG was useless when they got it, Abby might not be the only one who ended up dead by the end of the day.

Jess swallowed. A flicker in her mind made her wonder how she got caught up in the middle of all of this — the kidnapping, the bank robbery, trying to help Chase. Until that moment, she hadn't realized that her life was likely on the line too. She'd been so focused on getting Abby back that nothing seemed more important. Images of her house and her desk ran through her mind. Not that they were important in and of themselves, but they were just familiar. Would she ever be able to go back to them? Would she be able to go back to working for Charlie by the time the day was over? Jess shook her head, staring out the window, sighing. Suddenly, she felt lightheaded. She made her way back to Chase's stool and sat down.

He still hadn't answered her question. "Chase, how much time can you give us? We need to be able to travel to where they ask us to go, make the trade for Abby, wait for them to test it, and then get out of there before they figure out you doctored it."

Chase was flipping through a notebook on the edge of the lab table. He had a frown on his face, vertical lines crunched together between his eyebrows, "I don't know, Jess," he said with an edge to his voice, "How much time do you need? Two, three days? How much time is enough?"

"Don't get sarcastic with me. Remember, I'm here to help. I want to get Abby back as much as you do."

"I highly doubt that," Chase said, shooting her a look.

The words stung. It wasn't the first time that day that Chase had accused her of not caring about Abby as much as he did. Jess knew he was right, of course. It was his daughter, his flesh and blood. Abby was someone Chase could look at and see himself in, the shape of her eyes, the color of her hair, even a few of her mannerisms looked similar to Chase's. Jess didn't say anything. There was nothing to say. They both wanted Abby back. That was what was important.

Jess stared at the floor for a second and then back at Chase. "Listen, the way I look at it, we're gonna need at least three or four hours for the ABG to stay active before it becomes inert. Is that even possible?" She felt funny for asking him exactly the same question three times, but the reality was he hadn't answered it. There was a part of her that needed to know. With all of their lives hanging in the balance and no experience dealing with kidnappers, they had to do the best they could to think of contingencies. This was one of them.

Chase stood up and stared at the ceiling for a second and looked at Jess, "I'm sorry. I understand what you're saying. We do need to factor in travel time, the exchange and the testing, and our escape before the ABG degrades." Chase bent over, scrawling something in his notebook she couldn't see. "I think if I coat the inside of the vial with the dampening agent and then use two coats of the sealer, that should protect the ABG for long enough." He frowned and then scrawled a few more notes on the paper. When he stood up, the frown was still spread across his face, "The thing is, I need the ABG samples. All of this is a moot point without them. Did you hear back from Charlie?"

In the frustration of the last few minutes, Jess hadn't checked her phone. She walked back to the edge of the stain-less-steel lab table where she'd left it and looked at it. There was only a single text. It was from Charlie. "I'm sorry, Jess. I can't get you into Building B. I reached out to my contacts, but the DOJ has taken over the building for the next six months. They are doing some sort of top-secret research there, stuff that's well beyond my pay grade. You are on your own."

The words landed on Jess like she'd been punched in the

stomach. She blinked and looked at Chase, "Charlie can't get us into Building B. Said it's locked down for some sort of classified experiments by the DOJ."

Chase slammed his hands on the stainless-steel lab table, the vials and sensitive machinery rattling with the concussion, "Then what are we supposed to do?" he shouted. "It's not like I can pull this stuff out of thin air! The samples I need are in that building. That's the only way!"

Jess blinked and then stared down. Glancing back up, she said, "Are you sure the only way you can get the ABG to the kidnappers is by using those samples? There's no other way for you to fabricate it in time?"

"No. I'm telling you Jess, this stuff has taken me years to develop. The chemistry is really sophisticated. It's not like baking a batch of blueberry muffins."

"Can't we just go over there and show them your ID and tell them we need to get something?"

"No. They won't let anybody in there, especially on the weekends. I think that's when they run their top-secret experiments. Anytime I send something over there, they send one of the lab techs from Building B to come and get it."

"Can't you call someone? Do you have a friend or someone who works in that building who could go in and get the samples out for you?" Jess's heart pounded in her chest. She knew she was reaching, but there had to be a way to get in the building before it was too late.

Chase started to pace, sticking his hands in his pockets, "I only know one person over there very well. Her name is Juliet, but she works on the first floor in the files department. She doesn't work upstairs in testing. I think the credentialing is different. When the lab techs come over, they have a different kind of badge than Juliet has. It's like everything is segregated. You know, the whole right hand doesn't know what the left hand is doing."

Jess took a deep breath, trying to chase the headache that was forming at the back of her skull back where it came from. Everything seemed to be a blur around her. She closed her eyes for a second. When she did, all she could see was Abby's face smiling at her from that morning as she shoved a bite of pancakes in her mouth. A lump of sadness and fear formed in her chest. That poor girl, she thought. What is she going through right now? Was she alone? Afraid? Jess's mind refocused on the problem at hand. The ABG.

Before Jess could say anything else, she heard a phone beep, as if a text was coming in, but it wasn't her phone. Chase pulled his phone out of his back pocket and Jess held her breath. "Is it Abby?" she said while Chase was still tapping the screen.

Chase stared down at his phone, the color draining from his face. Jess looked at him, wondering what happened, her gut telling her that something had gone very wrong. "Chase? What happened?"

He didn't say anything, only slumping down on his work stool, holding the phone in his lap. Jess walked closer and took the phone from him, staring at the screen.

It was a picture of Piper.

It took a second for Jess's mind to adjust to what she was seeing. It was Piper's same face and same long blonde braid, but she was positioned in front of a black drape, a knife held to her throat, a man behind her, dressed in a ski mask, black jacket, and black gloves. There was nothing that could identify him. Jess's heart started to pound. The kidnapper was wearing the same garb as the kidnappers from that morning. Jess's breath caught in her throat. She whispered, "Piper."

"They have her, Jess. They have my wife, too."

16

Seeing the picture of Piper sucked all the air out of the room. For what seemed like hours, neither Jess nor Chase spoke, even though it was just a few minutes. Chase sat staring at the phone, at the image of Piper, the nick from the sharp blade pressed against her neck causing a trickle of blood to run down. Jess didn't say anything. She stared at the floor, her stomach in knots, wondering what to do. At that moment, Chase's entire family was being held by people that were willing to do whatever they had to in order to get the ABG. None of it made any sense. ABG was meant to save lives. Why do the kidnappers want it so badly? What about it made it valuable to Landon Walker, enough so that he'd have an affair with Piper and then kidnap her daughter to make a point?

"Chase, there's something we're missing here. Why do they want the ABG so badly? Something about this just doesn't make sense."

"Honestly, Jess. I don't have time to think about what they could possibly want the ABG for at this point," he said, staring at the computer screen in front of him. The problem was, they still hadn't solved the problem of how to get the ABG from Building B.

The only option they had for help in getting the samples out of Building B was Charlie and that hadn't worked. Charlie had no pull, no way to try to get the building open enough for Jess or Chase to go over and retrieve the samples. Jess chewed her lip and then got up, starting to pace. One thing she knew from being an intelligence analyst was that the most effective organizations were the ones that worked with the stuff they had in front of them. They didn't always have the best funding or the best resources, but they were resourceful. That was different. All of a sudden, she got an idea. "I'll be right back."

Chase didn't have a chance to respond. Jess ran out of the lab and went back down to the first floor, taking the steps. As she rounded the corner, her shoes squeaking on the highly polished tile as she ran, she spotted Sully. He was still sitting behind the security console, playing with his phone. "You're still here?" he said. "Thought maybe you and Chase had gone out the back entrance."

"No. I have a problem, Sully. Actually, Chase has a problem. The project he's working on, the samples were sent over to Building B for testing. They were supposed to be back last night, but they never showed up. Some problem with broken equipment, or something. Chase really needs them. It's an emergency. Is there any way you have access to Building B?"

Sully shook his head slowly, his head cocked to the side, "I wish I did. That place has been locked down for the last month or so. Some super-secret government stuff going on over there is what I heard."

Jess didn't need Sully to confirm what she already knew from Charlie. An idea crossed her mind, "Okay, well if you can't get us in that building, do you know anybody over there in that building who might be able to?"

Sully frowned for a second and then looked back at Jess,

"The only thing I can do is tell you that my friend Bobby is working security this weekend over there. At least, he's on the schedule. I can't get into that building, that's a fact, but Bobby works there all the time. Now, that's not to say he's got access to the area Chase needs to get to. But at least Bobby could let you in the door. How's that?"

Jess gave him a curt nod. It was the first good news they'd had in hours. "You're the best, Sully. Will you let him know we will be over in a few minutes?"

"Yeah, let me text him."

As Sully stared down at his phone, Jess glanced around the lobby. Everything about it was white and shiny, from the two-story glass windows to the white marble floors and the white walls. Everything about it spoke of cleanliness and precision, exactly what an organization like Trident Labs would want to portray to their shareholders and clients. But behind the doors and all the fancy ID badges, Jess was starting to wonder what was really going on. The fact that Charlie hadn't been able to access Building B with his level of credentials, many of which extended to personal friendships with some of the highest-ranking officials in the military, surprised her. Not that he'd use them to help her, but for some reason knowing Abby had been taken, Jess thought he would. There had to be more to what was going on at Trident Labs and more to the kidnapper's demand for the ABG. Before any more thoughts could form in her mind, Sully's voice cut through the silence, "All right, Bobby said he can get you into the lobby, but that's it. He's doing me a big favor. But he said to use the side entrance, the one that's attached to this building. He said he can't let you in if you come through the front entrance."

Jess was just about to walk away when Sully called behind her, "Listen, I don't know what they've got going over there, but be careful. Nobody's playing in that building right now, if you know what I mean." The look on Sully's face told Jess he was something more than just a run-of-the-mill security guard. His warning made her hands feel clammy.

"Thanks, Sully. We owe you. Both of us."

Jess ran back to the stairwell entrance, ignoring the beeping elevator in the background. Hopefully, the fact that it was a Saturday would help them with less of the regular staff hanging around.

Taking the steps two at a time, she ran to the second floor and pressed hard on the metal bar that kept the fire door closed, the snap of the bar on the door sending an echo of metal on metal back down into the stairwell as she made her way out into the hallway. She ran into Chase's lab, her eyes wide. Chase was still sitting, staring at his computer. His glasses were off. Jess didn't know if he was thinking or crying or having a major revelation about the ABG. "Chase!"

As he looked up, she noticed his face was pale, "Listen, I ran downstairs and talked to Sully. He can at least get us in the side door of Building B. I have no idea if that will help or not, but he has a buddy over there, named Bobby, who's ready to meet us. We gotta go now."

Chase put his glasses back on, "Getting us in the side door isn't going to help with anything, Jess. I've got to get into the fourth-floor lab where the samples are." He held up his ID badge, "My ID badge isn't going to get me access to any of those rooms."

"Well, then we're just going to have to break in."

Jess watched Chase. He stood up and stared at her as if she had suggested murdering someone. "Do you have any idea what you're suggesting? That building is completely secure. I don't have any idea how we can get up to the fourth floor, or even if I could access the lab if we could make it there. That's not to mention the armed patrols that run through that building. And if we get caught..."

Jess didn't let him finish, heat rising in her cheeks. "Okay, so what's your idea? Should we just run to the store and buy some juice that happens to be the same color as the ABG and try to pass that off?" She felt a surge of anger burn behind her eyes as she glared at him. "How else do you propose getting your daughter, and now your wife, back? Unless you prefer to just sit on your hands and wait till the kidnappers, this Landon Walker or whoever it is, calls again and then apologize because you can't get what they want?" Where the words had come from, Jess wasn't sure. She knew they were harsh, but part of her didn't understand why Chase would give up so quickly, leaving his daughter and wife to die at the hands of the kidnappers.

"You understand that if we get caught in that building, we will likely go to jail. Abby won't have any chance at all. Neither will Piper."

"And if we do nothing? How's that going to work out for them?"

Jess's heart was pounding in her chest, the adrenaline from arguing with Chase surging through her system. She wanted to help. He had to give her the room to do that. Could they successfully navigate Building B after Bobby got them in the door? There was no way of knowing. A lump formed in Jess's throat as she realized if half of what Chase was saying was true, it would be more than difficult to try to get up to the fourth floor. Probably impossible. It wasn't like they could just walk in the door, press the elevator button and sail up, cruising through to the lab, quickly stuffing the ABG in their back pockets. If the DOJ had the building locked down and Charlie couldn't even get access, they were facing difficult odds. And neither of them was trained for this kind of a mission. Jess swallowed, pushing the lump back down into her chest. She lowered her voice, "Seriously, Chase, do you have a better plan?"

He shook his head slowly, the muscles rippling across his jaw, "No."

"Then let's go."

. . .

JESS WAS the first one out the lab door. She turned and waited for a minute as Chase closed it behind them. She led the way to the stairwell she'd found and pushed the metal bar, the latch snapping open. Neither of them said anything, the only noise was their footfalls on the concrete steps. Down the steps and into the lobby, Jess saw Sully pacing back and forth in front of the security desk. "Perfect timing," he said, walking down a side hallway Jess hadn't noticed before. "Bobby just texted me. He said he's waiting at the side door for you."

Following Sully down the hallway, Jess noticed it was white with the same polished floors as the second floor had, but this time there were offices on either side of the hallways with small placards attached outside each doorway. "Emma Jones, Accounting," "Robert Blakemore, Finance," "Malcolm Randall, Human Resources."

At the end of the hallway, there was a single door, a fire exit with glowing red letters. Sully punched in a code in the keypad that was next to the door and swiped his ID. "Okay, I've disarmed the door and unlocked it. It'll stay this way for the next thirty minutes. I'm thinking you guys don't want to be clocked in and out of the building, so this is the best way." Jess saw Sully look at each of them for a second, "Listen, I don't know what's going on here, but good luck." For a second, Jess was surprised Sully hadn't asked more questions. Then again, if Chase had worked at Trident Labs as long as Sully had, then perhaps he knew what kind of a man Chase was — that it would have to be a dire circumstance for Chase to ask for a favor like this.

As they pushed the door open, Jess brushed past Sully and whispered, "Thank you."

Sully gave a single nod, "Keep an eye on your brother."

Out in the sunlight, the midafternoon light caused Jess to

squint. As her eyes adjusted to the heat and the brightness, she saw a carefully manicured river rock and stone pathway between the two buildings. Part of it went straight towards Building B just ahead of them, and part of it curved off, both left and right, into the adjacent parking lots. Stepping on the larger stones, Jess's heel caught on a few of the river rocks, their hard surfaces making a quiet grinding noise as they rubbed against each other. Chase had stepped out in front of her and was walking quickly towards Building B, stepping on each one of the stones. There wasn't much space between the buildings, maybe only twenty-five or thirty feet, Jess estimated. Why they were so close together, she wasn't sure, but she was grateful for it. Moving between the buildings would just take a few seconds, nothing more. That was, if they could get back to Chase's lab with the ABG.

As Chase reached for the door handle on Building B, it pushed open without him having to tug. Bobby. Jess paused for a second as Chase stepped inside, his back disappearing ahead of her. Bobby closed the door behind them with a click and then stopped. Jess took a second to look at him. He was considerably younger than Sully, with dark, gelled hair and a neatly pressed uniform that matched the one that Sully wore. "Welcome to Building B," he whispered. "This is as far as I can take you. The door will stay unarmed for the next half hour. I'm hoping that gives you enough time to get in and out of the building." Without saying anything more, Bobby walked away. Jess frowned for a second, wondering why Bobby hadn't asked any questions about why they needed to get in the building. Maybe he was just taking Sully's word for it? Maybe Sully owed him? Jess felt the muscles tighten at the back of her neck. They were on their own now. Bobby hadn't offered any information or any floor plans. He'd simply walked away.

Neither of them moved for a second. Chase looked at her

and then blinked, pointing, "I've only been in here one other time. I think the door for their stairwell is right over there."

"Chase, I just had an awful thought. What if there are surveillance cameras all over the building?"

"I don't think there are, Jess. Sully and I had lunch one time a couple years ago. He didn't tell me what goes on in this building, but he told me it's stuff that no one wants any record of. What that is, I don't know. Let's just hope it works in our favor."

As the information settled on Jess, she felt her heart start to pound in her chest, her breathing ragged, trying to fight the urge to run outside, anywhere to get away from what they were in the middle of. Abby. She had to focus on Abby. Watching Chase, he walked forward about five feet to a doorway and then pushed it open, just barely twisting the metal door handle. Jess followed, carefully closing the stairwell door behind her. Any noise could cause the security teams to come running. That was one thing they didn't need.

The stairwell in Building B was identical to the one that was in Chase's building. Same white paint, same gray, concrete steps with grooves cut into them to prevent slipping. Clearly, the buildings had been constructed around the same time. But the words Chase said hung with Jess. What was going on in Building B? If it was so secret that Chase didn't think they had surveillance cameras, that was a whole new level of covert operations, one Jess had never encountered even in her work as an analyst. She shook off the thought and followed Chase.

As they got to the first landing, Jess glanced up at the ceiling. There were no glass bubbles attached to the wall anywhere, the kind that was commonly used for building surveillance. So far, so good, she breathed.

Moving as silently as possible, Jess trailed Chase to the second floor. Her heart was still pounding in her chest. She was sure Chase could hear every beat. As she was about to put her foot on the landing for the second floor, she saw Chase hold his hand out and then duck down. He was moving smoothly, only glancing back at her occasionally. It was like he was in his own world. The stairwell door to the second floor had a glass window in it and a shadow passed by. Jess dodged behind Chase and then pressed her body against the wall as tightly as she could. As she glanced back up, she saw two men, dressed in the same black tactical gear she'd seen the kidnappers wear, pass by the window, one of them glancing inside. She held her breath, her lungs burning. If the security teams found them now, they'd have no chance of retrieving the ABG, no chance of saving Abby and Piper.

Still kneeling, pinned against the wall, Jess gritted her teeth. She counted to ten and then glanced up. It looked like the guards had passed by the window, but she and Chase would need to move quickly to get up the steps. The glass pane had a perfect view of the next flight, between the second and third floor. If they didn't move, they'd be caught for sure. Jess leaned forward, tugging at Chase. "Let's go," she whispered. Instead of waiting for him, she stepped in front, taking the steps two at a time, trying to make sure that her shoes didn't make any noise against the concrete.

As they rounded the corner on the next landing, Jess realized it was the same setup as the second floor, only this time it was the third. As she approached from below, she glanced forward, peering around and into the window. There was nothing to be seen, just a blank white wall on the other side. She nodded at Chase and started up the second half of the steps, getting them up to the third floor. "One more to go," she whispered to herself, checking behind to make sure Chase was still coming. As she glanced behind her, she saw him reach for the handrail, his hands shaking, drops of sweat beading on his forehead. She knew it wasn't the temperature. In fact, if anything, the stairwell was icy cold, the air conditioning running overtime to combat the Arizona heat. It was stress. As

Chase gripped the handrail, the metal from his wedding ring connected with the gray paint and metal on the rail, letting out a low, clanking sound. Startled by it, Chase tried to take the next step up, but missed, falling forward, catching himself with his hands on the steps above. Jess gasped. Though probably no one in the building noticed the noise, there was no need to alert anyone to their presence. Jess glanced around, her eyes wide. She motioned to Chase, waving him forward. If they stopped where they were, they were in full view of the guards as they passed.

As soon as they got to the next landing, Jess stopped for a second, staring at Chase. She mouthed the words, "Are you okay?"

Chase closed his eyes for a second, and then nodded, using the sleeve of his shirt to wipe the sweat off his brow. His cheeks were red islands in the middle of pale skin. Jess turned and moved forward. The higher they got in the building, the more tense she felt, like someone was crushing her intestines with a trash compactor. The adrenaline rush and her body sent a buzz to her ears and left her feeling lightheaded. Keep it together, Jess, she thought. You're almost there.

On the landing that spanned midway between the third and fourth floors, Jess stopped, leaning against the wall. "Do you know which lab it is? We're almost there."

"I think so. Like I said, I haven't been in this building in a long time. Not since before they secured it."

"Want to give me an idea what we're looking at before we barge our way into someplace we shouldn't be?"

Chase nodded, "It's the same layout as my building. You know, doors running along the hallway."

"Are they flush to the wall or are they inset?" The answer could make all the difference in terms of whether they had any place to hide, or not.

"Flush to the wall. All the doors open inward."

Not good news. There would be nowhere to duck into if security came down the hallway. They'd be spotted immediately. Jess sighed. "Okay, lead the way."

Jess stood behind Chase as he pushed on the metal bar, easing the door open. As she looked down the hallway, she realized Chase was right — the layout was exactly the same as in Chase's own lab building — the same polished white floors, white walls, and matching white doors on each lab. Each one seemed to have a keypad. As Jess stared down the hallway waiting for Chase to move, she heard a click. In front of her, about halfway down the hallway on the right-hand side, a woman left one of the labs, quickly turning in the other direction. Jess and Chase darted back inside of the stairwell, staying away from the window. The woman didn't look in their direction, staring down at her phone, the edges of her white lab coat swishing around the back of her calves. Her shoes made a quiet clicking noise on the tile as she disappeared around a corner.

A minute passed by. Jess glanced through the window of the fire door again. There was no movement down the hallway, no security guards, and no lab personnel anywhere to be seen. Chase pushed the door open again, this time letting Jess out and quietly closing it behind her. "The lab the woman came out of is the one we need to get into, I think."

"You think?"

"I told you, I haven't been in this building very much," Chase hissed, his eyes narrowed.

Jess followed Chase down the hallway. They'd gotten to the fourth floor without any trouble, but if they'd come this entire way and they were unable to get into the lab or the ABG wasn't there, that presented a whole new set of problems. Jess clenched her teeth, silently praying the security teams would be busy doing something else, even taking a coffee break, rather than patrolling the fourth-floor labs. She followed Chase down the hallway, walking as quickly as possible and trying to make no noise at all.

When they got to the lab door, Chase put his hand on the handle, giving it a twist and then a little nudge inward. Jess glanced around the door, noticing there was a keypad, but everything was green on the panel. Next to the keypad was a small optic display. Jess frowned for a second and then realized it was a retinal scanner. She hadn't seen one of those at Chase's lab. If what they were protecting was so valuable, why was the system disarmed? The more she was learning about Trident Labs, the less it made any sense at all.

She didn't have time to follow up on her suspicions. That would be for another day, that was, if they made it through the next few hours. Jess followed Chase inside. "Stay here," he whispered. "Let me know if anyone is coming, okay? I'm gonna look for the ABG."

Jess positioned herself just inside the doorway, where she could see through the glass window. After watching for a second, she turned and glanced around the lab, trying to figure out where Chase had gone.

The lab itself was significantly larger than the space Chase occupied, probably at least three times, she realized. There were stainless steel tables positioned around the perimeter of the room as well as two lines of them positioned down the center. The lab, though it was bigger than Chase's, still had the same buzzing noise of machines working in the background, the whirr of lab equipment beeping and processing materials. Although Jess had taken a lot of science classes in high school, she had no idea what the equipment was that Trident was using. It was stuff she'd never seen before.

Jess glanced back at the doorway, watching to see if anyone was coming. She leaned forward a little bit and thought she saw a shadow of black moving down the hallway. The guards. Her heart pounding, she ran around the corner to her left, trying to find Chase. He was standing at a bank of refrigerated units, bent over, the door open, clearly searching for the ABG. Jess tried to get his attention by waving at him, but he was looking so intently inside the unit, he didn't see her. Finally, she snapped her fingers. He glanced her way and she motioned for him to get down. Jess ducked between two stainless steel tables, squeezing herself in between the legs and the lower shelving units. She saw Chase do the same, using the stainless-steel table across from the refrigerated unit as cover. Jess held her breath, the blood pounding in her head. They waited, but there was no noise from the door. As she unwedged herself from between the stainless-steel worktables, she frowned, motioning to Chase to hurry it up, not that he needed any encouragement to do so. Jess slid back towards the lab door and glanced down the hallway. She saw the backs of the guards walking past the lab. They were looking inside each of them, but not entering. That was good news, at least for the moment.

Jess peered around the room. For a moment, all she saw was Chase's hand and then his forearm as he pulled himself out from under the table where he'd been hiding. Moving as quietly as she could, she walked over to him as he reopened the refrigerated unit, "Did you find it yet?" she whispered.

He shook his head no, "I don't know where they put it. They have like a thousand samples in here." He glanced back at the door. "Give me another minute or two. Go check the entrance, will you?"

Jess nodded and moved as quietly as she could back towards the door, nearly bumping into the corner of one of the worktables, catching herself before she rattled all of the equipment on it. Peering out the rectangular glass window in the door, she didn't see anything. Maybe the fact they were doing this on a Saturday was a good thing, she thought. Trying to get into the lab during the workweek would be impossible without alerting someone with all of the regular staff in the building. At

least on the weekend, it was a skeleton crew, or it appeared
to be.

Another minute went by and Jess glanced back at Chase.
He was reaching into one of the refrigerator units like he was
grabbing something. Jess couldn't see his face, but she hoped
he'd found what he was looking for. Leaning toward the
window, she took another look out the door, the tension in her
back nearly cramping her muscles out of nervousness. She
moved back around to where Chase was standing, watching
him move test tubes out of a tray. "Is that it?"

Chase pressed his lips together, "Yes, but there are only five
samples here. I sent twelve. We need all of them to get Abby
back."

"Are you sure there are only five in there?"

Chase nodded. "I don't know what they did with the rest of
them. They were supposed to take all twelve of them, test them
for compatibility with different blood types, specifically anti-
gens, and then return them to me. What are we going to do,
Jess? There aren't enough for the trade."

Jess pulled her phone out of her back pocket. They only
had about five minutes left before the doors would automatically lock on the two buildings. They had to move, and they
had to move now. "Let's take what you can get. We gotta get
outta here. The fire doors Bobby and Sully opened for us are
going to relock in like five minutes. We don't want to have to
parade out the front door of either of these buildings right
now."

Chase nodded. "Here, take a few of these samples. My
hands are so shaky I'm afraid I'm gonna drop them."

"What am I supposed to do with them?"

"I don't know. Hide them on your body someplace. It's not
like we can walk out of the building carrying them."

Jess grabbed three of the test tubes, nearly dropping one.
She bent over, pulling up her pant leg, pushing the test tubes

down into her socks. The vials were cold against her skin, but she didn't care. She knew she'd have to walk carefully so as not to jostle them and be careful not to break them if she bumped into anything, but it was the only place she could hide them. Someone would see them in her pockets, and she couldn't very well just hold them in her hands. "Let's go," she said, staring at Chase, who was still busy adjusting his own pant legs.

Darting back to the lab door, Jess tried to look outside. With the way the door was positioned, they only had a very small arc where they could see what was going on. Remembering the woman that had left the lab just a few minutes before, Jess cracked the door open, looking for any signs of guards or the lab technician. There was no one. It was a straight shot back to the stairwell. She waved Chase forward and gently pushed the door open. She half expected there to be some beeping or screeching of an alarm, as though someone had been watching them the entire time they were in the lab, but none came. It still surprised her that the doors weren't secured, but she didn't have time to think about it. Jess slipped out the door and started moving down the hallway, sticking close to the side wall, making her way for the stairwell. She could feel Chase behind her, the sound of his shoes on the floor, the heat of his body close behind on her back. As they got to the door, Jess heard voices. The guards. She could hear the rumble of their low voices bouncing off the empty hallways. Her eyes got wide, and she motioned for Chase to hurry up. He slipped through the stairwell door just ahead of her and they closed it, both of them smashing their bodies up against the walls on either side of the door so they wouldn't be seen if the guards decided to look through.

Jess's heart was beating loud enough she was sure they would either hear it or she was going to have a heart attack. Her mouth was dry. She felt like she'd spent the last hour chewing on sawdust, the graininess of the inside of her mouth not giving her any comfort. All she wanted to do was run down the stairs as fast as possible, hit the hallway on the first floor at a full run, and get out into the sunshine, into the open air where she could breathe again. But she couldn't. She had vials of ABG stuffed in her socks, as ridiculous as it sounded, and was trying to avoid guards that looked like twins of the people that had kidnapped Abby just that morning.

Taking a deep breath, Jess leaned forward and peered through the window that led back out under the fourth-floor hallway. The guards were gone, the sound of their low conversation having passed by her and Chase. She waved to her brother, who seemed frozen in time. "We've gotta go. There are only three minutes left." He nodded.

The exertion of just going down the steps in Building B left her breath ragged, the adrenaline pushing her body to its limits. On each floor, they stopped near the door with a glass window to check. Passing the third floor was fine. They paused again at the second floor, their backs plastered up against the wall as a small group of white-coated technicians walked by. Jess counted in her head. Other than the little group they'd just passed, they'd only seen one lab tech the entire time they were in the building. Sure, it was a Saturday, but it did seem a little strange there were so few people working in a situation where things were locked down doing such important research.

Neither she nor Chase said a word as they descended the steps, only using hand signals to say whether to stop or go. In her mind, Jess knew the most dangerous part of the trip was yet to come. Bobby wouldn't be at the exit waiting for them and she couldn't tell whether the door was locked or not. If it was and they opened it, all the fire alarms in the building would go off, sending everyone who was in the building scurrying out. It would definitely alert the guards to their presence given how few people were in the building.

As they made it to the turn between the second and first

floors, Jess picked up the pace a little bit. They were still trying to be quiet, not making any noise by talking, moving as quietly as possible to not make noises on the concrete steps. Jess peered out the glass door that led into the hallway. There wasn't much she could see. Just a little section of the wall on either side of the hallway. Luckily, the door pulled inward, so at least they had that as an advantage. She reached down and checked to make sure the ABG test tubes were still in her socks. They were.

Taking a deep breath, like she was diving underwater, Jess pulled the door open. There was no one there. She motioned to Chase to follow her. As she glanced at him, she saw how pale he was, as if all of the color had been drained out of his face, leaving him gray, his face showing barely any life at all. She just had to get him to the next building. Then everything would be okay. Her instincts as a sister kicked in. They had to protect each other.

Knowing the ABG was safely tucked in her pant legs, Jess opened the door. As she and Chase started moving down the hallway they pressed forward when they heard a voice, "Hey! That door is secured. You can't go out that way."

Jess wheeled around to see two guards standing behind her and Chase, about halfway down the hallway. Her mind raced. Where did they come from? "Oh, sorry," she called back. "I thought this door was unlocked."

"That's a fire door," the other guard said, narrowing his eyes. "Do you guys have your ID badges? I haven't seen the two of you around here before."

Frozen in place, Jess stared at the guards. One of them was a little taller than the other, with close-cropped sandy-colored hair. The other one was about three inches shorter with a huskier build and black hair. Neither of them looked like they'd shaved in a day or two, the shadow of beards forming around their jawline. They were both wearing the same identical black outfits — black cargo pants and work boots topped off by a long sleeve black shirt and a tactical vest. Each of the guards had a pistol on his hip and a rifle strapped to his chest, a crisp white ID badge clipped to the front pocket.

Jess glanced at Chase, barely able to breathe, not sure what to say. He only blinked and looked to be frozen in time. She noticed his arms and hands were limp; like he'd been doused with a cold bucket of water. She cleared her throat, "I left mine in the car." She glanced at Chase, "I think we both did. I'd be happy to go out and get it for you if you'd like."

For a second, Jess wasn't sure what would happen. She held her breath. The guards glanced at each other and then the shorter one narrowed his eyes again, "Somehow, I don't think that's the truth. I think you know you're in a secured building and that you're not supposed to be here. So, the question becomes, why are you here?" As the words came out of his mouth, Jess saw him tighten his grip on his rifle. He didn't aim it at her, but his grip was enough that Jess knew he was serious. "No, that's the truth. My card's right out front."

"Well, while we figure out what's in your car and what's not in your car, I think the two of you should come with us," the taller guard said, taking a couple steps toward them. "Come on, the security office is this way. "And, let me just tell you that if you weren't supposed to be in this building, then you may have just earned yourself a one-way trip to Leavenworth."

Leavenworth.

Leavenworth was a maximum-security prison in Kansas, the toughest of its kind. The idea of small cells with sliding doors trapping her inside for the rest of her life flashed past Jess's eyes. But there was nothing else she could do. Jess looked at Chase and started walking toward the guards. They couldn't be taken to the security office. They didn't have that much time if they wanted to save Abby. It was as if everything stopped. Jess realized her hands were sweaty. She wiped them on the side of her pant legs and balled her hands into tight fists. If the guards took them into custody, there would be no way they'd ever get Abby back. If the kidnappers were watching the building, they would somehow find out that Jess and Chase had run into the security there, or the police would be called. Either way, Abby, and likely Piper would be dead.

As Jess took a couple steps closer to the guards, she spotted something on the wall. A small red box. An idea flashed through her mind. Lunging, she reached for the wall, pulling the small handle for the fire alarm down. A second later, lights started blinking all over the building, a siren wailing. "What did you do?" one of the guards groaned. He reached for the back of her arm, gripping it tightly. "If we didn't think you were guilty before, you are definitely guilty now."

The guards started pushing Chase and Jess down towards the main hallway. As they walked through the lobby, she saw Bobby at the door, waving people out. There was just a handful of them. For a second, Jess thought that maybe Bobby recognized her and Chase as they walked with the guards. She was sure he did, but he didn't say anything and didn't try to help. Not that his word would have meant anything at all. He'd probably get fired for letting them in. Jess thought that maybe the guards would take them outside with the fire alarm blaring. That was her hope at least, but they didn't. Pushing them forward, they passed the entrance to the main lobby and headed down a separate side hallway, one that was dark.

"Where are we going?" Jess asked.

"You'll see..." one of the guards said.

17

D etective Jamison Saunders was tired of sitting at the office. It wasn't doing him any good. If there was anything he'd learned as a detective, it was that cases were solved in the field. Sitting in the office wouldn't do him any good. He'd been back for only about an hour, studying the videotape from the bank robbery that morning. The problem was, it didn't tell him much more that he didn't already know -- there was more to the story than the Montgomery family wanted to let him in on.

Picking up the keys to the car the department let him drive while he was on duty, he stood up from his desk, leaned over to log out of his computer, and then walked toward the door giving Ferguson a wave as he headed out. Ferguson was on the phone, so he didn't bother to ask Jamison where he was headed off to.

Outside, Jamison stopped for a second in the sunshine, sighing. The day definitely had not gone the way he thought it would, that's for sure. First a bank robbery, then a missing child, then getting blown off by the family. That wasn't a normal day, not in his book. He normally dealt with car thefts and store break-ins, with the occasional domestic violence issue, but most of those were handled through a separate set of detectives in their division. All he could keep thinking was that something wasn't right. It didn't sit well with him. He'd decided to go after a position in the detective bureau after a three-year-old had been hit by a car, the vehicle fleeing the scene. A week later, Jamison put a physics professor in handcuffs. She'd been drinking at the bar with her colleagues after making tenure.

But this case was different. Usually, the families were more than happy to have him help. Not so with the Montgomery clan. They'd iced him from the beginning. He rolled his neck to the side. In a way, it made it more exciting, knowing that he'd have to convince them he was worth trusting. He knew he was. He just had to help them see it so he could assist them in getting Abby back.

His car was parked near a stand of trees. From above, he could hear the chirping of birds hanging out on the branches or in their nests. Which ones, he couldn't tell, the tiny foliage too dense for him to see much past the leaves. A slight breeze had picked up, though it did nothing to cool the heat. The breeze blew the hot air around; like someone had turned on a giant blow dryer to bake the city of Tucson just a little more. Jamison knew that people who visited the area for the first time were surprised by the dry heat, especially northerners who were used to more humidity and a fair amount of snow. Some liked it, some didn't. But Jamison did. It was what he knew. He couldn't imagine waking up in the morning and having temperatures below zero and having to trudge through the snow just to get a cup of coffee. He'd take heat any day over that.

As he walked toward the car, he noticed there was a team of landscapers working in the beds around the police station. They seemed to be spraying weedkiller between the plants, covering the little sprouts of unwanted plants that were peeking up between the rocks used to keep them down in the first place.

A few always seemed to make it through, he thought. It was the same with the Montgomery case, he thought, unlocking the car and getting in. Details were peeking up, but not enough for him to see the whole landscape. As soon as the engine turned over, the air conditioning started blowing, the air first lukewarm, then rapidly cooling the interior of the car.

Pulling out of the parking lot, Jamison tried to make sense of the Montgomery case, to put the pieces together in a way that might make sense. He knew he was missing something. But what? He turned the wheel of the car toward Chase's house. Maybe now that a few hours had gone by they'd be more interested in talking to him. At least that's what he hoped. He knew there was something going on, but it was like someone had draped a veil over the situation. He could only glimpse parts of it, the rest of it murky and foggy. The information from the bank seemed to be relatively clear — the kidnappers came in, they made a lot of noise, they secured the hostages, they pulled Abby out of line and then they wriggled their way down a tiny tunnel and escaped. No money taken, only Abby. It was a targeted hit. Nothing more. Jamison shook his head a little, realizing at least the kidnappers wouldn't be charged with stealing any money from the bank if they were caught. Not that it would help their case much. Breaking into a bank was a big deal, especially in the eyes of the FBI. Last he heard, they were still all over the South Ridge Bank, looking for evidence. He was sure they'd be there for hours. Maybe they'd had more luck talking to Chase and Jess?

The first place Jamison stopped was Chase Montgomery's house, the same wide, low ranch set on a perfectly manicured lawn that backed up to a golf course he'd been at hours before. It was a typical, upper-middle-class piece of Tucson real estate. Walking to the front door, he knocked and then rang the doorbell, announcing, "Tucson PD," as he waited.

No one answered.

Jamison furrowed his eyebrows. The fact that no one was home seemed strange. Weren't the Montgomery's waiting for a call from the kidnappers? He stopped and listened. He could hear the screeching yip of a small dog barking, probably the same one he'd spotted that morning when he talked to the Montgomery's the first time. Jamison decided to walk around the perimeter of the house, a knot forming in his chest. What if the kidnappers had decided to come back to the house and kill the family? As Jamison passed the garage doors, he felt his heart rate increase. He moved his right hand onto the butt of his gun and kept it there, without drawing it, just in case. As he eased around the side of the house, he saw three bikes leaning against the house, closest to a door that looked like it led into the garage. He peered through a small window that gave him a view into the garage space. No cars. There were only a few assorted tools, a rake, and a couple shovels, leaning against the opposite side of the garage wall. He kept moving.

Turning the corner around the back of the house, he could see a few golfers out on the fairway, their golf cart parked underneath the shade of a clump of trees. He glanced at them and kept moving, looking in each of the windows on the back of the house. The first windows looked to be the master bedroom, and then the kitchen and living area he'd been in earlier that morning. Pressing up against the glass, he scanned the floors, looking for bodies. There were none that he could see. He frowned, taking his hand off his gun. None of the doors or windows on the back of the house had been jimmied open. There was no broken glass. It was as if it was a typical Saturday, with a busy young family out running errands or getting lunch or shopping. It wasn't the kind of response he expected from a family whose daughter had been kidnapped.

Jamison walked around the far side of the house, much more relaxed, but still glancing in the windows. It was strange to him that no one was home. He pressed his thumbnail into the pad of his index finger, feeling the nail bite into the skin. As Jamison started to walk down the driveway, he heard a voice, "Hello? Is everything okay?"

An older woman with a tuft of gray hair on the top of her head and a pair of Birkenstocks on her feet was standing at the junction of the driveway and the sidewalk.

Jamison walked over to her, "Hello. Tucson PD. There something I can help with?"

The woman shook her head, looking confused, "Is everything okay with Chase and Piper? I saw you walking around the house."

"And you are?" Jamison didn't want to give the woman any unnecessary information without knowing who she was.

"Shirley. I live across the street," she pointed. "I only live here half the year. I go home to Pittsburgh in the summer to see my grandkids." The hint of a frown passed over her face, "Is everything okay? I can hear Roxie barking in there."

"Yes, of course. I was just coming over to follow up on a case with the Montgomery's. It doesn't appear that anyone is home, though. Everything is secure. Nothing to worry about. I'll give them a call later." He didn't want to give Shirley any information about the case. It wasn't his news to tell.

"I could've told you they weren't home. I don't know about Chase, but Piper, that's Mrs. Montgomery, she left here a couple hours ago. Haven't seen her since. Do you think their dog, Roxie, is okay?"

"Thanks for that. I'm not sure about Roxie, but I can tell you the house is secure. Nothing seems disturbed. I'm sure they're just out running errands or maybe they went to go get lunch. It is Saturday, after all," Jamison lied.

"Okay, well I have a key and their alarm code. I think I'll go get Roxie. Maybe she has to go for a walk."

For a second, Jamison considered having Shirley open up the house so he could have a look around, but he didn't have a warrant and no probable cause, and none of the Montgomery's were home. If he did go in, Shirley would likely report every detail of his visit to the entire development. That was an easy way to end up in hot water. "Do you have an arrangement with the Montgomery's to let Roxie out?"

"Yes, of course. I have a little dog, too. His name is Toby. Roxie and Toby are friends. Piper lets me stop by and pick up Roxie so the two puppies can walk together. It's very sweet."

Jamison nodded, tiring of the conversation, "I'm sure. Well, thank you very much for the information. I'll let you go gather up Roxie. Have a great walk."

As Jamison walked back towards his car, Shirley turned and gave him a little wave, heading across the street. At least he knew the Montgomery's weren't home, and Piper had left approximately two hours before. Nosy neighbors gave great information.

Getting back into his car, Jamison started it up, the police radio chirping in the background about a traffic stop on Palmdale Boulevard and then another downtown. Jamison checked his phone before putting the car into gear. There were no texts, nothing new from Ferguson or anyone else. Jamison stared at the Montgomery's house for a second, wondering if the FBI had stopped by to talk to them and found the house empty. That would certainly frustrate their attempts to get information from them, he thought, shifting the car into reverse and pulling it out of the driveway.

Jamison turned down the Montgomery's street and headed out of the development, wondering what to do next. There were really only a few options — he could go back to the department and do paperwork and wait for something to happen, follow up on another case he'd been assigned, or he could take another drive out to Trident Labs and see what was going on there.

Jess and Chase had made their wishes clear. They didn't want his help, but Jamison didn't feel good about their decision.

How could he? Chase's daughter was somewhere out in the city with people who looked to be methodical and equally dangerous. Not following up – whether they wanted the help or not – seemed like dereliction of duty. Sweat formed on his forehead even with the air conditioning in his unmarked sedan on full blast.

At the stop sign, he made his decision. The other cases could wait. Whether or not Jess and Chase wanted his help, he needed to try. He turned the car toward Mesa Boulevard and Trident Labs. About a mile down the road, the radio in his car chirped to life again, "We have a fire alarm at Trident Labs in the Mesa industrial Park, 73250 Industrial Road. Fire has been dispatched. This is Building B of the Trident Labs complex. Responding units, please identify."

The drone of the dispatcher's voice rang in Jamison's ears. Trident Labs. Was this a coincidence? Jamison grabbed the radio, "Dispatch, this is D577, show me responding."

"Copy that, D577."

Seating the microphone back on the radio, Jamison flipped the lights and sirens on his unit and gunned the engine, feeling it roar to life under his foot. The traffic cleared in front of them, the only obstacle a slight pause at each intersection. The last thing he needed was to get T-boned by some unaware driver as he was speeding to Trident. About a quarter-mile ahead of him, he saw a batch of red lights. The fire department. His heart raced and he chewed his lip. How was it possible that there was a fire alarm at the same building where the Montgomery's had been found earlier that day? Questions flooded his mind, questions about what Jess and Chase were really doing. They were clearly avoiding talking to him. Why were they keeping what happened to Abby a secret? It just didn't make any sense to him. Sure, the kidnappers had threatened to kill her if they got the police involved, but that was normal, par for the course. Even in the movies, kidnappers did that. It didn't mean keeping the police out of it was the smart play. That was the thing that surprised him the most, he thought, as his tires screeched around the corner into the industrial park. These seem like smart people, but they weren't behaving in a way that was smart.

Pulling up in front of the building behind the fire trucks, Jamison sat for a second, staring out the windshield. This wasn't the same building Jess and Chase had been at. It was the one next door. His gut told him something wasn't right. He gripped the handle that opened the driver's side door. What it was, he still didn't know. But he needed to find out.

18

___

Jess and Chase made it halfway down the dark hallway with the two security guards gripping their arms when another man, dressed the same as the guards, came out of an office on the left side of the hallway, a frown plastered from ear to ear. "What are you doing?"

The shorter guard answered, "This woman is the one that pulled the fire alarm. I don't think they're supposed to be in this building. We were bringing them into the office for questioning."

Jess stayed quiet, watching the interaction. The two guards that had them stumbled over their words. It had to be their supervisor. From the look on his face, he wasn't happy.

"It doesn't matter who pulled the fire alarm or not. Everyone has to evacuate. You know that's the procedure. Take them outside like everyone else. Once the fire department clears the building, you can question them, okay?"

The guard started to answer, but the other man, clearly his boss, interrupted, "Don't give me a hard time, Hoffman. Just do what you're told and follow procedure."

Jess felt her body relax just a smidge as she realized they were going outside and not into some dark holding cell. She felt the guard holding her arm, who she now knew was named Hoffman, turn her and Chase back toward the center of the building, toward where Bobby was ushering people out of the building. By the time they crossed the polished, white marble lobby, the first two firefighters had entered the building, decked out in full turnout gear, oxygen tanks on their backs, their masks hanging down on their chests. Jess glanced in their direction and Hoffman tugged on her arm, "Come on. Let's go," he said, pulling her toward the exit.

At the door, Bobby held it open for them, giving Jess and Chase not much more of a look than anyone else that exited the building. As they passed, he said, "Please exit the building and go to the opposite side of the driveways so the emergency vehicles have room to work. Thank you." To Jess, it sounded like a perfectly rehearsed line, one that Bobby had read in some manual somewhere. She glanced back at him, hoping he would say something or do something to help them get away from the guards, but all he did was widen his eyes and stare at her; as if to say there was nothing he could do.

In front of the building, it was chaos. Although there weren't as many safety vehicles as earlier that morning at the South Ridge Bank, there were still plenty. As Hoffman dragged her across the driveway, she counted four ambulances and five fire trucks. Four police cruisers had pulled up as well with a few more behind that Jess couldn't get a good look at. Jess scanned the crowd, wondering if there was some way she and Chase could get break free. Her breath was ragged. If they could just get loose from the two guards, they could probably slip into the small crowd of people and get the ABG back into Chase's building. She wanted to reach in her back pocket to check the time but didn't dare. She was afraid Hoffman would take her phone away from her.

They had just reached the other side of the parking lot when a voice cut through the noise of the small crowd assembled under a tree with small, pointy leaves, "Hey there! Let me talk to you for a second."

Jess turned to see a man wearing jeans and a shirt with a badge on his belt approaching them. Saunders. A million questions flooded her mind. How did he know they were there? Did he find Abby? What about Piper? She didn't ask, afraid to say anything, her heart tightening in her chest.

The two guards, Hoffman and the one with no name turned towards Saunders. "Sir, please stay back. We have these two in custody for questioning because of the fire alarm pull in the building. It's official government business."

Saunders came a few steps closer, his eyebrows raised, "Really? Are you sworn police officers or federal agents? I'm assuming you have permits for all the firearms you're carrying?"

"Private contract security for Building B. We were brought in by the DOJ." No name guard had a smug look on his face as he dropped the Department of Justice name to Saunders, adjusting the grip on his rifle.

"Let me see your credentials please?" Saunders said.

Jess turned her gaze to the guards, who looked at each other as if they were confused. "We don't carry credentials."

"Well, then we have a little problem. See, this building sits on land that belongs to the City of Tucson. I'm a sworn law enforcement officer within that jurisdiction. I, unlike you, have credentials. I also have authority. And last I checked, falsely pulling a fire alarm is a local law infraction, not a federal law, not even a state law. So, if you claim this woman is the one that pulled the fire alarm, then I need to talk to her and her accomplice."

Jess glanced back at Hoffman, who'd loosened his grip on her arm. She felt the blood running back into her hand as she shook it a bit trying to get the feeling to come back. Until he let go, she didn't realize how hard he was holding it. He narrowed his eyes, as if calculating whether he wanted to continue pushing Saunders. Hoffman glanced at the no-name guard and then at Jamison, "All right. When you're done questioning these two, I'd appreciate it if you'd bring them back to the security office here in the building. We do have a few questions about why these two were in the building in the first place since they didn't belong there. We're concerned there was a theft or something else."

"Will do." Jamison settled his eyes on Jess and Chase, "Okay, you two. Let's go have a talk about pulling fire alarms."

As Jess took a couple steps away from Hoffman, she could finally breathe again. It was like she'd been stuck in a teeny tiny space, almost claustrophobic. As she followed Jamison, she took in a deep breath and bent over, pretending to check her shoelaces. She felt for the vials of ABG she'd hidden in her socks. They seemed to be there and in one piece despite the jostling of being buried in her socks.

Jess and Chase followed Jamison without saying anything. Jess checked over her shoulder a couple times, checking on Chase, whose face was a whole new level of pale, his eyes unfocused, staring at the ground. She looked for the guards who brought them outside. The two of them were standing in the same spot where they'd dragged Jess and Chase, staring at them as they walked away, glares on their faces. Jess knew they were more than just run-of-the-mill security guards. But Jamison hadn't flinched at coming to get her and Chase, even with how heavily armed Hoffman and his partner were. That still left Jess with questions about what was actually going on in Building B and why such heavy security was needed. What if the security team at Building B was former special operatives, the same type of people that Charlie told her about that worked for Zeta Tactical Consulting and Colonel Harrison Foster? The kidnappers from the bank robbery this morning carried themselves the same way as the ones that were watching over Building B, with the same alpha male aggression. The thought sent a shiver down her spine. When this was all over, Jess made a note to talk to Charlie about it. They had to figure out what was going on.

A few seconds later, Jamison led Jess and Chase behind one of the firetrucks where his blue car was sitting, the flashing lights still going off near the visor under the windshield. Jamison turned to face them, "Okay, now that I've rescued you from whoever those guys were, would you like to tell me what is going on? Jess, did you pull the fire alarm?"

Jess stared down at her feet for a second, wondering how much to tell Jamison. "Yes, I did pull the fire alarm," she said, swallowing, "But, that's really all I can tell you at the moment. We have to go."

As she glanced at Jamison, she could see a wave of frustration across his face, the muscles in his jaw tightening, "Chase, would you like to add anything to that story?"

Chase shook his head, staring at the ground. "No."

Jess pulled her phone out of her back pocket. It was nearing three o'clock. Time was running out. Butterflies formed in her stomach, "Listen, Jamison. Thanks for the rescue from those guys, but we really have to get back to Chase's lab. There's something important we have to do." She knew the words rang hollow.

Jamison started to answer when Jess's phone rang. A mixture of dread and hope filled Jess, her fingers clumsy as she fished her phone from her pocket. Turning away from Jamison, she answered the phone, feeling out of breath. "Charlie?" she said, turning away.

"What's going on, Jess? Can you give me an update?"

Speaking as quietly as she could with the hum of police and firefighters around the building, just gave Charlie a quick update, telling him about how Chase figured out a way to make the ABG inert, but they had to break into Building B in order to get the samples back. She told Charlie about the guards at Building B and how they'd nearly gotten dragged into the security office when she pulled the fire alarm and how Detective Saunders had shown up and taken them into custody. "The thing is, Charlie, we only have five vials of the ABG."

"And you need twelve?"

"That's right. And complicating matters," she whispered, "I don't know if Detective Saunders understands what's going on. I'm not sure he's gonna let us go back into the building."

"Give him your phone."

Feeling confused, Jess blinked and then mumbled, "Charlie?"

"Just do it."

Jess pulled her phone away from her ear, tapping the button to put it on speaker. She turned towards Detective Saunders and Chase. Chase had his eyes focused on the ground. He wasn't moving. "Detective, my boss would like to speak to you."

Jamison furrowed his eyebrows and then took a step closer to Jess, "This is Detective Jamison Saunders of the Tucson Police Department. How can I help?"

"Detective, my name is Charlie Burns. I'm the Executive Director of the North American Intelligence Institute. As Jess said, I'm her boss. Listen, I don't know how much these two have told you, but we have a critical situation here, one that involves a little bit more than you might think."

"Are you talking about the abduction of Abby Montgomery?"

"Yes, but there is more to this case than just that."

Jess's eyes got wide as she realized Charlie was going to tell Jamison everything that was going on. Holding the phone in her hand, she looked at Chase. He was staring at her. Jess leaned toward the phone, interrupting, "Charlie, if we tell Jamison what's going on we're going to put Abby's life in more danger!"

"Jess, you're going to have to trust me here. I know that's what the kidnapper said. They always say things like that. You two need help. I'm doing what I can on my end, but you have to trust me."

Conflict raged inside of Jess's chest. Everything in her wanted to tap the end button on the call and stuff her phone back in her pocket, pulling Chase away and running back up to the lab to get the samples put together as fast as possible. Abby's face surfaced in her memory. That poor girl. Jess took a deep breath and sighed, closing her eyes for a second, "Okay, Charlie."

"Detective, Chase has been working on a revolutionary medical treatment that could save literally hundreds of thousands of lives in our military. What he's working on is mission-critical to our national security. It's as simple as that. What the kidnappers want is samples of the formula. Why? We don't know. But they've gone to great lengths to target Chase, his family, and his sister in order to get what they want."

Jamison looked confused, "So, what does this have to do with you? I thought Jess was an intelligence analyst."

"She is. And I run the organization she works for," Charlie said, his voice suddenly becoming stern, "But I do a lot more than that. I've been in touch with the DOJ and my military contacts at the highest levels of government, you'll just have to trust me on that. I'm going to tell you right now what needs to happen. Are you ready?"

"Okay."

By the look on Jamison's face, Jess wasn't sure he was buying what was going on. But at least he was listening.

"I'm going to be forthright with you here. Jess and Chase

called me several hours ago to see if I could get access for them into Building B. The DOJ, unfortunately, has that building locked down to an extraordinary level. They are running some sort of top-secret research that I am not allowed to know about. It's nearly Presidential-level access. Do you understand what I'm saying?"

"I think so," Jamison mumbled.

"Good. So, when I was unable to get access for Jess and Chase to get into the building to retrieve the samples of Chase's product, they decided to take matters into their own hands. They did no damage to the building. The only thing they did was retrieve the samples that Chase had sent over for testing that had not been completed. When they were intercepted by guards, Jess did what she needed to do, which was to pull the fire alarm. There is a tight clock from the kidnappers on how quick they expect delivery in order to do the trade for Abby's life, and now Piper's. All of this to say, you are welcome to follow them around for the rest of the day if you'd like, but I need those two back up in Chase's lab, and I need them up there right now."

Jess chewed the inside of her lip. She'd never heard Charlie talk to anyone the way he was talking to Detective Saunders. How he would react to someone being that bossy, she didn't know. She watched for a moment. Jamison stared at the ground as if he was concentrating. What she could see of his face seemed relaxed, like he was just absorbing the information as he went. There was nothing excitable about him. Jess liked that.

It didn't seem that Charlie was going to give Detective Saunders any choice. "Chase? Are you there?"

Chase cleared his throat, "Yes. Mr. Burns, I'm here."

"This is what I need you to do. Go back up to the lab. Take the samples you have and make them work. Do you understand?"

"Yes."

"And one more thing, Chase. I'm not totally convinced that Landon Walker and his crew, if that's who has Abby, want your product for good purposes. While you are working through getting things packaged up, I need you to start thinking about what other applications there might be for the formula – both tactical and medical. Does that make sense?"

"Yes, sir."

"Jess?"

"I'm here, Charlie."

"I want you to work on the same thing. Whoever these people are, they have a reason they want the ABG. I don't believe for one skinny minute that it's because they have kind hearts. People who will go to the lengths this crew has gone to target Chase and his family, they've got no good written all over them. Figure out what they want the ABG for. Call me in one hour with an update."

As Jess pushed the end button on the call, she swallowed, glancing at Detective Saunders, waiting. Jamison had no idea who Charlie Burns was or the extent of his contacts. Would he let Jess and Chase go back to the lab?

Jamison looked at the ground for a second, slowly shaking his head, "Okay, I have no idea what that was, but is that guy on the up and up?"

Jess nodded. "I think at this point in his career the only person he can't get on speed dial is the President himself. He's worked in the intelligence business his whole career. I didn't want to bother him with the abduction. He's up to his eyeballs in Washington power politics." Jess thought about the words as they came out of her mouth. She should have gone to Charlie right away. She stared at the ground. She knew why she hadn't, though she couldn't bear to say it out loud – she was ashamed that she needed the help. How had she lost her niece?

"And you agree the only play to get Abby back is to give them this stuff, whatever it's called, the ABG?"

Jess nodded, "From the first text, that's what the kidnappers were demanding in exchange for Abby's life, and now Piper's."

"All right. Since I don't have any other leads, we're going to go with yours. Let's go back up to Chase's lab, or office, or whatever it is. I'll come with you guys. Jess, maybe you can fill me in on this Landon character that Charlie mentioned."

As they started to walk, Jamison grabbed Jess's arm, "By the way, where is the ABG right now?"

"In my socks."

Jamison shook his head from side to side, "You get a ten for creativity if nothing else. Let's go."

Jess led the way back to the building, the adrenaline still pumping in her system. The four ambulances that had been positioned outside of Building B had left. Jamison's blue car was still parked at the curb behind a single fire truck and the Battalion Chief's SUV. As they crossed the driveway, Jess saw a single police officer talking to the two guards that had brought Jess and Chase outside. Hoffman, the shorter of the guards, pointed toward Jess and Chase as if trying to get the police officer to stop their progress back to Chase's lab. Jess saw Jamison turn back to the officer and flash his badge. She glanced back just in time to see Hoffman's shoulders slump.

Back inside of Chase's building, Sully was standing behind the console when they came in, "Everything go okay?" he asked, leaning his hands on the counter.

Jess didn't stop moving to have a conversation. Time was running out and they needed every minute they could spare. "We're going back up to the lab, Sully. Can you buzz us through?"

"Sure. Who's your friend?"

Jamison angled his body so Sully could see the badge on his belt. "Detective Saunders, Tucson PD. I'm going to be hanging with these guys for a while if you don't mind."

"I don't mind at all. Have at it."

In the elevator, Jess felt her heart pounding in her chest even though they were doing nothing but waiting. She could barely catch her breath. Her throat was tight and her chest constricted like someone was hugging her too tight. The whole day had come crashing down on her in one moment. Spots started to form in front of her eyes, and she felt her breathing get ragged. As the door slid open to the second floor, she bent over, putting her hands on her knees, trying to take a couple deep breaths. "Jess? Are you okay?" Chase said, holding the door of the elevator open for her.

"I'm okay, just a little lightheaded."

Jess felt a hand under her arm. It was Jamison. "Here, let me help you."

With a tug, Jess felt Jamison guide her off the elevator, "Is there a place she can sit down?"

"The conference room," Chase said. Jess could hear his voice but for some reason, it seemed far away.

Jess felt her body move through the hallway and over the doorway into the spot where her computer was still sitting. She heard the wheels of a chair being rolled near her and felt the seat come up under her. "Here, sit down," Jamison said. As Jess eased herself back into the chair, she put her head between her knees. Trying to take deep breaths, she heard Jamison, "Chase, is there a bottle of water we can get for her? Is there a vending machine or something where we can get her candy or a granola bar, or something?"

Jess heard feet moving on the tile. It was probably Chase she realized. A second later, she heard Chase come back in the room, "Here. I have more water if she needs it and I can find more granola bars, too."

The spots in front of her eyes hadn't gotten any better, but when Jamison offered her the bottle of water, she took it, trying to take a few sips. "Just try to relax, Jess," he said.

From the corner of her eye, she saw Jamison stand up. He

passed out of her view. "Chase, go back to the lab. Do what you need to do. All that stuff Charlie said. I'll stay here with Jess. Don't worry. I'll let you know if she needs anything. Where will you be?"

"Right across the hall."

"Wait..." Jess reached down and pulled up her pant leg, reaching for the three vials of ABG she'd stuffed in her sock. She was afraid to look up, worried she would pass out, "Here," she said, extending the vials toward Chase. "Don't forget these."

As she held them out, Jess felt the touch of warm hands. Whether it was Jamison's or Chase's, she wasn't sure.

As soon as Chase left the conference room, everything was quiet. She only heard the rattle of the wheels of another chair being pulled close to her. Jess sat up and took another sip of water, feeling the cool liquid run into her stomach. She blinked a couple times and then looked at Jamison. He was staring at her, but not in the way that she expected. He had kind eyes. "Here. Try to take a couple bites of something."

Jess took the granola bar from him and broke off a small piece, trying to chew it. "I'm sorry. I don't know what happened. All of a sudden, my heart just started to pound and then I felt lightheaded." She fought back feelings of embarrassment. How would she be any good to Abby if she passed out?

Adrenaline. That's what happened."

Jess took another drink of water, "So, in addition to being a detective, you're a doctor, too?"

Jamison chuckled, "No, but I've been on the department long enough to see exactly what adrenaline does to people. It's not good. We have lots of officers that once they get into some sort of a crisis situation have to be transported to the hospital along with the victims. When your system gets charged up with adrenaline, it can be hard for it to come down. Drives your blood pressure up and throws your whole system into chaos."

"I guess I'm just not used to this much excitement in one

day," Jess said. As her body started to calm down, she realized she had work to do. Charlie asked her to figure out why Landon Walker and his crew wanted the ABG so badly. Questions started to churn in her mind, like the ocean in the middle of a storm. "I've got to get back to work. We're running out of time," Jess said, struggling to her feet.

"Take it easy, Jess," Jamison said. "Before you go back to work, I want you to sit for another minute. While you're doing it, tell me about this Walker character your boss mentioned."

Taking another bite of the granola bar and trying to chew it, fighting back a wave of nausea, Jess sighed, "Okay. Here's what we know. I did a thirty-day search on LPRs in the greater Tucson area searching for Chase's and Piper's cars."

"License plate readers?"

Jess nodded, "Yeah. NAII has access to them around the globe. My access is only domestic because that's the type of projects I work on. Anyway, I did a search, figuring that whoever took Abby was using surveillance. Like, pro-level surveillance. I didn't find anything on Chase's car — he went all the normal places you'd expect, Abby's school, the drugstore, home, and here at the lab. But Piper's car was a different case."

Jamison crossed his ankle over his knee and leaned back in the chair, "What do you mean?"

"Well," Jess sighed, "When I did the analysis on Piper's vehicle, I realized she'd been out to a remote area called Saguaro Pass a couple of times. Based on the maps I have access to, there's nothing there. It's just a little parking area off of a two-lane highway that wraps around the mountain. But that wasn't what was really interesting. As I kept looking, I found out that she had been to Desert Springs a lot in the last thirty days, like ten times. At first, I thought she was going out there with girl-friends, but then I realized the frequency was too much. So, I pulled video surveillance from the local businesses and saw her."

"And you did all of this just this morning?"

Jess nodded, a couple of them black spots forming in front of her eyes again. She took another sip of water and a bite of the dusty granola bar, "Yeah. It didn't take too long. This is the kind of stuff I do every single day. Anyway, I found Piper on the video surveillance. She was with a man."

Jamison reached into his pocket and pulled out a notepad, "This Walker person, right?"

"Correct. I didn't know who he was at first, so I did a screen-grab, ran facial recognition and it came back as Landon Walker. That's when Charlie called me."

"Why's that?"

"Well, I used a few of NAII's resources that I really didn't need to this week. Charlie keeps a pretty close eye on who is accessing what kind of intelligence. So anyway, he called me just as I found out that Landon Walker was dishonorably discharged from the Army and now works for a company called Zeta Tactical Consulting. Charlie and I think Landon's boss, Colonel Harrison Foster, is the one behind all of this."

"Who's Foster?"

"A retired Army Colonel. Someone that Walker used to work for. From what Charlie told me, Foster was someone the Army couldn't dishonorably discharge, but they were happy to get rid of. Now he runs his own private security firm."

Jamison scowled, "Why do they want the ABG?"

Jess realized that the conversation had led her right back to the spot Charlie had asked her to investigate — why Walker wanted the ABG in the first place. "That's the part that's confusing. This product, the ABG Chase has developed, Arterial Blood Glue, it's designed to save lives, not hurt them. Why would private security contractors need access to it? And why would they go to the extent of abducting Abby, and now Piper, in order to get it? It just doesn't make any sense."

Jess watched as Jamison stood up and started pacing, "So,

what you're telling me is that you were all targeted in order to get to Chase, in order for these private security contractors to get access to a classified product that is not on the market as of yet. Is that correct?"

Jess nodded, "That's right. But what we don't know is why."

19

L andon was tired of staring at Abby and Piper. Piper had quieted down considerably after Landon held the knife to her neck. But who wouldn't?

Landon twisted in his chair back towards the screens that Baker was monitoring. There was no movement on them, save for an occasional truck that passed by the building. Landon glanced over at Reinhardt, who had put away his sunflower seeds for the moment. He seemed to be picking at something with his nails. A glint off of one of the overhead lights told Landon it was his K-bar knife. There was a constant tick, tick of the knife against something hard. The noise felt like someone was drilling fillings out of Landon's mouth. Before he could tell Reinhardt to stop, Baker interrupted, "Hey, boss?"

As Walker turned, he saw Baker pointing to one of the monitors that were displaying images from the surveillance cameras they'd installed in the parking area of Trident Labs. During their planning cycle, Landon had recommended they get someone in the building to tap into the surveillance already built into the labs where Chase worked, but Foster thought it was too risky. Organizations like Trident had a robust security presence. They settled on surveillance in the trees outside the building, placed by a crew pretending to be there to do landscaping.

"What's going on?" Landon said, squinting at the screen.

Baker paused for a second, tilting his head a little bit, listening to the police scanner on the desk. "Sounds like a fire alarm was pulled at one of the buildings."

Landon leaned back in one of the chairs in front of the command center, resting his elbows on the armrests and intertwining his fingers. This was an interesting development to be sure. He watched as the first fire truck rolled in and a small stream of people came out of one of the buildings. "Is that the same building Chase Montgomery works in?"

Baker pulled the binder across the surface of the desk and flipped it open, looking through a few papers that had been carefully placed in plastic sheet covers. "No. It doesn't look like it is. He works in the main building. From the map we have here, it looks like this is a different building, Building B."

"Any chance those buildings are connected? The last thing we need is to have Chase interrupted while he's trying to get the ABG for us." Landon frowned. Delays were unacceptable, especially on a mission as important as this.

"No, sir. They are close together, to be sure, but not connected."

Another minute went by and then Baker pointed at the screen again, "Sir? Aren't those our targets?"

Landon stood up, pushing the desk chair behind him, leaning forward on the edge of the wood, resting his weight on the palms of his hands. "Zoom in."

Landon heard the mouse click a couple of times and saw as the surveillance camera zoomed in closer to the front door of the building where the fire alarm had been pulled. Two people, a man and a woman, were being escorted out of the building by what looked to be security personnel. Landon raised his eyebrows, "Is that them? They have some serious firepower power in that building. Did we know anything about that?"

Baker flipped a few more pages in the binder and then shook his head, "No. There's nothing about that in here. I guess they didn't do much research on that building since Chase doesn't work there. Probably figured it was siloed."

Landon tried to remain calm. Gaps in intelligence like this were the ones that could doom any operation in seconds. He stared at the screen, watching the security people walk across the street with Chase and Jess, a hand on each one of their arms, keeping them under control. "What did you do to get yourselves in trouble?" Landon muttered, staring at the screen.

He watched for another second, leaning back in his chair and taking a sip of water from a bottle that was half empty. Nothing seemed to happen for a moment, just a few firefighters dressed in their gear walking towards the front of the building. They didn't seem to be in any hurry, which was a good sign, Landon thought. Probably a fire alarm malfunction, or something like that. To top it off, with it being Saturday, there was virtually no one in the building, so it wasn't as though there were a ton of people to move out of the way while the fire department investigated. "Can you zoom in more? Get me a look at their faces?"

Landon heard the roll of a mouse on the surface of the desk and then saw the picture enlarge. Landon had only caught a glimpse of Jess that morning at the bank, just enough to confirm her identity before they put the hood on her, but the person who was standing with the guards was definitely her based on the images he'd seen. The same dark wavy hair, the same athletic figure. Her brother Chase was caught up in the same image. His hair looked rumpled, as though he'd spent the last few hours running his hands through it. The fact that he looked distressed was a good sign. Maybe they would get the ABG today after all.

Landon licked at the inside of his bottom lip, pulling at a little piece of dead tissue with his teeth, staring at the screen. "Is this real-time, Baker?"

"Yes, sir. You're seeing it as it happens. Did you need me to roll it back for you?"

"Nope. Keep it running." Another minute went by. Landon watched as Jess searched the parking lot with her eyes; as if she was trying to figure out how to get away from the guards. Chase didn't do the same. He just stared at the ground, completely submissive, as if he was lost in his own world. That was good. Maybe Chase was thinking about Abby. Desperate people did desperate things. Hopefully, Chase was desperate enough to give them the ABG.

Landon watched for another minute, taking in the scene. The psychological profile they'd done on the Montgomery family looked to be spot on. Jess seemed more assertive, while Chase seemed more inwardly focused and not as confident. Landon glanced over at Piper, who was still huddled in the corner of the cage with her arms around Abby.

Baker zoomed the view out, giving them a better look at what was going on in the parking lot. A mass of emergency vehicles had parked near the front entrance of the building, but nothing seemed to be happening very quickly. From behind one of the fire trucks, a man appeared, walking directly toward the crowd. He had on a pair of jeans and a shirt. He was aiming directly for Jess and Chase. Leaning a little forward on his chair, Landon saw the man had a pistol on his hip. "Son of a gun," he muttered. Landon pointed to the monitor, "Is that a police officer?"

"No idea, sir."

Landon stood up again, feeling a little bit of heat move through his body. If the police got involved in this case, it could potentially slow everything down to a snail's pace. First, it would be the local police jurisdiction and then the FBI would get involved. Not that they weren't already. He watched as the police officer walked over to the two guards. Within about thirty seconds, the guards had dropped their hands off Jess and Chase. Landon watched as Jess inched her way away from the guard that was holding her, moving closer to the police officer as if he was a safe harbor. Landon flicked the nail on his right thumb with his index finger, thinking. As part of the ransom demand, they'd told the Montgomery's not to involve the police, that they'd kill Abby immediately if that was the case. But the Montgomery's had no idea whether Landon and his crew knew about police involvement or not. Strategically, he would let this play out, at least for a little bit. Maybe Jess and Chase were just using the police officer as a way to get away from the guards that were holding them. That would be a smart play. That would be what Landon would do if he was in the same situation.

"Should we do something, sir?"

Landon shook his head slowly, "No. Let's let this run for a little bit. See what happens. That guy is clearly a police officer, but I don't want to act too quickly. Let's see where this goes."

Before Baker could ask any other questions, Landon's cell phone rang. Foster. "Sir?"

"Calling for sit rep, Walker. What's going on?"

Landon swallowed, "Well, currently, the two targets are in custody by some heavily armed private security guards in front of the Trident Labs building. I don't know why that is. A police officer has just walked to intercept. We still have Abby and the wife in custody. They are both healthy and unharmed." Landon almost told Foster about the cut to Piper's neck but decided not to. It was inconsequential, really.

"Didn't you tell them no police?"

"Of course, sir. That was already preloaded in the scripts the team put together. We just played them. We didn't alter them at all. But you have to think with a bank robbery, there's going to be all sorts of law enforcement working the case."

"Any sign of the FBI?"

During their mission briefing, Foster seemed to be more worried about the FBI than the local law enforcement presence. That was for good reason. The federal agencies were much more well-funded and well-trained than the locals. "Not much, sir. From the surveillance cameras, we saw them arrive at both the house and the lab building, but they had no luck at either. By the time they arrived at the house, the family was already gone. Apparently, either the security staff at the lab building didn't know Jess and Chase were upstairs, or they wouldn't let them in." Landon shook his head and furrowed his brow, pacing back and forth. "I do want to add one note, sir. The guards that have Jess and Chase right now are heavily armed. Rifles, pistols, and full tactical gear, minus helmets. It's kind of strange, if you ask me."

"And these are the guards from Chase's building?"

"No, sir. They appear to be from the building next door." Landon realized there was noise behind Colonel Foster. "Sir, are you in the ops center?" The headquarters of Zeta Tactical Consulting looked like a simple office building from the outside, but the reality was there was an armory, ops center, and a couple of floors of analysts and mission planners available to the teams at all times, plus a medical bay and racks where the guys could get some sleep either before or after missions. It was like a mini military base that no one would ever suspect by the looks of the outside of the building.

"I'm headed back there now. Had a meeting to attend. Listen, that's not why I called. We've got a team rolling out for the Middle East at midnight tonight. I need that ABG. I need time to process it and get it ready to go with my guys for the buyer and our teams. Landon, you're going to have to speed up the timeline. It's four o'clock there now, correct?"

Landon looked at the time in the corner of the computer screen in front of him, "Just about, sir."

"See if you can push up the timeline. Let's get these people moving."

"Sir, I'm not sure I'm going to be able to get them to move any faster. We gave them a six o'clock deadline. That's only a couple hours from now. That's not fast enough?" Landon didn't want to argue with Foster, but the timeline was already tight. Any variations on the delivery could change things dramatically. And not for the good.

"Walker, this is not a discussion. See if you can get these people moving a little faster. Do what you need to do. That's an order."

Foster hung up without saying goodbye. Landon stood for a second, staring at his phone, his mind racing. He just wasn't sure how much quicker he could get Jess and Chase moving. If he was unable to get them moving, he knew what the consequences would be. Plenty of operatives had disappeared from Zeta Tactical Consulting. It was "the law of the wild," as Foster called it. Landon had no inclination to get either he or his team caught up as a casualty because Chase Montgomery was inept. Landon stared back at Baker, "What's going on with our police officer?"

"While you were on the phone with Foster, the police officer got them away from the guards. I saw them reenter Chase's lab building. What's going on inside of there, I have no idea."

Landon glanced over at Piper. She was still sitting, huddled in a ball next to her daughter, her eyes closed. Landon stared at her for a second from where he was seated and then narrowed his eyes, pushing himself up out of the chair. Taking long strides, he went over to the cage, staying outside of it. "Piper," he called.

She didn't answer, keeping her eyes closed. Landon gave

her until the count of three to answer. When she didn't, he nodded to Reinhardt, who unlocked the padlock. With one smooth move, Landon charged into the cage and grabbed her by her braid, yanking her up, tearing her away from Abby. Landon heard the jingle of the chain being reattached, hearing a low moan from her throat as Reinhardt secured the cage behind him. "When I speak to you, respond to me. Is that understood?"

Piper jutted her jaw out at Landon, her head at an unnatural angle with the grip he had on her hair, "Sir, yes, sir," she said sarcastically.

The fact that Piper had the nerve to be so mouthy infuriated Landon. He let go of her hair and slapped her across the face, her head spinning to the right as his palm connected with her cheek. Piper dropped to her knees, holding the side of her face with her hand. "It doesn't pay to be difficult," Landon said. He glanced at Reinhardt, "You and Alvarez take her out back." Landon saw Baker watching him from the command center, "Baker, stay where you are and watch the feeds. Let me know if anything changes." Baker gave a curt nod but didn't say anything.

Reinhardt and Alvarez pulled Piper to her feet, half walking, half dragging her out of the warehouse through the rear entrance. Landon turned back just in time to see Abby, who had stood up, her fingers entwined around the chain-link of the cage, her eyes wide, watching them as they took Piper away. At least she had the sense to stay silent, Landon thought. She was way smarter than her mom. Must take after her dad.

Landon followed Baker and Alvarez out the back doors of the warehouse. There wasn't much there, just a three-sided concrete pad with buildings on either side of it, with access to the single loading dock the warehouse had. There was some litter against the edge of the building, some old fast-food wrappers that hadn't made it into the single dumpster that was at the back of the building.

The afternoon had become hot and even more dry than usual. Just stepping out into the sun caused Landon to sweat, little beads of perspiration gathering on his head. But the heat didn't bother him. It was nothing compared to Afghanistan. He was focused on Piper. Alvarez and Baker stood Piper up, turning her towards Landon as he emerged from the inside of the building. "Listen, our timeline has shortened. I need you to call your husband and tell him to get us what we need. I need it now. I can't wait any longer."

Piper didn't look up at him, just staring at the ground. Landon could see the side of her face bright red from the sting of the slap. "No," she whispered.

"Excuse me?" Landon growled. Rage built inside of him.

Piper lifted her head slowly, staring at him, "I said no," she said slowly, spacing each word out.

Landon moved towards her, positioning his face just a few inches from hers, "Do you understand what's at stake here? Do you want to be responsible for whether Abby lives or dies?"

"I'm not going to help you!" she screamed in his face. "You are a dirty, filthy liar! Let me out of here right now!"

Landon took a step back, surprised at her reaction. "You can scream all you want, but if you look around, you can see there's no one here. No one is going to hear you. No one is going to come and help." A smug smile spread over his face. These were the moments he lived for; when he knew he had the upper hand, the life and future of his captives up to him. "This is very simple, Piper. I'm going to dial your husband's number. You are going to tell him to get the ABG for me now. And then, when he does, I will return you and your little wavy-haired daughter to your precious little home so you can go about living your boring life."

Piper struggled against Baker and Alvarez for a second, her

face reddening. The men held her firm. Landon saw a couple of tears roll down her face when she realized she couldn't get away and there was no one there to help her. "All right," she whispered.

"That's what I wanted to hear."

Landon pulled his phone out of his back pocket and opened the encryption program that would allow him to contact Chase without the call being tracked. There was only one number saved in the program. It was for Chase. A moment later, the call connected. Landon put it on speaker. Two rings went by and Chase answered the phone, "Hello? Abby? Piper?"

"It's Piper..."

"Oh my God, honey, are you okay? Where are you?"

Landon didn't give Piper a chance to answer, "We need the ABG in one hour. I'm gonna text you in thirty minutes with the drop-off location. Be ready."

"You said we'd have until six. That means you wanted it at five!" Chase stammered.

"Plans change. Be ready." Landon said.

"I have to finish prepping the ABG. I need all the time that you gave me. I promise I'm going to get it for you."

"That's not good enough. Do you want your family to suffer?"

"No, but..."

Landon didn't give Chase a chance to answer. Holding the phone in his left hand, He pulled his pistol out of the holster and gave a curt nod to Alvarez and Baker, leaving Piper to stand by herself. He raised his gun at her face and pulled the trigger before she could register what was about to happen to her. Piper's body fell backward in a small pile, a single red mark in the center of her forehead. "That was your wife. Don't make me do the same to your daughter. I'll be in touch in thirty minutes."

Landon ended the call and re-holstered his gun. He looked

at Baker and Alvarez, "He was better off without her, believe me," he shrugged. Nodding toward the dumpster, Landon said, "Throw her in there. I'll let the cleanup crew know there's a body." Landon turned on his heel and walked back into the building.

20

Jess sat, stunned. When the call came in from the kidnappers, Chase ran across the hallway from the lab, holding his phone in front of him. This time, the voices weren't masked with the fake, female AI-generated voice. It was clearly a man. And clearly Piper. The call was quick and to the point. They wanted the ABG within the hour. Chase stood in the doorway, staring down at his phone, trying the best he could to negotiate for more time. Jess watched Jamison as he motioned for Chase to keep them on the phone to tell them he needed more time to prepare. When the shot rang out and the call ended, Chase slumped down to the floor against the wall in a pile, not moving.

Jess glanced around the room. It was just three of them. The muscles in Jamison's jaw rippled as he shoved his hands in his pockets. From where Jess was standing it looked like the skin had tightened over his entire face, a mask emerging. For a second Jess wondered how many times Jamison had been in this kind of situation, the echo of the single shot ringing in her ears even though it was through the phone. She replayed the conversation again in her mind. The kidnappers tightened the timeline. They heard Piper's voice. Then they heard the shot. Jess got up out of her chair, the muscles in her jaw tightening, kneeling over Chase, "Chase, we don't know what happened. Let's not make any assumptions. It was probably just a warning shot — something to try to get you to move a little faster."

Jamison agreed, "She's right, Chase. We don't actually know what happened. The best thing you can do is get the ABG ready. We have less than an hour at this point." He stared down at his phone, "I'm going to go brief my lieutenant."

Chase looked up, the rims of his eyes read, "No, Detective. You can't..."

"Sorry, Chase. No matter what the kidnappers say, I still have to do my job. And believe it or not, the best thing for you and your family is if I do just that."

Jess moved her body so she was sitting next to Chase, both of them leaning against the wall. Neither of them said anything for a moment, the weight of the phone call laying heavy over them. "Do you think Abby's still alive?" Chase whispered.

Jess glanced at Chase. The heat of anger filled her chest. Who were these people to think they could take Abby? She swallowed, the memories surfacing of how guilty she felt and how many nights she agonized over losing the relationship with her brother. She closed her eyes for a second. Today wasn't the day to make the same mistake, and it wasn't the day to cave in. She had to be strong for the two of them, stronger than she'd ever been. There wasn't a lot of time left. She looked over her shoulder at him and grabbed his hand giving it a squeeze. When she let it go, she said, "Chase, we have every reason to believe Abby is still alive. For that matter, Jamison is right about Piper. We don't know what happened. It's very likely Walker and his crew just let one round fly to scare you. From what I can see, they did a good job. Listen," she said, turning toward him, putting her hand on his knee as they sat on the floor, "right now we have to work off the information we have. That's what I have to do in my job. That's what you have to do in yours. The information we have is that they need the ABG. Figuring there's going to be a little bit of drive time, we need to have it ready in less than half an hour. That's what we can do to help Abby right now. Do you understand what I'm saying?"

Chase took off his glasses and used the sleeve of his shirt to wipe his face. Whether it was sweat or tears from the shock of the phone call, Jess wasn't sure. He struggled to his feet, offering Jess a hand. She stood up and looked at him, "Are you okay? Ready to move forward?"

He nodded, letting out a long breath. "Yeah. I just finished coating the inside of the vials when the call came in. They were all set up on the dryer so I can add the ABG. I should be able to load what serum I do have into them in the next few minutes. The thing is," Chase stopped for a second and stared at the floor, his body angled, ready to walk out of the conference room, "Jess, I'm not sure I have time to figure out why these guys want the ABG. I have to agree with your boss. There's no way somebody would go to all these lengths, even pretending to kill my wife, just to save lives. It doesn't make sense. It's not logical."

Jess nodded and sighed, "I know. It doesn't make sense to me either." She glanced back at her computer, trying to be positive even though her gut wasn't that optimistic, "Don't worry. I'm sure Charlie is working on that angle right now as we speak. I'm gonna get on my computer while you load up the ABG and see what I can figure out. Either way, if the ABG becomes inert, it won't matter." Jess had the beginning of a thought as Chase walked out of the conference room. She called after him, "Chase? What about the formula? They wanted the formula, too!"

Chase tilted his head to the side, "Don't worry about that. I have that done already."

"Will it work for them if they try to replicate it?"

A small smile crept over Chase's face, the first one Jess had seen all day, "Nope. And they'll never know why."

Alone in the conference room, Jess sat down at her computer, opening the lid, waiting for it to warm up again. She was trying to corral her thoughts to get her mind working in the right direction, but it felt like a stampede of wild horses had run over her body in the last few hours. She uncapped her water and took a sip, reaching for the granola bar again and taking another bite. It tasted terrible, but at least she knew it would keep her blood sugar up enough so she wouldn't pass out.

Jess stared at the wall in the conference room, her eyes unfocused. She felt so bad, so weak. How could she let Chase down like this? Deep inside her, she'd tried to be rational about Abby's kidnapping, to know that things were out of her control, but there was still a part of her that felt like the whole day had been her fault. She'd wanted it to be fun for Abby. That was the whole point. But the robbery, the kidnapping, and then having to tell Chase, and then Piper being taken — everything had gotten out of control. No matter what she did, Jess felt like it was her fault. She swallowed, balling her hands into small fists. She realized they were clammy, damp from the rush of emotions cycling through her body. "Come on, Jess," she whispered, trying to derail the thoughts that threatened to get her completely off track. "Chase needs you." She knew she was putting a lot of pressure on herself, but she knew in her gut that if she didn't stay strong, they would never see Abby again. It was up to her.

Jess keyed in her password on her computer and started doing a few random searches on the type of injuries that Chase was trying to prevent. Using the NAII databases, Jess quickly found thousands of reports of military men and women who'd been killed by gunfire that hit them in the neck, the shoulder, or the groin. Those were all locations in the body where there were junctions of large arteries, femoral, brachial, and carotid. As she read a few of the reports, scanning them for the high-level details, she realized what Chase was trying to accomplish. She found one report of a Marine sniper who was positioned on a hillside in the Kandahar province of Afghanistan. He'd been there for forty-eight hours, waiting for a convoy of arms dealers to come through the area. The way the report read, he wasn't the only sniper there. The arms dealers had positioned their own overwatch security to help the arms dealers get down the road. The way the spotter reported it, the sniper moved his rifle into position and the sun must've caught a glint of the scope he was using. A second later, the spotter reported hearing a whoosh and then seeing his partner drop. A round from across the valley had nicked his neck. There was blood gushing out. Jess leaned forward as she read the rest of the report. Although the spotter had medical training and medical supplies, there was no way for the spotter to stop the pumping of blood that drained the life out of the sniper in under two minutes.

Jess blinked. She had heard Chase explained this to her earlier, but somehow reading a real-life account of what had happened changed things in her mind. She tried to imagine the spotter and how frustrated and scared he must have felt, knowing there was nothing he could do for his friend. If Chase's product worked the way he said it did, then the spotter could simply have pulled a dose out of his vest, applied it to the wound, and called for a medevac. For a moment, Jess's mind fast-forwarded to the Marine chaplain showing up at the sniper's house, his wife answering the door, knowing what the visit meant. Chase's product could save lives, that was for sure. Jess had no doubt about that.

But that didn't change the fact that Walker and his crew, or whoever they were, couldn't simply want the ABG to save more lives. It just didn't make sense. No matter how she looked at it, there was no way they would go to this length in order to get their hands on what Chase had developed. What could they possibly want with the ABG?

Jess did a few more searches on arterial injuries in the field and found pretty much the same report. It didn't matter whether it was military or local law enforcement or even construction accidents that involved arterial damage, for that matter. Arterial injuries were something that took a lot of lives every year. Jess stared at the screen for another minute and then got up and started to pace. Her gut told her she was missing something. There was something about the theory Chase was using that wasn't fully fleshed out. She ran through the details in her mind again. She knew the idea behind the ABG was to quickly close the wound. How did he say that would get done? Clotting, she remembered.

Jess sat down at her computer and did a few minutes of research on clotting. Millions of articles popped up within just a few seconds. Jess's eyes got wide. Scanning a few of them, she quickly realized that with the modern-day sedentary lifestyle most people followed, blood clots were becoming more and more prevalent, taking lives in the form of pulmonary embolisms or even devastating strokes. People would get an ache in their leg, assume it was just a pulled muscle or pinched nerve when it was really something called DVT, Deep Vein Thrombosis. If one of those clots broke off and made its way to another area of the body, like the heart, lungs, or brain, it could do devastating damage. Jess's mind started to put pieces in order. She reached for the granola bar and broke off another bite. As she was thinking, Jamison walked back into the room, "What's going on here?"

Jess held up her hand, licking her lips. She was onto something, but she just couldn't quite figure out what. She heard the chair next to her squeak as Jamison sat down. She scrolled through a couple more of the articles in front of her when she ran across a small excerpt from a graduate student at the University of Wyoming who'd written a piece called, "Clotting Factors in the Human Body: All Good or All Bad?"

As Jess scanned the article, she saw that the graduate student had provided an overview on the difference between how clotting helped at the surface of the skin versus the damage it did on the inside. It was basic medical knowledge, but it was something Jess needed to hear. "That's it," she whispered.

"What's it?" Jamison said.

Jess pushed herself up out of the chair and ran across the hall into Chase's lab. "Chase! What would happen if ABG got into the inside of the body? Not the outside. I know that you mean it to solve the problem of the arterial wounds. But what if it got inside, like into the bloodstream?"

Chase was hunched over his workbench, putting teal stoppers on the top of test tubes, small ones filled with a red liquid. He frowned for a second and then glanced at Jess, "Well, it would do exactly the same thing as on the surface of the skin. It would create a clot." As the words came out of his mouth, he stared at her, his eyes open. "Are you saying...?"

"I think so. I'm wondering if the kidnappers want to use the ABG as a weapon. I don't know how they would deliver it, though. But if they could get it inside of someone instead of using the ABG on the surface of the skin, it would kill somebody nearly every time, right?"

Chase nodded, putting the last teal stopper on the vial. "Yeah, for sure. It's one of the first concerns I had about the design. This stuff is designed to clot. That's its entire function. So, yes, if it got inside of the body there would be a problem. On all the tests I've run, we've only used surface wounds from cadavers. Larger scale testing is the next step. There's been no internal leaking of the ABG into the body. But, if you delivered it directly inside, or if it had access to blood vessels, there's no telling where it could go."

Jess stared down at the floor. How would someone get the ABG to the inside of the body? How would they do that in a military setting? Her mind began to race, ideas popping up. She looked up at Chase and blinked, "What if someone ingested it? Like in a drink?"

"The same thing would happen. They would suffer from a massive esophageal clot."

Jess chewed her lip. That would work if the kidnappers were targeting individuals for assassination, but that was one body at a time. A thought started to form in her head, "Chase, what about ammunition? What if the ammunition was coated in ABG? What would happen then?"

Chase was loading the vials into a carrier with a handle when she said the words. He stopped. He stared off for a second and then looked back at Jess. "You're thinking that if ammunition was coated with ABG and it penetrated the skin instead of being used on the surface? Is that what you're asking me?"

Jess nodded, "What would happen?"

"Well, it's entirely hypothetical, but the ABG is still designed to clot."

Jess shook her head, frustrated. "You aren't understanding me. If the ABG got inside the body because of a gunshot wound, would it make a clot that could then travel around the body?" As soon as the words came out of Jess's mouth, she knew she was onto something.

Chase didn't answer for a second, his gaze focused on lifting the test tubes in their carrier into a small soft-sided bag that looked a lot like what Jess used to carry drinks to a picnic. The tray disappeared inside, Chase zipping the lid closed before turning and looking at her. "That's exactly what it would do." He sounded resigned to the fact that on the surface ABG could heal. Inside the body, it could kill.

Jess didn't wait for Chase to say anything more. She darted back across the hall, grabbing her phone. She dialed Charlie, "Charlie?"

"Yes? Do you have an update?"

"We think the kidnappers may have killed Piper but we're not sure. I'll tell you more about that in a minute. I think I figured out why they want the ABG."

"Go on..."

One of the things Jess appreciated about Charlie was that he didn't interrupt her train of thought. He'd worked with analysts long enough to know that once their brain got chugging along on a problem, it was best to let them keep building their momentum, like a locomotive moving along a railroad track. Stops and starts with too many questions could derail the entire process. "So, we know the ABG is designed to create clots at the surface of the skin, right?"

"Correct."

"So, I did some research on clots. There's a big difference between clots on the surface of the skin, which protect us from infection and start the healing process, versus clots that are on the inside of the body, which can be life-threatening, causing things like strokes and pulmonary embolisms."

"And you're thinking..."

Charlie was doing a good job leading Jess through the conversation, she thought, sitting down in one of the conference room chairs and taking a sip of water, "So, what I'm thinking is if they were able to deliver the ABG to the inside of the body, it would, without fail, create a clot, which could be devastating."

"And how would they do that?"

"Ammunition."

"What are you talking about?"

Jess stopped for a second, collecting her thoughts. The ideas were coming faster than she could get them out, "Well, it's just a theory at this point. It's nothing Chase had even considered until just a few minutes ago, but it is possible, according to Chase, that if somehow ammunition was coated with the ABG, if it managed to connect with a person and got inside the body, it would clot whatever it hit. That clot could cause devastating damage."

There was silence on the other end of the line. From working with Charlie for so many years, she knew he was thinking. A second later, he said, "All right, I'm with you so far. Can you flesh that out a little bit?"

Jess shook her head, "I don't know, Charlie. It's just the beginnings of a hypothesis."

"But if you and Chase had to guess, what do you think?"

"If you take what we know about Colonel Foster and Zeta Tactical Consulting — the things you've told me about how you think they have ulterior motives, and the company does more than just executive protection and asset transportation — then I think there's a very high probability they might want the ABG for nefarious purposes. If that's the case, and if they somehow found out that Chase was developing the ABG and figured out another application for it, say assassinations, that would be big business. There are plenty of bad actors across the globe that would be more than happy to pay Colonel Foster and his team to take care of people that are causing them trouble."

"I'm on board with that. From what we know about Harrison Foster, he's a bad actor all unto himself. Go on. Tell me how you think this might work."

"If Foster's team got a hold of the ABG and they were somehow able to harness it and get it inside of people's bodies, it would kill them. Blood clots kill. We know that science backs it up. Let's say they were able to coat a nine-millimeter round with the ABG, they shoot someone in the gut, and then the ABG gets inside the body…"

"... then instead of the ABG saving their life, it would kill them."

"And even worse," Jess said, starting to pace, "what if they coated a knife with it or put it in someone's drink? Or, what if their target was in a prison and they were able to get a shiv to someone that was coated with ABG? Instead of the person simply getting stitched up and spending a couple days in the hospital, they'd be dead within a couple minutes, a clot heading to their heart or lungs. Charlie, we have to find a way to stop them. They can't get the ABG. They just can't!"

Charlie whistled, "This is worse than I thought. Was Chase able to package up the ABG samples in a way that would make them inert?"

As Jess was talking, she saw Chase come out of the lab. He must have heard Charlie's question. As Jess looked at him, he nodded. "Yeah. He took your idea and made it work. We've got the twelve samples and the formula ready for them. Chase somehow altered the formula so it won't ever work for them, but they won't know that on the face of it."

"So, what's the next step?"

"We have to wait for the kidnappers to get a hold of us." Jess checked the time on her cell phone. It looked like fourteen minutes until they would text them the information on where to meet to do the trade. "We've got a few minutes left before they're supposed to call. And Charlie, there's one more thing."

"What's that?"

"They have Piper. A little while ago, they called Chase and he heard her voice. That's when they updated the timing on everything. But then, we heard a gunshot. We didn't hear Piper's voice after that." The words trailed off as they came out of Jess's mouth. She swallowed, feeling the bile rise in the back of her throat. While there was certainly no love lost between her and Piper, seeing how devastated Chase was at the thought of his wife being murdered tightened her heart into a tiny knot.

She pushed back thoughts of Piper laying on the ground some-where and Chase and Abby trying to go on without her.

Charlie's voice lowered, "Jess, do we have any evidence that it was anything more than a warning shot?"

"No."

"Then let's not borrow trouble, okay? One step at a time. I know you have a lot of experience on the analytical side, but not as much in operations. I know this is your family, but you've got to stay clear-headed right now. I need you to do exactly what you do in an analysis, which is one step at a time. There is no way for you to process this thing as a whole. All you can do is take the next step."

"And the next step is to wait for contact from the kidnappers."

"Correct."

Jess hung up with Charlie with the promise that as soon as the kidnappers relayed the details for the meet she'd pass them along. She wasn't sure exactly what Charlie could do to help, but she now knew Charlie had his fingers in a lot more than she ever suspected.

Jess sat down in one of the conference room chairs and closed her eyes for a second, steeling herself for what was coming. Her gut told her they would be on their own. Chase was standing in the doorway, leaning against the frame, staring down at the floor. Jess heard a rustling at the door. She opened her eyes. Jamison was back. "I've updated my Lieutenant on exactly what's going on. Once you get the details for the meet, he's gonna roll our SWAT team. We aren't going to use any of the normal road guys for this. The SWAT team is highly trained in covert operations."

Chase glanced up, his eyes wide, "I'll bet they aren't trained as well as this crew. They could get all of us killed!"

Jess licked her lips and glanced between the two men. Chase was about to break, the stress of the day taking its toll on him, but he was right. She glanced at Jamison, a frown forming on her face, "What about the FBI? Have they gotten wind of this?"

Jamison shook his head, "No. Ferguson isn't too fond of the FBI. They've made his life pretty difficult at times. When I asked him to keep it quiet, he was all about that. He said he'd brief the SWAT commander and get them ramped up and ready to go. He's always said our local guys are better than the FBI anyway. They have a better sense of the terrain."

Jess wasn't sure exactly how true any of that was, but just knowing that Jamison had managed to convince his lieutenant not to get the FBI involved made her feel better. It was bad enough that the police were involved at all, not to mention how much of a disaster things could become if the feds showed up. Hopefully, the FBI would stay at the bank and take their time to process the scene while they were handling the trade to get Abby back.

"What do we do now?" Chase said.

Jamison glanced in his direction, taking up a spot leaning against the wall, "We wait."

21

Landon was getting antsy. Normally, operations involved a lot of moving around. There were planes and boats and trucks in order to get to the destination to access their target. They usually spent an hour, maybe two or three, on target and then they left, leaving nothing more than their shadows passing across the ground. It hadn't been that way with this operation. Spending all day sitting in a dark warehouse had put him on edge. Landon got up from the command center where Baker was still watching the video feeds from the Montgomery's house, the outside of Trident Labs, and the outside of the warehouse. Landon started to pace. He folded his arms across his chest, staring at the ground, counting his steps. Five one way and then a quick pivot and then five the other. He scratched the side of his face and looked at Baker, "Are we ready to send them the coordinates for the trade, Baker?"

"Yes, sir."

The trade location had been predetermined by Foster and the planning team as they worked with Landon. It was a park near an entrance to a freeway. They'd chosen Hacienda Park for a few reasons. Landon ran over them in his mind as he kept pacing. There were still a few minutes left before they would send the information to Chase Montgomery's phone.

Running through the plan in his head, Landon remembered sitting in the ops center at Zeta Tactical Consulting, the room mostly dark, except for a bank of screens against one wall and work lights over the table where they were sitting. The team had just finished lunch and Foster wiped his mouth before starting the meeting again. That afternoon they had talked about three or four possible exfil plans, ways to get the team out of the area after getting what they wanted from the Montgomery family. One of the first options put forth was to have the team hop on the freeway and go over the Mexican border. Foster had a lot of contacts in Mexico, especially with the cartels. They would be more than happy to help one of Foster's groups get away from the Arizona police and the border patrol. "I don't like that idea," Walker had said at the time. "Too many variables. Too many people involved."

The team spent the rest of the afternoon wrestling with options and finally had settled upon a little park that was five miles from the warehouse where he was standing right now. Hacienda Park was hardly ever used, based on the surveillance information they had from a satellite cruising overhead. The good thing about it was that there were five different entrances and exits. That made it just difficult enough for any prying eyes to figure out which way they were coming in or going out. Better yet, it was only a half-mile from the closest freeway entrance. They would use that as a red herring. Most local law enforcement, and Landon had to assume at this point that even though the Montgomery's had been told not to involve the police, interaction with the Tucson police officer in front of the Trident Labs building had resulted in them knowing exactly what was happening, weren't skilled enough to stop the exfil of an experienced team like Walker's. There were also three small airports in the desert within twenty miles of the park. Foster already had planes stationed at all three of them, flight plans filed as if they were moving legitimate travelers to different places in the country. One of them was scheduled to fly to California, another one to Wyoming, and the third one to Texas. Once Landon and his team made the trade, they would go directly to the closest airport, unless they were being tailed, in which case they would substitute one of the other airports, knowing that would give them enough time to escape whoever was chasing them. Foster and his team had also pre-positioned substitute vehicles in a couple parking garages nearby. It would be easy enough to dart in, jump out of the vehicle they were driving and grab a different one, quickly pulling out onto the street and resuming their journey, shaking whoever was following them.

As Landon ran through the details, he had to give Foster credit. Somehow, the man always came up with newer and more clever ways to get his teams in and out of difficult situations. And he had no issue spending the money to do it. Checking his watch again, Landon tried to calculate how much an operation like this would cost. It had to be in the millions of dollars, Landon realized. By the time Foster paid for their salaries, plus all of the needs they had for the operation — everything from weapons and tactical gear to the mechanic's garage Foster bought in order to give them access to the bank — Landon knew the cost was steep. And it wasn't like Foster was paying Landon and his guys the same rate they got paid in the military. They were all in the multiple six figures, with bonuses for their effectiveness and efficiency based on the number of successful operations they were able to complete. The flipside was that failure to perform could be deadly. If they didn't deliver the ABG, they were all as good as dead. The people that wanted the ABG wouldn't take no for an answer.

Landon checked his watch again. It was time. "Baker, send it."

"Copy that, sir."

A moment later, Baker gave Landon a curt nod. The message was on its way. Landon and his team wouldn't need the full thirty minutes to get themselves and Abby out of the building and to the location. Their goal was to arrive approximately three to five minutes after the stated time, and it was close by. All they needed was enough leeway to make sure that the Montgomery's were already there waiting for them. Landon didn't like standing around and waiting for his targets, especially in a case like this. In and out. That was the goal. With any luck, the trade should take less than three minutes. Foster had set them up with the testing kit that would give them the information they needed in order to make sure that Chase hadn't substituted something else for the ABG. Foster even had a chemist standing by to quickly check the formula Chase was supposed to provide. If everything went well, they'd hand over Abby and be on their way. At least, that was the hope.

22

Charlie picked up the phone on his desk, starting a secure line, realizing his hands were clammy. There was someone he needed to update, someone who had the resources to help. Charlie wasn't sure if he would, but based on what Jess had said, this was an issue of national security.

A voice answered after just a few seconds "Dumont."

"Admiral, Charlie Burns from NAII. Sorry to bother you on Saturday, sir."

"That's no problem, Charlie. I was just outside tending to my basil plants. What can I do you for?"

Charlie had gotten to know Admiral Dumont as part of the work NAII had done for the military. Charlie wasn't sure if he'd actually call them friends, but they were on their way to being so. They discovered a mutual love of great Italian food and even better bourbon. "I have a little bit of a situation I wanted to bring you up to speed on. See if there are any options you'd like me to explore."

"And, since this is a Saturday, this is in regard to national security?"

"Yes, sir."

"I'm all ears."

Charlie took two minutes to give the admiral a quick overview of exactly what was going on — the carefully planned bank robbery that morning at South Ridge Bank, the way the Montgomery family had been targeted, the fact that the kidnappers had Abby and possibly killed Piper already, and the demand for the ABG and the formula.

The Admiral cleared his throat, "And you believe that whoever has taken this young lady, and you believe it to be that retired colonel — what did you say his name was?"

"Foster."

"And you believe he and his goons are the ones that are doing this? He is the one that wants the ABG for his own use?"

"Yes, sir. Based on some recent information I got, he's been in talks with some of our favorite characters from Yemen, Turkey, and some other countries on the top hits list."

The Admiral grunted, "Sounds like my basil might have to wait."

"I'm sorry about that, sir. What would you like me to do?"

"Stay by your phone."

CHARLIE WAS DOING EXACTLY what Admiral Dumont said and staring at his computer screen at the same time when one of the analysts burst into his office, "Boss, I think I've got something on the Montgomery kidnapping."

The analyst, a young woman wearing torn jeans with her hair up in a ponytail approached his desk, pointing at the computer, "May I?" she said.

Charlie got up, giving her room to work. Carla hadn't worked for Charlie for very long. They'd brought her in from a program that tried to recruit some of the best black hat hackers in the country into white hats, giving them legitimate jobs where they could use their skills instead of working as cyber-criminals. It had been a rough three months. She and Charlie had some harsh words every couple of weeks as he tried to help her adapt to a new way of life. Breaking her of her lone-wolf habits had been tough, but if she'd found something about Abby, then in one moment, she'd prove herself to be an important part of the team. "What did you find?"

"The information you sent over to me; I checked this girl's school records. Seems she's quite the soccer player. I hacked into the sports team information and then followed the trail over to her coach."

Charlie frowned, "You hacked the soccer coach?"

Carla nodded. "You wanted information, right? You'll see why in a second. Anyway, it turns out the soccer coach is really into analytics. Even for middle schoolers. Can't say I really understand that, but this woman keeps detailed notes on every-thing. She just had the team run their forty times."

"What does that have to do with finding Abby?" Charlie was losing his patience.

"Give me one sec and I'll show you." Carla's fingers flew over the keyboard and an array of screens popped up all at once. Charlie blinked, surprised at the way his computer reacted.

Carla pointed at the screen as she pulled one of the docu-ments forward, "See here? The coach used the same type of RFID trackers they use for cross-country runners to track the girls' forty-yard dash times. The girls must have them attached to their running shoes."

Charlie shook his head a little bit. He wasn't a runner, but he knew people that were. Even for local races, the runners would be issued a little plastic chip that attached to their laces. It tracked when they crossed the starting line and when they crossed the finish line, instantly recording their times down to the hundredth of a second. "So, what are you saying here?"

"I'm saying that with any luck Abby has that pair of tennis shoes on this morning. Let's take a look. If she does, I can probably figure out where she is." As soon as the words came out of Carla's mouth, she pulled up another screen and typed in a long code plus a whole string of numbers. "This will take just a second."

Charlie watched as she worked. A map of the United States pulled up on Charlie's screen. Within a second it had started to narrow down the location, zooming in on Arizona and then Tucson. "Hold on, it's searching. Let's just hope she didn't leave this pair of shoes at home," Carla muttered, tapping her finger on the desk, her long purple nails making a clicking noise while they waited.

"There!" Carla pointed. She zoomed in a little bit closer. "That doesn't look like the Montgomery's home address to me." The RFID chip pointed to an area just outside of Tucson proper, an area Charlie wasn't familiar with, but then again, he was in Washington.

"What is that place? How far out is it from the lab where Chase works?" Charlie's heart was beating fast in his chest. Knowing where Abby was meant they finally might have the upper hand. Now, if they could only get to her in time. He checked his watch. If Jess and Chase hadn't already gotten the trade-off information, they would soon. That was, if there was a trade-off actually planned. Charlie hoped they weren't being played, but if they knew where Abby was, that was better intel than them heading over to some remote location where Walker and his crew had the advantage. What they knew for sure was that Walker and his team wanted the ABG. There was never any guarantee of the Montgomery family -- any of them -- walking away alive.

"It doesn't look like their house," Carla said, staring at the screen.

"No, it does not. Get me that address right now."

23

J ess and Chase were checking the vials in the cooler one more time, going over the plan with Jamison when Jess's phone rang, "Charlie?"

"I know where Abby is." With that kind of information, it didn't bother Jess that he didn't say hello.

"What? How did you figure it out?"

"One of the new girls from the hacker program figured it out. Abby is wearing an RFID chip on her tennis shoe. Carla said the coach was using them for tracking their forty-yard dash times."

As soon as the words came out of Charlie's mouth, Jess realized what he was saying. They'd all been so proud of how fast Abby was. It never even occurred to Jess that if Abby was wearing the same shoes she ran in they could track the chip. "She was able to find her?"

"Yes. I've got the address. I'm gonna send it to your phone."

"We were just about to leave to go to the meet. Shouldn't we do that and follow their instructions?"

"I don't know, Jess. That's gonna have to be your call. I'm not on the ground with you, so I can't say. All I know is we have a confirmed location on Abby right now. I can't say that we'll have anything better anytime soon. Once they have her on the move, there's no guarantee of what will happen."

"Okay, thanks. Send that address." Jess started to run the scenarios in her head as she hung up the phone.

"What was that about?" Chase asked.

"One of the hackers on Charlie's team found Abby. We've got a location." Jess's phone chirped. It was a message from Charlie, the address attached with two simple words, "Good luck."

JAMISON STARED AT JESS, "Send it to me. Right now. I'm gonna roll SWAT to that location."

"But we're supposed to be going to the meet right now. What if they've already left?" Chase said.

Jess pulled up the mapping feature on her phone and then ran directions between the address Charlie just sent her and where they were supposed to meet Landon and his crew. She checked the time. It wasn't far. It would only take Landon and his crew a few minutes to travel between the two locations. "Unless they want to get a head start on us, they're probably still there."

Without saying anything, Chase scooped up the ABG vials and ran into his lab, coming out a second later, darting down the hallway. Jess could hear the jingle of his car keys as he passed. She grabbed her cell phone and ran after him, "Chase! Where are you going?"

"I'm going to go get my daughter and wife back."

Jess took off after him running for the stairwell, leaving Jamison still in the conference room. She flew through the door and jumped down the steps, trying to keep up with him. As she heard the door on the first floor pop open, she saw it click into place as she got to the landing on the first floor. She caught a glimpse of Chase, but he was still ahead of her. Running across the lobby, she saw him rush out the front doors, toward his car. The screech of tires caught her attention. Chase ran right in front of a car that was trying to pull into the parking lot, having to slam on its brakes to avoid hitting him. Chase barely broke stride, only giving a little wave and running for his car. By the time Jess caught up, he'd already started the car and was backing out of the spot. "Tell me where we're going," he yelled, shifting the car into drive and slamming on the accelerator, the car lurching forward with a squeal of tires.

Jess pressed her hand against the dash, holding herself in her seat as she got her seatbelt on. Once it clicked, she pulled up the mapping program on her phone. "Get on the freeway. Go south. Down two exits and we'll get off. It's not far. This says it's an eight-minute drive."

Chase passed three cars going well above the speed limit down Mesa Boulevard. He merged onto the freeway so fast, Jess was worried he was going to lose control of his car and flip it. "Chase!" Jess shouted. "We're not going to do Abby any good if we die in a car accident on the way there."

Her comments didn't deter Chase's wild driving at all. Jess breathed a prayer under her breath, hoping they would get to Abby's location safely and without getting killed or pulled over by a state trooper. As she watched the desert fly by, Jess realized they'd left Jamison behind without even talking to him about what to do. After wiping her palms on her jeans, Jess sent him the coordinates for the building they were going to. She just hoped that SWAT would beat them there and that Landon and his team hadn't left with Abby yet. If they were in transit to the location where they were supposed to meet up and Jess and Chase didn't show up with the ABG, Jess didn't know what would happen. Jess swallowed, trying to push the bile from the back of her throat back down into her stomach. Whether it was from nervousness about getting Abby back or motion sickness from the way Chase was driving, she wasn't sure.

Chase got off two exits south of Mesa Boulevard, taking the ramp onto Parkland Avenue. "Turn right," Jess said.

The tires on Chase's car screeched as they went around the corner. Jess grabbed a hold of the handle that was near the top of the passenger side window, trying to keep herself straight in her seat. She sucked in a breath, feeling her stomach lurch again. Glancing down, Jess saw they needed to make another turn, "Chase, you have to slow down. We have to make some turns here. If you're going too fast, we're going to miss them." Jess glanced down again, trying to see where they were on the map. The next turn was a left. "We're looking for 33rd Avenue." Jess looked up ahead of her. There wasn't a lot going on in this area of Tucson. It looked to be mostly industrial, a cluster of older buildings that had signs in front that read things like, "Tucson Tool & Die," "Baker Restaurant Equipment, and "Southwestern Fertilizing Service." She squinted and stared at the buildings, not recognizing anything. Jess pointed to 33rd Avenue as it came up, and Chase turned the car to the left. "Chase, what's the plan when we get there? They're expecting us to meet them at Hacienda Park, not at the building."

The muscles rippled across Chase's jaw, "I'm going to go in there, get my daughter and my wife and give them the ABG. Then, I'm getting back in the car and taking my family home."

"We don't have any backup."

Chase glanced at her, his eyes searing her with a whole new level of anger, "We don't need backup, Jess. We have what they want. They have what I want. It's that simple. They'll give me the girls back. I'll give them the ABG. We will walk away and go on with our life." He glared at her, "Either you'll help, or you'll stay in the car. Your choice."

It wasn't that simple. The odds that Chase would march into the building and get what he wanted wasn't something Jess would bet on, but there was nothing else she could say. She'd seen Chase in this mood before. Single-minded and stubborn to the point of stupidity. As she held her phone, she realized her hands were shaking a little bit. She just hoped that Chase's belief that Landon and his team would do the right thing was correct. She wasn't sure it was.

24

J ess and Chase had run out of the building so fast that Jamison hadn't had an opportunity to talk to them about the trade for Abby. All he had was the address Jess had forwarded to him. By the time he ran out of the lab building and got to his car, Jess and Chase were nowhere to be seen. He quickly sent a text to her, hoping she would take a second to read it, "Jess, don't go into that building by yourselves. These people are dangerous. I've got SWAT on the move as we speak." It wasn't exactly true, but he was about to make that call.

"You got something?" Ferguson said as he answered the phone.

"I'm sitting in the Trident Lab's parking lot. I've got a location on Abby Montgomery."

"How?" Ferguson asked as Jamison put his car into gear.

"Something about a hacker that Jess's boss knows. You don't want to know."

Ferguson chuckled, "Sounds like I actually don't. What's the play?"

"I need you to roll SWAT to that address. I just texted it to you. Chase and Jess took off out here like he'd been lit on fire. They aren't waiting for the drop."

"You've got to be kidding me!" Ferguson bellowed.

"I know."

"What do these people think they're going to do when they get there?"

Jamison put his phone on speaker and set it on the seat next to him, heading down Mesa Boulevard. He hit the button for his flashing lights, clearing the traffic in front of him, "I have no idea. Chase is a real scientific guy. Not a ton of street sense, if you ask me. He probably thinks he's just going to charge in there, hand them the stuff they want and get his daughter and his wife back. I'm not sure that's the case." Jamison glanced down at his phone hoping that Jess would reply to him.

"I'm gonna get SWAT moving right now. Let's hope they can get there before the entire Montgomery family gets killed. Try to keep them under control, okay?"

"I'll do my best," Jamison said, pressing his lips together. He could only help as far as Jess and Chase would let him. If they were already in that building when he got there, there was no telling what might happen. Jamison ran through the scenarios in his head. The biggest problem was that Landon was not expecting Jess and Chase to show up at the building where they were holding Abby. Landon was expecting to see them at the park. If Jess and Chase were law enforcement that might be a strategic advantage. But they weren't. They were completely unprepared, and as far as Jamison knew, had no background in dealing with these kinds of situations. They were running on pure adrenaline and the need for justice.

Jamison's mind raced as he turned onto the freeway, following the squawk of the GPS on his phone. Jess was a little better, he reasoned, since she worked in intelligence analysis, but that didn't mean she had any real-world experience, anything that might help her in dealing with armed mercenaries. Jamison shook his head a bit, gripping the steering wheel tighter. For that matter, their own SWAT team might be outgunned and outmaneuvered. This whole scenario was likely to blow up like a box of Fourth of July firecrackers if they weren't careful. Jamison pounded his fist on the steering wheel. Why had he not stopped them when they ran out of the building? Anger flooded through him. It was his responsibility to protect people. Now people he was trying to take care of got away from him. In his gut, he knew he wasn't responsible for the choices Chase and Jess were making, but that wasn't how he felt. He had sworn to serve and protect the people around him. And that's what he was trying to do. But if they ran off ahead of him without letting him help, his hands were tied.

"Let's just hope SWAT gets there in time..." Jamison whispered.

25

Abby shifted on the little metal bench bolted to the floor inside the cage. She'd been sitting there for what felt like hours, the hard metal sending cramps down the back of her legs and into her back. She wasn't used to sitting for so long and especially not on something so hard. Most of her sandwich was sitting on a dirty paper towel on the floor. A couple of flies were dancing on the surface. Abby blinked back a couple of tears. She didn't know what'd happened to her mom. They'd taken her outside and she didn't come back. Abby heard the shot. Thinking about it, she swallowed, hoping they just moved her mom someplace else. Maybe they just did that to scare her. Abby had seen that in a movie one time. It had been a story about a kidnapping, just like what was happening to her. The kidnappers wanted to scare the person they'd taken so they took someone else, pretended to kill them, and hid them away in the bathroom. Maybe that's where my mom is, Abby thought, trying to console herself. Maybe she's in the bathroom. Maybe she's figured out some way to get a hold of my dad or the police so they can get us out of here.

The whole day had been a blur. The only clear memory she had was having breakfast with Aunt Jess that morning. From the minute they walked into the bank, nothing made sense anymore. Only fragments of memories were coming back — the loud noise of gunshots, the scratchy feel of the hood over her head, the smell of dirt as the men made her crawl through a tunnel, and the greasy smell of the van they put her in. Abby stared down at the flies that had gathered on the sandwiches again. They seem to buzz around and land every few seconds, trying out different parts of the bread and meat that were left. Abby nudged the sandwich farther away from her with the tip of her shoe, a wave of nausea gathering in her stomach. There was no way she could eat, especially now that she had no idea what happened to her mom. Abby looked down and realized that her right hand was shaking. She stared at it, willing it to stop, but it didn't. A lump of fear formed in her throat. All she wanted to do was go home, crawl into bed and hug their dog, Roxie.

Abby glanced up. She hadn't really made eye contact with any of the men since they got her to the warehouse. She'd only been out of the cage one time and that was just to use the bathroom. The tall guy, the man in charge called him Reinhardt, had gripped her arm tightly as he walked her to the back of the warehouse opening the door and looking inside before giving her a little shove and closing the door behind her. "Hurry up," he'd said. Other than that, all Abby had done for hours was sit and stare at the floor. She was afraid to look too closely at any of the men, afraid of what they might ask her to do. She tried to make herself small, but it was hard. She felt like one of the animals at the local zoo in a cage. Abby shifted on the bench a little, trying to put her weight on the other side of her body hoping the cramps in her back would stop. She glanced down at her hand again. It was still shaking.

From over her right shoulder, she heard voices talking.

They were low, almost too soft for her to hear what they were saying. Two men stood at the bank of monitors. They'd been there all day long. The only time either of them left was when one of the men had come to the cage to get her mom. One time, her mom had come back, blood on her neck, her face pale and sad. The other time, she didn't. Abby felt a fresh set of tears form in her eyes. She sniffed, not wanting them to come out.

The men working at the monitors caught her attention. She glanced to the right, keeping her eyes on the floor, but tilting her right ear, hoping to hear a little more of the conversation. All she could hear were snippets of words -- "Time is running out," "They need to get us what we want," and "I hope Chase is smarter than that." Abby's heart started to beat faster in her chest. Maybe the men were getting worried. Maybe her dad would find her after all. He was the smartest person she knew. He always had an answer for problems. She just hoped he could find her in time. That someone would. Doubt flooding over her, she fought the urge to scream and rattle the cage door, telling the men to let her out, but Abby sat frozen on the metal bench, willing her hand to stop shaking.

26

Jess and Chase were two minutes out from the building where they believed Abby was being held when Jess finally got Chase to get the car under control, "If you don't slow down, we're gonna pass the building. They might see us," she pleaded with Chase, who finally let up on the accelerator. Jess sighed, feeling part of her stomach return to where it was supposed to be, the wave of nausea lifting a little.

"Which building is it?" Chase said, leaning over the steering wheel.

Jess stared at the GPS on her phone and then looked for the numbers on the building. There weren't many buildings in the area and most of them looked to be closed. A couple of them had large for-sale signs on them, commercial real estate that had been the victim of a downturn in one way or another. The buildings in the area were brick and cinder block, not at all consistent with the type of architecture that the rest of Tucson had, Jess thought. The structures looked more like they came from the Midwest in an area where manufacturing was a priority, not in the middle of the desert. "There!" Jess said, pointing straight ahead of them. "I think that's it," she said, looking down at the GPS. She watched the distance count down and the arrows pointing to the building on the screen.

In front of them was a two-story brick building that looked much like it had been built in the 1950s. It was nothing more than a square box with a few windows scattered here and there. A small steel awning covered the front door. There was a large for-sale sign posted in the front of the building, mounted onto two staunch wooden posts. A matching sign had been hung near the roof, with the name and a phone number in case someone was interested in purchasing it. "Looks like it's abandoned," Chase said, stopping just down the street from the building.

"I'm sure it is," Jess said. "You wouldn't want to try to hold a hostage in an occupied building, would you?"

"I guess not."

Jess stared at Chase for a moment. He seemed extraordinarily calm given what they were about to do.

On the side of the building, Jess saw a door and what looked to be a garage bay, something that was big enough to move trucks in and out of, something the size the kidnappers could have moved Abby in. Next door was another building that looked like it had been constructed at the same time, the same color brick and design. There was no for-sale sign on that building, just a small sign on the front lawn that said Paint-Works. "I've never been in this part of Tucson before, have you?" Jess whispered.

Chase shook his head.

"Okay, so what do you want to do?"

Chase reached around into the backseat where the cooler with the ABG was sitting, still upright despite Chase's driving, "I'm gonna walk up to the front door and see if I can get my family back."

Jess swallowed, her heart pounding in her chest. She looked

at her phone for a second as Chase opened the driver's side door. She looked at the text she'd sent to Jamison, seeing he replied and told her to wait. Glancing up, she realized Chase was already approaching the building. "We're going in," she typed, quickly sending the text and shoving her phone in her back pocket.

Getting out of the car, Jess realized there was no way she could let Chase go in all by himself. In some ways, she'd gotten them into this mess. She had to see it through until the end, no matter what that meant, no matter the consequences. Gritting her teeth, Abby's face emerged in her mind again, the image floating away as Chase slammed the car door. Getting out, Jess felt the late afternoon heat radiating up from the road, pressing up through the soles of her tennis shoes. She looked around. There was no traffic, no road noise from vehicles passing by. The area was largely abandoned, only the whisper of a breeze rustling the grass in the background.

Jess walked toward a small sidewalk in front of the building. Chase was already halfway up it by the time she closed the car door. As she trotted to catch up to him she felt every fiber in her body tingling.

By the time she caught up with Chase, he was already at the door. He used his fist to pound on it, "Open up! I know you have Abby in there!" Chase stopped for a second, bending over, pulling a fistful of the vials of ABG out of the bag, wrapping his fingers around them and holding them up to a small window next to the steel door. "I have what you want. Now give me my wife and my daughter!"

Jess stood back just a little, her hands sweating, waiting to see what would happen. A second later, the door cracked open, a short man dressed in black tactical gear from head to toe motioning them in.

Chase disappeared inside. Jess looked back over her shoulder at the car. Everything in her wanted to run back to it and hide, waiting for Jamison, or someone, to come and help. But she knew she couldn't leave Chase. She was the only backup he had. She swallowed and followed him inside.

For the most part, the building was dark. Jess stood just inside the doorway waiting for her eyes to adjust. The interior of the building was empty, save for the equipment and the setup for the kidnapping. Her eyes were drawn to bright lights in the corner where she saw a chain-link cage with bright lights hanging over it. A small figure was huddled in the corner. Abby. The breath caught in her throat, anger surging in her chest. She was alive and looked to be unhurt. But before Jess could yell for her niece, she heard a voice to her left. "Pat them down," a man growled.

Landon Walker.

Jess knew exactly who it was. He looked exactly like the image she'd identified with facial recognition just a few couple hours before. He had a pistol drawn out of its holster, black gloves on his hands. It was pointed directly at them. Jess glanced around the room. There were three other men in addition to Landon, a taller man, and then two others that were similar in size to him. Jess tried to remember if they resembled the people she'd seen at the bank. It had to be the same crew. She felt the hair stand up on the back of her neck.

A voice drew Jess's attention as she felt rough hands pass over her body. They weren't polite. "They're clean, boss."

Landon stared at them, cocking his head. "Well, you must think that you're awfully clever finding us here as opposed to waiting for the drop."

Neither Jess nor Chase said anything.

Landon let the pistol slump down to his side, but he didn't holster it. At least that was a step in the right direction, Jess thought, relieved he wasn't pointing it at her anymore. "I'm guessing you are here to get your family back, Mr. Montgomery?"

Jess squinted at Landon. She was surprised by the relaxed tone of his voice. It was as if they'd been caught into a spider web, and Landon was the spider. A shudder ran through her body. They were standing in front of four armed mercenaries with nothing but hope to defend them.

Landon glanced at Jess, "You must be Jess," he said, staring at her. "I think we met briefly this morning at the bank; if you could call it that."

The way the words landed on Jess, she knew he was taunting her, challenging her to respond. She didn't. Landon finally re-holstered his gun, and started pacing back and forth in front of them, "I can see that we need to make some adjustments in our mission planning for the future, huh, boys?" He nodded at the other three men. "A couple of civilians managed to get past our planning. We'll have to talk to Colonel Foster about that. He won't be pleased." Landon stopped for a second and stared at Jess and Chase. Jess caught a glimpse of Chase, who was still holding the vials of ABG in his hand, his knuckles white from gripping them so tightly.

Landon stopped for a second, looking at both of them, "So, I suppose we should try to make the best out of a bad situation, don't you think? You have something I want. I have something you want," he said, nodding at Abby. Landon looked straight at Chase with a challenge in his eyes, "Oh, don't you worry, Dad. Your little girl is unhurt. We haven't done anything to her at all, at least for the moment."

"Where's my wife?" Chase hissed.

"I'm not exactly sure, to be honest. She was here at one point, wasn't she?" Landon glanced at the other men, half a smile pulling on his cheek. Jess knew Landon was mocking them. No one moved.

Jess held her breath. It was taking every bit of her self-control not to bolt out of the door behind her. Landon was dangerous, far more dangerous than she'd ever expected. Not only did he have military training, but he was likely a sociopath. He was playing with them, batting at them with his long claws, like a cat with a mouse cornered. They were just play toys to him, something to be enjoyed. Questions started to fill her mind. Would he actually make the trade? Why wasn't Piper with Abby?" Jess swallowed.

"I see you've brought something to trade with, Mr. Montgomery," Landon said, giving a short nod. "Is that the ABG?"

Chase was still holding the fist of vials. Jess closed her eyes for a second, hoping that Chase didn't grip them so hard that it broke them. "Yes. Let's get this done," Chase said.

Jess watched Chase as he spoke. It was like they were stuck in a slow-motion movie. Jess moved her eyes down Chase's arm. The knuckles that were holding the strap on the cooler were white. His other hand was balled into a fist, his lips pressed together into two white lines. It was the four mercenaries against the two of them. Chase was holding his own, but for how long, Jess wasn't sure. Landon turned to her, "Are you expecting someone else to show up, Jess? Is that why you're looking at the door? I can call you Jess, right?"

Jess didn't answer, knowing that whatever she said he would use against her. She just stared back, locking eyes with him, a fresh wave of anger surging through her.

Landon looked back at Chase, "I can see your sister is a fighter. Sounds a lot like your wife, huh?" Landon folded his arms across his chest, "Yeah, Piper is a real fighter, especially in bed." He cocked his head to the side, "I wouldn't have taken you for a guy that likes such an aggressive woman. What are you, mild-mannered on the outside but you like it rough when the doors are closed?"

Jess watched Chase, willing him to stay calm. Landon was using tried and true psychological warfare techniques, ones that Jess had read about over and over again in her work, to try to break them down, but had never experienced. She sucked in a breath, trying to separate herself from the words coming out of Landon's mouth, knowing they'd have to stay clear-headed. If they weren't careful, she and Chase would end up locked in the same cage as Abby. The only advantage they had was the fact that Chase was gripping the ABG in his fist.

Landon must have seen her pressing her lips together. He turned back to her, "Would you like to say something? Did you want to comment on your brother's sex life? I mean, I'm here, I'd be happy to make a go of it with you if you'd like. The bathroom isn't big, but we could make it work."

The other three men chuckled under their breath; as if listening to Landon tear apart Jess and Chase was some sort of sport. Probably to them, it was, Jess realized. She pulled in a breath slowly, willing her body to relax. Landon could clearly read signs of tension in a body. The last thing she wanted to do was give him any indication she was weakening. They'd never get Abby back if that was the case.

Jess didn't bother answering. She glanced at the cage. Abby had gotten up from her spot on the bench and was standing at the front, her fingers looped through the chain-link. Abby was staring right at them. Jess wished there was some way she could tell Abby things would be okay. But she couldn't. Worse yet, there was no way to promise that. Jess swallowed.

Chase straightened up, "Do you want this ABG or not?"

Landon raised his eyebrows, "Is it really the ABG? What happens if I test it?"

"It's the ABG."

Landon blinked and stared at Chase, "Do you know what will happen if it's not really the ABG?" Chase stood, unmoving. Landon didn't give him time to answer, "There are several options if it's not really the ABG you've brought me, since the two of you were nice enough to join us here at our facility," Landon said, extending his hand as if he were giving them a tour of the local art gallery. He continued, sarcasm dripping from his voice, "We could simply take you with us. Now, I would have the option of leaving your sister and your daughter here. Oh, and your wife, too. If we can find her, that is. We can drag you off to one of our facilities and have you re-create the ABG for us at which point we will decide whether to let you go or not." Landon glanced at the other men as if there was really an option to be discussed. "The other option would be that we kill all the women in your family in front of you and take you with us. Or, depending on my mood, we could just kill all of you and leave your bodies here. This building is abandoned, so there is no real telling when someone might show up to help. I have noticed there seem to be a lot of flies. They do a thorough job on a dead body." Landon furrowed his eyebrows in mock concern, "That's a problem, isn't it? I think they eat eyes first." He turned to stare at Jess, "I'm assuming you're the one that figured out where we were hiding? You're an intelligence analyst, correct?"

Jess didn't say anything. The anger in her chest was building. Landon was working on the two of them, grinding away at whatever sense of normalcy they had, bit by bit. He was pushing them towards a reaction, one they couldn't control. She had to stay calm if she wanted to keep her wits about her.

The tension in the room was growing moment by moment. One of Landon's men shifted the rifle on his chest, lifting it a bit higher. Next to her, she could hear Chase's breath going in and out, almost like he was panting. She said a silent prayer that Chase would stay under control. It was their only hope.

When Jess didn't answer, Landon stopped talking. A stalemate. Landon looked back and forth at Jess and Chase a couple of times as if he was calculating what to do next. From the computer set up behind them, Jess heard a couple of quiet beeps, the hum of the air conditioning in the warehouse kicking on, cool air filtering down and touching her skin.

Landon's eyes narrowed, "Throw her in the cage with the

kid," he growled. He pointed at Chase. "Bring him over to the command center. Let's get this ABG tested. Baker, send a message to Foster. Let him know we've been invaded and ask for orders."

One of the men grabbed Jess by the arm, his grip so tight it pinched her skin. He gave her a shove and pushed her towards the cage, never letting go of her. As she drew closer, she saw Abby, who had slunk back to the corner, perched on the metal bench, her knees pulled up to her chin. The man who held Jess pinned her up against the cage with his body as he unlocked the padlock where Abby was trapped. Jess could smell his sweat and his breath as he pressed up against her. He didn't use his hands, but his body was enough. She could feel the hard shell of his Kevlar vest across his chest and back, the corner of it digging into her side. Once he got the chain off the door, he shoved her inside with enough force that she tripped, having to catch herself on the back of the cage. Behind her, she heard the rattle of the chain being looped back around the gate. She watched as the man put the lock back into place, sealing her inside.

As soon as she regained her balance, Jess reached for Abby, wrapping her in her arms, "I am so sorry, honey," she said, letting go of Abby long enough to look at her face. Glancing at the rest of her, Jess said, "Are you okay? Did they hurt you?"

Jess could see Abby was blinking back tears, "No," she whispered.

Hugging the girl close to her, Jess glanced at the inside of the cage. There were two sandwiches and two bottles of water on the ground, uneaten, flies buzzing over the top of them. Letting go of Abby, Jess pushed the food away with her foot, under the gap in the fencing and outside of the cage. No one would be eating those. The shock of joining Abby as a hostage settled on Jess. She frowned. "Abby, where's your mom?" she said quietly. Glancing around her before Abby answered, Jess noticed that Landon and his crew had dragged Chase away. She thought she could hear low voices in the background, but under the bright lights of the cage, it was difficult to see. It looked like all of the men were with Chase. They probably figured Abby and I aren't going anywhere, Jess realized.

Abby grabbed Jess's hand, her fingers cool and clammy against Jess's warm skin, "I don't know, Aunt Jess. They took her out one time and brought her back. She had a little cut on her neck. She wouldn't tell me what it was from. Then, the same guy came and got her again. They went outside, I think. She didn't come back after that. Maybe they brought her in a different way and put her someplace else?"

Jess didn't want to be the one to tell Abby that her mom might not be alive anymore, but she needed to find out how much Abby had absorbed of the situation. "Okay, that's good information. You could do my job for me! Tell me what other details you can. Did you hear anything? See how many people went outside with your mom?" Jess was treading lightly. Abby had already been through so much. There was no reason to traumatize her more, especially if nothing was confirmed. Maybe Abby was right. It was possible Landon stowed Piper somewhere away from Abby just to keep her off balance.

Abby stared down at the ground, chewing her lip, "I think three of the guys took my mom outside. The one that put you in here stayed with me. He just sat on that chair over there and ate sunflower seeds. It was gross. He spit the seeds out on the floor."

Jess glanced toward where the chair was. Sure enough, there was a smattering of shells on the ground. At least it was better than chewing tobacco, Jess thought. "Okay, that's good. What else? Did you hear anything else after they took your mom outside?" Jess knew she was fishing, but if they were able to get out alive, Abby was going to need help. The details in her memory might be able to help her heal.

"I heard a loud pop. I wasn't sure what it was."

Jess stroked the back of Abby's hair. Apparently, Abby didn't want to think about the fact that it could've been a gunshot. If she wanted to describe it as a loud pop, that was okay. Denial was okay for now. "That's good, Abby. Really good." Jess looked behind her. There was still no sign of Chase or the men. And there was still no sign of Jamison. They were all alone.

27

L andon didn't know whether to be furious or grateful. The fact that Chase and Jess Montgomery had shown up on his doorstep with the ABG was like Santa delivering presents on Christmas. On the other hand, there was a serious flaw in their mission plan. Clearly, there was no need for them to go and stage at Hacienda Park, and as far as he knew, all of their exfil plans were still in place. Following as Baker and Alvarez dragged Chase over to the table where they had the testing equipment ready to go to the drop, Landon shook his head a little. Who shows up to confront a bunch of mercenaries without a weapon? Either Jess and Chase were naïve, or they were more brilliant than anyone he'd ever encountered in his career. Which one, he wasn't sure just yet. He pushed the thought to the back of his head. What was important now was that Chase had done what Landon asked — he'd shown up with vials of something he claimed to be the ABG. Whether it actually was or not remained to be seen.

On a table behind the command center in the corner of the warehouse, Baker opened up a small test kit. He'd been trained during their mission prep to run the test on the ABG. With

Baker's background in bomb disposal and chemical warfare, he was the perfect one to do it.

Alvarez pulled a chair over and pushed Chase down into it. Chase was still gripping the vials of the ABG in his fist like a grenade. Landon tried not to snicker. What was he going to do? Smash them on the floor? If he did, that would get him and Abby and Jess exactly the same treatment he'd offered Piper. The one-shot cure.

Alvarez pulled the cooler out of Chase's hand, almost having to pry his fingers off of the nylon handle, "Come on, man. Your way out is to let us test this. Don't make it more difficult than it already is." Finally, Chase let go of the handle of the cooler. Alvarez took it from him and set it on the table next to Baker, opening the lid. Landon looked inside. He saw a test tube tray that had vials sitting in it, their teal stoppers still in place. Off to the side was a sheet of paper. Landon pulled it out. It was filled with notations and chemical markers he didn't understand. He shoved the paper at Alvarez, "Take a picture of this and send it to the chemist. Let's see if this stuff is for real."

As Baker took one of the vials out of the cooler, Landon stood back, his arms crossed over his chest, studying Chase. It wasn't very often that he got to interact with his target. Usually, it was get in, get them secured or eliminate them, and leave. Not a lot of time for chitchat. But, with the mission prep for this operation, he'd gotten to know the Montgomery family. He still didn't understand why Piper would choose a man like Chase. From the way it looked to him, Chase was too quiet and too bookish, the kind of guy who had no hobbies and no interests outside of his test tubes and microscopes. Definitely not the kind of person Landon would want to hang out with.

Scanning his men working silently, Chase was frozen in his chair, Landon shook his head, amazed at how calm he was about this entire mission. It had to be all the standing around over the last few hours. He pressed his lips together, realizing if he got too relaxed, he'd lose his edge. He needed his edge. It was the only way to survive. The most important part of the mission was coming up — getting out of Tucson and to one of Foster's safehouses. He had two favorite parts of every mission — the moment they left and the moment they got to the safe house. There was something about turning in all of his equipment and watching money getting transferred into his bank account that was satisfying. It was like making a touchdown in football. They'd spend days or weeks or months driving the ball down the field and once they crossed that line, the feeling of victory was sweet.

"How long does the test take?" Landon asked.

"Well, it depends on which test you want me to run. The quick test takes three minutes. But, if you want to be sure, I have another test they gave me that takes fourteen."

Landon looked at the time on his watch. Since Jess and Chase had been kind enough to show up at the warehouse, they weren't under as much time pressure. They were well hidden, no one knew where they were, and Foster had provided multiple plans for them to get away. Better to be sure. "Go ahead and run the longer test. We've got a few extra minutes. I'd rather be sure than show up at home base with the wrong stuff."

Baker nodded, "Roger that."

As Baker lined up three of the vials of ABG on a test tube tray, getting out a variety of clean test vials and chemicals, Alvarez came back, standing shoulder to shoulder with Landon, "I sent the formula. Just waiting on a response."

Landon nodded. They were at a crossroads. If Chase had brought the ABG, they faced one set of options. If he'd tried to trick them, there was another. Landon would know what path to take in the next few minutes. "Let's hope this stuff is the real deal," he said. Failure was not an option.

28

J ess had been sitting in the cage for what seemed like about five minutes when her phone chirped. The only problem was she couldn't get to it. The soldier that shoved her into the cage had made a big show of reaching into her back pants pocket, taking the time to grip her backside as he pulled her phone out. It was sitting on the chair where the man who was eating the sunflower seeds had been watching Abby all day long.

Jess stared at the empty chair where her phone was sitting. She and Abby had been quiet, not saying anything to each other for a couple minutes. Jess sat with her arm protectively over Abby's shoulder, pulling her close. She kept wondering if Abby would ever get back to normal. Jess closed her eyes for a second, taking a deep breath. It's not the time to figure this out, she told herself. When she opened them, her phone chirped again. A few seconds later it chirped for a third time. Jess stood up from where she was sitting, going to the side of the cage that was closest to her phone, trying to see what was happening. She prayed it was Jamison or Charlie trying to find them.

Jess glanced to the other side of the warehouse. It was too

dark to see where they'd gone. With the men on the other side of the warehouse testing the ABG, Jess realized she could probably climb the chain-link fence and drop down on the other side, but she was sure the rattle of the fencing as she climbed up would make enough noise they'd come running. Probably not the kind of chance to take, she thought to herself, sitting back down next to Abby. She'd have to wait for her opportunity.

Jess's phone went off again and then stopped. A shrill beeping pierced her ears. It was coming from the command center. She jerked her head to the side, staring at the computers. There was a red line across each one of the screens. She heard footfalls in the background, the noise of heavy boots running on the concrete floors of the warehouse. Jess blinked a couple times. What was happening? Her heart started to pound in her chest, and she reached over and grabbed Abby's hand. "Whatever happens, run outside. Don't wait for me and don't wait for your dad. If somehow you get free, go outside and find someone to help you. Do you understand?" Abby nodded, her eyes wide, filled with terror. Jess couldn't be sure that help was coming, but the fact that alarms were sounding in the warehouse told her something was happening.

Jess took two steps over to the gate, watching the door. A shadow passed in front of it and then another. Jess gave the gate a little push, trying to see how wide of a gap there was. Was it enough for at least Abby to squeeze out and get away? As Jess pushed on the gate, she saw that the kidnapper that had locked them in hadn't completely closed the padlock. From where he was standing, it probably looked like it was closed, but it was just hanging. Jess's eyes got wide. Just as she was about to reach through the gate and take the padlock off, she saw Walker and his men moving around the building. They'd grabbed rifles and had taken positions near the command center. They didn't seem overly concerned about Abby or Jess.

They were probably protecting the ABG and Chase, Jess realized.

Before Jess could do anything else, the door she and Chase had walked through cracked open, the tinny sound of something metal dropping on the ground. "Abby, get down!" Jess shouted, covering the little girl with her own body. The light and sound of the flash-bang grenade nearly blinded her, the ringing in her ears deafening. When Jess opened her eyes, she saw shadows moving around the building, the sound of gunfire. All she could do was protect Abby with her own body. The noise of guns going off echoed on the brick walls of the warehouse. The concussion of each shot thudded in her chest, the noise making it impossible to hear.

Jess knew that she and Abby were sitting ducks in the cage. If they weren't caught in the crossfire, Landon or one of his crew might use them as a human shield to try to get away. They couldn't stay there. Jess gritted her teeth and motioned for Abby to stay on the floor. She crawled over to the gate on her knees and reached up, loosening the lock. It fell to the floor at the same time as shots rang out. Jess dropped to the ground, covering her head with her arms. A second later, the volley stopped and Jess pushed on the gate, the rattle of the chain falling away. She glanced up. The gate was open. The door that would get them outside was maybe forty feet from them. She knew how fast Abby was, but no one was fast enough to outrun a bullet. There was no possible way to know what Walker and his crew were prepared to do.

As another volley of gunfire roared through the building, Jess covered her ears, shivering under the noise. Still on the floor, she realized the gunshots seemed to be coming from the back corner of the building. Whoever had come in had driven Walker and his crew away from the cage. Why they hadn't stopped to rescue Jess and Abby, she wasn't sure, but Jess knew they couldn't wait. She jumped to her feet, extending her hand behind her toward where Abby was still flat on the floor, "Abby, come on!" she yelled. Jess pushed at Abby from behind, "Run for the door. Go as fast as you can. Don't stop!"

Jess took off after her, sprinting as fast as her cramped legs would carry her. Shots rang out overhead, forcing Jess to duck and cover as she ran for the door. Abby got there two strides ahead of Jess. As she pushed the door open, the bright sunlight from the long afternoon streamed through the door. Outside, there were a dozen vehicles. Jess scanned the crowd. Jamison. He was dressed in the same tactical gear that Walker's crew had on, but with his badge hanging around his neck. Abby stopped just outside of the door, looking confused. "Over here," Jess said, grabbing her hand and dragging her to Jamison.

As soon as Jess and Abby got to Jamison, he grabbed them, pulling them behind one of the armored vehicles. He looked at Jess, grabbing both of her arms and staring at her, "Are you okay? What's going on in there? Who is in there?"

"It's just Walker and his crew. Plus, Chase. I don't know where they are. It sounded like they were in the back corner of the warehouse, so Abby and I ran. The guard didn't lock the padlock on the cage the whole way, so we were able to get out. Is that the SWAT team in there? They didn't come to get us. Where's Chase?"

"I don't know where Chase is," Jamison said slowly, "and no, that's not SWAT. When I got here, there was someone in military fatigues that told me to stand down. He said they'd handle it. Something about a matter of national security." Jess glanced back toward the building. The door she and Abby ran out of was half-open, but it was impossible to see inside, the bright light outside drowning the darkness within. From where they were standing behind the armored vehicle, Jess could hear the occasional rattle of gunshots firing. How anyone had any ammunition left, she didn't know. When she'd seen Landon and his crew that morning, it was clear they were ready for a fight. She didn't expect it would take as long as it did for them to settle this. "Chase is still in there," Jess said, staring at Jamison. Her chest was tight. It felt like every muscle in her body had been made shorter, the stress and strain causing pain to surge everywhere. "Who did you say is running this operation?"

Jamison pointed a couple more vehicles away from the building. "Right behind there. There's a guy, I don't know his name. He got here just as I pulled in. Told me the military was taking over jurisdiction."

Jess glanced at Jamison, "Stay with Abby!" Jess ran off just in time to hear Jamison's voice behind her, telling her to stay put.

She didn't.

Jess darted between a couple of other men dressed in fatigues that were waiting by the back of one of the other vehicles, their combat helmets on, their rifles strapped to their chests, American flag patches on their shoulders. Behind the truck where Jamison had pointed, the doors on the back of the vehicle were open. It was something that looked like a cargo van, with steps that led inside. The interior had three people -- two of them were seated at remote computer monitors that had been bolted to the inside of the van. There was someone else inside, pacing back and forth, his fingers interlocked behind his back, staring at the floor. As he glanced up, he gave Jess a little nod, "You made it out. How's your niece?"

Jess shook her head, knitting her eyebrows together, "Who are you?" she said, not answering the question.

"Lieutenant Commander Mitchell. I'm running this op."

There were a couple of murmurs behind Mitchell from the two people monitoring the situation inside. One of them pointed as Mitchell stopped to stare at a computer screen. He glanced back at Jess, "We're doing our best to get your brother out. The guys in there are some of the best in the business."

Confusion washed over Jess, "I don't understand. Who are you? Who sent you?" Jess glanced behind her, seeing the Tucson SWAT team huddled behind another vehicle just down the block, "Why are you handling this and not SWAT?"

"Matter of national security. By order of Admiral Dumont and the Secretary of the Navy."

As soon as Mitchell said the Secretary of the Navy, all the pieces fell into place. Charlie and the secretary were golf buddies. Somehow, Charlie must have called in a favor. Jess nodded and glanced at the computer screens, "Where's my brother?"

Mitchell shook his head, "I can't see him at the minute. My guys have body cams on, but..."

Jess didn't wait for his answer. She sprinted toward the building as fast as her legs could carry her. She ran down the sidewalk, cut across the scrubby grass, and got to the door, pulling it open. She heard Jamison's voice yelling behind her, telling her to stop, telling her to come back and hide behind the vehicle. She couldn't. Chase was still inside. Landon had taken enough of her family. He wasn't going to get Chase.

Just inside the door, Jess crouched down. It was so dark inside the building, she wasn't sure how anyone could see at all. The military must have cut the power when they breached. Jess hadn't noticed. She was so busy trying to get Abby out of the cage that it didn't matter, light from outside casting a long enough glow for her to see how to get out. Now, things were different. She waited for a second, trying to see what was going on. From over her left shoulder, she heard more gunshots, two or three, by her count. She sucked in a breath, her stomach in a knot. What was she doing? She was unarmed in a building where people were chasing each other with live ammunition. This wasn't paintball. But she had to find Chase. She couldn't leave him behind. Last she saw, he was with Landon. What if they still had him as a hostage? There was no telling what Landon and his crew would do to Chase if they were able to escape with him. She swallowed. She might never see her brother again.

Jess inched her way along the wall, staying low, hoping the darkness would cover her. She knew all of Lieutenant Commander Mitchell's guys had headsets on. She'd heard the audio when she was standing at his command center. She could only hope Mitchell radioed them, letting them know she was in the building so they didn't shoot her. From where she was, she could see the cage where Abby had been kept all day long, the door pushed open, the abandoned food off to the side. As she pushed herself along the wall, she could see the outline of the command center, all of the monitors dark. There was no way for her to know how big the warehouse was, or how many rooms it might have. She decided her best bet was to stick to the perimeter. At least there was a chance she could find some cover if she did.

Jess made it to the corner of the building, pausing for a minute. She listened. The only thing she could hear was her own ragged breathing. She inched her foot forward, trying not to make any noise. She couldn't see anyone, only hearing the occasional rattle of gunfire. For some reason, it seemed close and yet far off at the same time. There had to be more to the building, Jess realized, picking up the pace a little bit. She stood up, bent over, dodging behind a few metal barrels as she made her way around the corner. This part of the warehouse was unfamiliar. Ahead of her, a few windows from above showed the outline of another wall and a few doors that were open ahead of her. Maybe those are offices, she thought. Jess pushed her way forward, getting to the first office door. She peered inside, just in time for more gunfire to erupt, over what sounded like her right shoulder. She ducked down again, a lump forming in her throat. A second later, they dissipated.

Voices seemed to echo off the walls, but they seem to be far away.

There was nothing in the first office, Jess realized as she ran through the door, ducking down on the other side. Nothing except for an old desk and chair that had been abandoned. Crawling around the other side of it, a head of hair appeared on the other side. Jess drew back until she realized the person was on his back. It was one of Landon's men. Jess inched forward toward him. His eyes were fixed on the ceiling. She waited for a second, trying to see if his chest moved up and down. Was he just unconscious? Or dead? Jess waited for another second, a shallow breath catching in her throat. She leaned over, scooting toward him. He wasn't breathing. She put two fingers on his neck, surprised that his skin seemed to have cooled already. No pulse. He was dead. She looked at him for a second, wondering which of Landon's crew had died. A second later, she realized it was the man that sat outside of the cage while she was in it, the one with the sunflower seeds. Jess thought maybe his name was Reinhardt or something. "One down, three to go," she whispered, moving past him.

On the other side of the office, there was another doorway. It opened up to a massive space, one that Jess didn't know even existed while she was in the building before. Chains attached to pulleys hung from the three-story ceiling, a couple of mechanic's lifts positioned off to the side, their metal frames jutting up out of the ground. At the far end of the space, she could see a flight of steps. Leaning forward, Jess noticed they looked to be metal and ran the entire way up to the roof of the building, connecting to a catwalk that spanned the length and width of the ceiling. Jess knelt back behind the wall in the office, blinking, trying to get her bearings. She glanced around the corner again, just in time to see a few dark forms moving, the eruption from the end of their guns lighting up the space with an incandescent red glow that only lasted for a second as the ammunition exploded from the end of the barrel. The noise was so loud Jess covered her ears as it bounced off the high ceilings. She could barely think straight.

Jess crawled around the corner again. From over her shoulder, she saw another body on the floor. Staying low, she ran over to it, wondering if the person was alive or dead. The shadows made it hard for her to see. She dropped to her knees as another volley of bullets sounded, a few of them whizzing right over her head. Dodging behind a couple of crates, she hid, looking at the outline of the person who was down. It looked like Chase, she thought. Was it? If it was, she had to get to him. Her heart started to pound in her chest. Chase had to get through this. Abby needed her dad. She needed her brother.

Jess didn't dare stand up with bullets flying overhead. She crawled on her hands and knees, grit from the floor pressing into her palms, trying to get close enough to see if the person curled up on the floor was one of the soldiers or Chase. She stopped for a second, peering around the back corner of the crates she was hiding behind. Glancing up, she noticed that black writing had been stenciled on the side of each crate, but it was impossible for her to read it in the darkness. As another blast of gunshots fired, she stared at the body, realizing there was just enough light as the shots fired to see the shirt on the body looked like it belonged to Chase. She swallowed. He wasn't moving. Jess waited for a second, listening. Every muscle in her body was tense. As soon as the volley stopped, she crawled as fast as she could over to the form on the floor. From five feet away, even in the darkness, she could see it was Chase. "Chase," she whispered. "Are you okay?"

Chase didn't answer. As Jess got to him, she realized there was a puddle of blood underneath his head, coating his hair. She rolled him on his back. He blinked at her, his hand covering a wound on his neck. It was gushing blood. Chase looked at her, his eyes wide, "ABG," he said, his voice garbled with blood collecting at the back of his throat, "My pants."

Jess stared at him, "What do you mean?" Chase didn't answer. Jess leaned over him, trying to see where his neck had been injured. Panic rose inside of Jess, knowing she had maybe a minute, if that, to try to help him. Frantic, Jess used her hands to pat him down, trying to figure out what he was saying about the ABG. He slid his right heel along the floor, setting his foot flat. He whispered something, but she couldn't make it out. She felt down the leg he'd put on the floor and then to his sock. There was a lump in it. She lifted the cuff, finding one of the vials of ABG still stuffed in his sock. Glancing at it, she realized it was one of the test tubes they grabbed from Building B just a couple hours before. Chase must have brought it with him into the building in case something happened. How Landon's guys missed it, Jess wasn't sure. Maybe Chase had more street smarts than she thought he did.

"Got it," she whispered as another volley of bullets raged overhead. She ducked down, still holding the vial in her hand. Pulling the stopper off, she replaced Chase's hand with her own. The blood, dark in the shadow, started to ooze between her pale fingers. She knew she only had a second to pour the ABG onto the wound. Whispering a silent prayer that Chase's invention would work on the man that created it, she parted her fingers just enough to pour the ABG into the wound. She poured slowly, not exactly sure where the hole was. After using about half the vial, she rolled Chase onto his side. He was going in and out of consciousness, his eyes closed, murmuring about Abby in a whisper, the blood loss clouding his thinking. Pulling her hand away, Jess could see where the damage had been done in his neck a little bit better. She poured the rest of the ABG on the spot, and waited, holding her breath.

From behind her, she heard movement. She covered Chase's body with her own, as two black outfitted people came her way. If these were Landon's men, she knew she was dead and likely Chase, too. Her heart pounded in her chest as she heard one of them speak, "It's okay, ma'am. We're here to help. Let's get the two of you out of here. We've chased Landon and the rest of his men to the back of the warehouse."

Jess rolled off of Chase's body. One of the men was unfolding something that looked like a tarp with handles. She realized it was a sling the men could use to get Chase out of the building. The man that spoke to her whispered, "Are you okay? Are you hurt? Lieutenant Commander Mitchell sent us in here to get you out."

"I'm okay," she whispered. "But Chase, he's got a neck wound. I used ABG on it."

The man nodded as his partner pulled on a set of surgical gloves and stared at the wound. He squinted, putting his face close to the wound. "It's closed," the other soldier said, "but I can tell by the blood on the floor he's lost a lot. We gotta get him outta here and to the ambulance now."

The men rolled Chase's body onto the sling, one of them looking at Jess, "Okay, we're going move him. I want you to follow right behind me, okay?"

Jess nodded, standing up, waiting for the volley of gunfire to start again. She kept her shoulders hunched low behind the two men as they lifted Chase up on the sling, one man at his head, the other man at Chase's feet. Jess followed and made it as far as the entry to the offices when she heard gunfire again. All of them dropped to their knees for a moment, waiting for it to pass. One of the men seemed to be listening to the radio, probably getting more information from Mitchell as they waited. "Roger that," he whispered into his headset. The soldier glanced at Jess, "the Commander said we can move. Walker and the rest of his crew are still in the back of the warehouse with our team. Let's go."

Jess stood up, ready to follow the men and Chase when the

gunfire started again. She turned, just in time to see shadows moving along the back of the warehouse, dodging between the barrels and crates that had been left there by whoever used to own the building. The building was probably owned by Colonel Foster or someone affiliated with him, just like they'd done with the mechanic's garage. There was no telling how many properties Zeta Tactical Consulting owned throughout the world, using them as needed to stage crimes or as safe houses. Balling her hands into fists, Jess realized that somewhere in that warehouse, Landon Walker was still running around, probably with the rest of the ABG. Her chest clutched. That man had tried to single-handedly take down her entire family. Abby would have mental scars she'd have to deal with for years, it would be a miracle if Chase survived, and Jess still had no idea what happened to Piper. Was she alive somewhere in the building? If she wasn't, how would Abby and Chase go on without her?

The questions swirled in Jess's head. Every option was unthinkable. As the men started to move forward, Jess hung back, leaning against the doorframe staying in a crouched position. She knew she should follow Chase out to the ambulance and stay outside with Jamison and the military until things were safe, but something kept her where she was standing, her heart pounding in her chest, her breath ragged and her hands shaking. She couldn't tell at that moment whether it was fear or fury, but it didn't matter.

Jess glanced at the men who had Chase on the sling. They were only a few feet ahead of her. One of them looked behind and nodded his head, encouraging her to follow.

She didn't.

Running back into the area where the warehouse expanded into an open space, Jess crouched again behind the crates where she'd first spotted Chase. The pool of his blood was still on the floor. She could make out the murky outlines from the bit of light that was pouring in from the windows above. Gunfire erupted again around her. Jess stayed in place for a moment, trying to figure out where the assault was happening. She covered her ears, the noise of the rifles going off nearly deafening her. As she glanced up, she saw what looked like two of Landon's people crouched behind barrels at the other end of the warehouse. A third person stood at the bottom of the stairs, hunkered down. From what she could make out, it looked like he had something hanging on his wrist. Jess leaned forward, staring, trying to make it out. It had to be Landon. He must have the ABG with him, she realized.

The gunfire settled down for a second. Jess was just about to run forward when she saw two of Landon's men, hiding behind barrels, start to fire again. It was rapid, preventing any of Mitchell's men from moving forward, the rattle of bullets not stopping. Jess saw Landon start to run up the flight of metal steps. Where was he going? Without thinking, Jess crouched down and ran to the corner of the building and then turned left, staying low, hunched behind a few more crates. She had to get to him before he took the ABG and got away. Her mind raced with possibilities. Was Colonel Foster going to land a helicopter on the roof to rescue Landon and the ABG from Mitchell's men? Jess set her jaw, staring forward. In her gut, she knew it was now or never. Either she made a move to get to Landon or she'd have to turn tail and go back outside to see what was going on with Chase and Abby.

Jess glanced over her shoulder, looking back the way she came. In that instant, she knew she couldn't live with herself if she didn't do everything she could to protect Chase's invention. Landon and his crew had tried to ruin their lives. It couldn't be allowed. She needed to get the ABG back and get justice for her family.

Bent over, Jess took off, running, trying to avoid any stray bullets coming from Mitchell's men. As she did, she looked up, seeing Walker running up the metal steps. He was already on the second leg of the three flights leading up to the catwalk. From where she was stopped, she could see there was one more flight above the catwalk, with light streaming in. The roof. She took off running again, skidding to her knees as bullets flew overhead. A second later, she took off again, ending up behind two of Landon's men. They were so focused on what was going on in front of them that they never noticed she was hunched against the wall. She stopped for a second, trying to catch her breath. Her lungs were burning. She glanced up. Landon was at the catwalk. Just ahead of her, Jess could see the first few steps of the metal rungs of the ladder. Staying low, she sprinted for them, taking the steps two at a time, trying to stay out of the gunfire. Every inch of her body was burning up from running so fast up the steps. As she got to the catwalk, she looked down. There was still gunfire going on between Walker's men and Mitchell's. She glanced up, seeing a shadow moving above her. Landon was up there with the ABG. Gritting her teeth, Jess ran up the last flight of steps, poking her head out through the opening in the roof. Walker was nowhere to be seen.

The roof was cluttered with a maze of mechanicals for the building, the blazing heat from the day had gathered on the roof, hovering above the space. Jess's feet slid on the loose gravel as she ducked behind a large air conditioning unit. It was humming, sending cool air down into the building. Jess glanced around the corner and saw Landon standing at the edge. He was turned sideways as though he was looking for something off in the distance. Jess squinted, wondering if he was waiting for a rescue from Foster.

Jess ducked behind a few more protrusions from the roof — a set of pipes, another condenser, and some other mechanicals she couldn't identify — using them as cover. Moving as quietly as possible, she stayed low, trying to get close to Landon. She could see he was holding the cooler in his left hand, the strap wrapped around his wrist. He had a pistol dangling from his right hand. He didn't seem concerned at all about the gun battle that was going on below him. He simply stared off into the distance, waiting.

Emerging from behind a metal box installed on the roof, Jess stood up, calling him, "Walker! I want that ABG back." Her breath was so ragged, she barely got the words out. Watching him, she realized her heart was pounding in her chest and her mouth was bone dry.

Landon turned slowly towards Jess, a smirk on his face, "Jess Montgomery. You are the last person I expected to find on the roof with me. You want the ABG? Come and take it!" A sneer formed on his face as he pulled his pistol.

"All you need to do is drop the ABG. Just hand it over to me and I'll take it back where it belongs, back to Chase."

Landon raised his eyebrows, "To your precious brother? He has no idea what he's created with the ABG. He's nothing but an idealist." Landon glanced down at the ground and then glanced back at Jess, "Actually, if he survives the day, I'll bet that this experience is good for him. Your whole family, you're all a bunch of do-gooders. It's time you toughened up. Well, except for maybe Piper. At least she liked to have a little fun."

The words felt like a punch in the gut. Jess knew Landon was taunting her again. Chase did have people's best interests in mind. Whatever Piper had done, that was between them. "There is nothing wrong with what Chase has done. You and that perverse organization you work for think you can take anything you want and destroy lives in the process. That's just not going to be the case. Not today." Before Landon could say anything else, Jess took off at a sprint, charging at him, aiming for the wrist that held the ABG. Walker caught her with a punch to the stomach that doubled her over. Jess felt all of the air leave her lungs as she collapsed on the roof. From the corner of her eye, she saw Walker toss the cooler ten feet away, where she couldn't get to it. She laid on the roof for a second and then stood up again, lunging at his legs, hoping to tip him off balance. He dodged her and she ended up falling on the roof, skidding on her knees, the gravel digging into her skin.

"What are you going to do, Jess? I could shoot you and put you out of your misery, but I'm finding this kind of entertaining. You don't have a gun. You don't have any training. I could do this all afternoon."

Before Landon could say anything else, Jess stood up and charged at Landon again, this time wrapping her arms around his waist, trying to wrestle him to the roof. She heard his gun clatter as he dropped it, pulling her towards the edge of the roof. In her ear, he hissed, "It's a long way down, Jess."

Jess couldn't breathe, panic rising in the back of her throat. As he dragged her to the edge of the roof, she caught a glimpse of some pipes out of the corner of her eye. She caught one of them with her heel and then wrapped the other leg around them, preventing Landon from pushing her over the edge.

On her side, Jess's head and shoulders were over the edge of the building. She glanced down, some gravel from the roof dropping the three stories below, raining on the sidewalk. Terror rose in her throat. The only thing preventing her from falling was the strength of her legs, which were burning. "Almost there, sweetheart. It'll be a fun ride down," Landon said, kicking at her legs, trying to get them to come free. Jess twisted away, lunging for Landon's gun, which he'd left lying in the gravel after it fell. In one move, Jess landed on top of it, covering it with her body, grabbing at the grip. She felt Landon jump on her back, punching her in the back of the head and the kidneys, trying to roll her over. She saw spots, the pain in her body was excruciating, the breath leaving her lungs. Jess reached her hands around the grip of the pistol underneath her and tried to roll away. As she did, Landon ended up straddling her, landing a punch to her face. More spots formed in front of her eyes. Without thinking, she lifted the gun to his chest and pulled the trigger.

Landon's eyes went wide as his body collapsed on top of her, the full weight of him pressing down. Jess's hand was still pinned underneath her, the gun still wrapped in her fingers as he died. Barely able to breathe, her eyes wide with panic, Jess wriggled out from underneath him, leaving his body face down on the gravel, the pistol still in her hand.

"Over here!"

Jess heard yells coming up onto the roof, the sound of boots on the roof. Without thinking, she crawled on her belly to get the cooler with the ABG, wrapping the strap around her wrist as two of Mitchell's men approached her. She curled herself into a ball, hugging the cooler to her chest, Walker's gun still in her hand. One of the men knelt down in front of her, pulling off his helmet. "You're okay, Jess. We're here to help. I need you to let go of the pistol, okay?"

She stared at the soldier in front of her, the tip of his rifle resting on the gravel as she stared down at her hands. They were covered in blood. Walker's blood. She opened her fingers just enough to let go of the pistol, still clutching the cooler of ABG to her chest. She closed her eyes knowing she'd gotten Chase's ABG back.

The next few minutes were a blur. The two men on the roof became four and then a team of medics joined them. As one of the medics examined Jess, he looked at her, "Are you able to stand?" She nodded, whispering, "I think so."

The medic looked at her and nodded. "Good. We're gonna help you get downstairs. Walker beat you up pretty good. We've got an ambulance standing by. They'll get you checked out."

As Jess stood up, feeling the strength of the two men lifting her, her legs felt wobbly, pain in her head burning from where he'd punched her. She glanced to her right. Landon's body had been covered with a yellow tarp. How long it would stay on the roof, she wasn't sure.

The medics guided her back down the metal stairs, a team of paramedics meeting them at the bottom of the steps with the gurney. Jess sat down slowly, feeling every ache in her body. She felt straps being secured around her as she leaned her head back and closed her eyes. The wheels of the gurney rattled on the concrete floor as it passed back through the space, through the offices, then to the area where Abby had been held. Jess opened her eyes enough to see techs working on the command center, the bright lights over the cage having been turned back on again.

As they pushed the gurney out of the door, she heard Abby's voice, "Aunt Jess! You're okay!" Jess looked up in time to see Abby and Jamison standing at the foot of the gurney.

She nodded. "Okay enough. Where's your dad?" Jess said, her eyes going wide. "Is he okay?"

Tears rolling down Abby's face, "They said you saved his life. You used his invention to help him."

Jess nodded. "He's a clever man, your dad. He had just enough in case of an emergency." Jess reached out her hand and squeezed Abby's. "It's all over, honey. Everybody's okay." As the words left Jess's mouth, she realized that she hadn't seen Piper. She felt confused for a moment and then glanced at Jamison, who shook his head ever so slightly. Jess closed her eyes for a second, biting her lip.

The paramedics rolled Jess's gurney over to the back of an ambulance, where they put a blood pressure cuff on her and started an IV, looking for wounds. Jamison had stayed right by the gurney, Abby trailing behind, "Where's Chase?"

"Over there," Jamison said, pointing. "He wouldn't let them take him to the hospital until he knew you were okay."

As Jess glanced over toward the ambulance, she saw Abby standing nearby, holding her dad's hand. Jess looked at Jamison, "What happened to Piper?"

"Mitchell told me they found her body in the dumpster behind the building. Single-shot to the head."

Jess turned her head to the side, tears rolling down her face. The day had been too much. Jess had done more that day than she ever thought she could. But Abby was safe and the ABG was back where it needed to be.

Her dad was right. She was stronger than she thought, Jess realized as they loaded her into the ambulance, the doors slamming closed.

EPILOGUE

After a few hours of sitting in the emergency room, Jess was released with a black eye and two broken ribs, plus some scrapes and abrasions from wrestling with Walker. Chase had been rushed to surgery to repair his carotid artery. The doctors had received a full briefing on the phone about ABG from Charlie before they worked on him. When the surgeon came out to talk to Jess and Abby, he shook his head, "I have to say, in all my years as a surgeon I've never seen anything like this. What your brother has developed is a game-changer for us as medical professionals." Jess reached down and squeezed Abby's hand, looking at her, "You should be proud of your dad."

Abby stared at her lap, "I am. I'm proud of you too, Aunt Jess. You're kind of a badass!"

Jess turned her head to look at Jamison, who had stayed with them while they were waiting on the results of Chase's surgery. They all broke out in laughter, including the surgeon, which was a welcome relief after having to tell Abby about the death of her mom.

"Your brother will need to stay with us for a couple days.

You should probably go home and get some rest. We gave him medication to help him sleep. It sounds like you all have had a very busy day."

Jess nodded and tried to stand up, feeling a little woozy. Jamison grabbed her under her arm. The pain medication they'd given her in the emergency room made her feel a little lightheaded. She frowned and looked up at him, "Could Abby and I get a ride back to her house? I don't think I should drive."

Roxie was barking at the door when Abby and Jess arrived home. Jamison followed them in. They'd stopped and picked up a pizza on the way back, not that anyone was hungry after the day they'd had. Jess had invited Jamison to join them. He said the department had assigned him to stay parked in front of the house for the next couple of days, just to make sure there weren't any other repercussions from Walker's crew or Colonel Foster. Jess was more than happy for the company. After a text from Charlie, Jess knew there wouldn't be any. Charlie and the Secretary of the Navy were taking care of Zeta Tactical Consulting and the sketchy experiments going on in Building B at Trident Labs.

Exhausted, she slumped down on the couch, a piece of pizza on a paper plate, Roxie sitting patiently by her feet, waiting for a bite of crust. Jess stared at Abby and Jamison, who were gathering up drinks and napkins. Jess reached up to touch her eye. It was swollen and felt hot, but the doctors told her there was no long-term damage. The doctors said it just needed time.

They all needed time.

Can Jess figure out why cybercriminals are targeting her before it's too late? Click here to check out The Patriarch Code now!

A NOTE FROM THE AUTHOR...

Thanks so much for taking the time to read *The Trident Conspiracy*!

After reading *The Trident Conspiracy*, I hope that you've been able to take a break from your everyday life and join Jess on her adventure to get justice for Abby. There are more stories to come! Check out the next few pages for a preview of the next book in the series, *The Patriarch Code*, or click here now to get it now!

Enjoy!

KJ

P. S. Would you take a moment to leave a review? They mean so much to indie authors like me!

THE NEXT BOOK IN THE ADVENTURE — THE PATRIARCH CODE

Intelligence analyst Jess Montgomery thought her life was finally going the right direction.

With a good job at a DC think tank, her niece safely returned to the family after a traumatic kidnapping. and the glow of the newly married life, Jess thought everything was good.

But ransomware attacks are popping up all over the nation, with millions of dollars being demanded in return, the exposure of top-secret government technology, energy and lives on the line.

Jess Montgomery gets the call to work on the case. She doesn't realize getting involved has put a target on her back. The hackers will stop at nothing to achieve their global goals, even if it means eliminating anyone who is in their way, including her...

Jess is drawn into a web of lies, betrayal and deceit before she realizes it. Can she escape and find the hackers before it's too late?

If you like books by Mark Dawson, Lee Child or L. T. Ryan, you are going to love the Jess Montgomery Thrillers!

Click here to get it now!

AN EXCERPT FROM THE PATRIARCH CODE

Jess stood frozen in the space between the family room and the kitchen for just a moment, leaning her hand on one of the backs of the kitchen chairs for support. She felt dizzy with uncertainty. Stop being so emotional and use your head, Jess, she thought to herself. She blinked a couple of times and then started moving. Her stomach clenched, threatening to throw up what was left of her breakfast from a few hours before. She swallowed, chasing the bile back down where it belonged. Something more than just the break in was troubling her. What that was, she didn't know.

Jess could only work off of the facts she had. She closed her eyes for a second, shifting her mind into analyst mode. Just the facts, Jess. Focus on the facts. What she knew was that her house had been destroyed. It was no longer safe to stay here. She also knew that her husband, the person who was supposed to love her and protect her, wasn't. He had more unexplained absences over the last six months than she was comfortable with. He was distant. As much as she didn't want to admit it, they were hardly speaking. She had no idea what was going on or why. And then there was the receipt from a hotel that didn't have a reservation from him, the mud on his pants and the blood on his boots. Sure, those could be easily explained by a training exercise, but then the call from Molly resurfaced in her mind. Apparently, people from the department thought he was out sick. If he was lying to them, he was probably lying to her. Jess set her jaw. Something was going on. Something she couldn't explain. All she knew in that moment was that she couldn't stay at the house.

Unlock all the Jess Montgomery adventures now by visiting the series page!

Made in the USA
Las Vegas, NV
07 July 2023

74332495R00171